FIGHT OR FLIGHT

Books by Fern Michaels

Fight or Flight
The Wild Side
On the Line
Fear Thy Neighbor
No Way Out
Fearless
Deep Harbor
Fate & Fortune
Sweet Vengeance
Fancy Dancer
No Safe Secret
About Face
Perfect Match
A Family Affair
Forget Me Not
The Blossom Sisters
Balancing Act
Tuesday's Child
Betrayal
Southern Comfort
To Taste the Wine
Sins of the Flesh
Sins of Omission
Return to Sender
Mr. and Miss Anonymous
Up Close and Personal
Fool Me Once
Picture Perfect
The Future Scrolls
Kentucky Sunrise
Kentucky Heat
Kentucky Rich
Plain Jane
Charming Lily

What You Wish For
The Guest List
Listen to Your Heart
Celebration
Yesterday
Finders Keepers
Annie's Rainbow
Sara's Song
Vegas Sunrise
Vegas Heat
Vegas Rich
Whitefire
Wish List
Dear Emily

The Lost and Found Novels
Secrets
Hidden
Liar!
Proof

The Sisterhood Novels
Backwater Justice
Rock Bottom
Tick Tock
19 Yellow Moon Road
Bitter Pill
Truth and Justice
Cut and Run
Safe and Sound
Need to Know
Crash and Burn

Books by Fern Michaels (cont.)

Point Blank
In Plain Sight
Eyes Only
Kiss and Tell
Blindsided
Gotcha!
Home Free
Déjà Vu
Cross Roads
Game Over
Deadly Deals
Vanishing Act
Razor Sharp
Under the Radar
Final Justice
Collateral Damage
Fast Track
Hokus Pokus
Hide and Seek
Free Fall
Lethal Justice
Sweet Revenge
The Jury
Vendetta
Payback
Weekend Warriors

The Men of the Sisterhood
Novels
Hot Shot
Truth or Dare
High Stakes
Fast and Loose
Double Down

The Godmothers Series:
Far and Away
Classified
Breaking News
Deadline
Late Edition
Exclusive
The Scoop

E-Book Exclusives
Desperate Measures
Seasons of Her Life
To Have and To Hold
Serendipity
Captive Innocence
Captive Embraces
Captive Passions
Captive Secrets
Captive Splendors
Cinders to Satin
For All Their Lives
Texas Heat
Texas Rich
Texas Fury
Texas Sunrise

Anthologies
Tiny Blessings
In Bloom
Home Sweet Home

FIGHT OR FLIGHT

FERN MICHAELS

KENSINGTON
PUBLISHING CORP.

kensingtonbooks.com

"Thus the emotion of fear is associated with the instinct for flight, and the emotion of anger or rage with the instinct for fighting or attack."
—Walter Bradford Cannon, *Bodily Changes in Pain, Hunger, Fear and Rage*

Prologue

Patriots' Day, 2013
Boston, Massachusetts

Katherine Celeste Winston glanced at her watch. Two thirty. She'd promised Adam she would wait until he whizzed past the winning pennant displayed at the end of Boylston Street. If his stats were correct, and she had no reason to doubt them, he should be running past soon. The enormous crowd of onlookers had gathered at the finish line, waiting for their peeps to raise their arms high in the air, or maybe dance or collapse once they'd completed the race. The lucky winner had crashed through the winning line about three hours earlier. Katherine knew Adam wasn't going to win, he just wanted to best his previous time.

She was tired, and the crowds were starting to overwhelm her. As a rule, she didn't place herself in a position where she would be in large groups. However, she couldn't always dictate the circumstances of life. Of course, she knew the Boston Marathon crowds were estimated to be around one million along the twenty-six-mile route from Hopkinton to Copley Square. She'd inched onto Boylston Street, merely a few blocks from Copley Square. It had taken her two hours, wending her way through hundreds of other marathon enthusiasts, before she'd found an ideal spot to watch for Adam, number twenty-six-thousand . . . something. She couldn't recall the last three numbers; it wouldn't matter as Adam's height and rusty hair would stand out amongst the other runners. While it wasn't a perfect spot, it gave her a decent enough view of those hoping to complete the race.

Sandwiched between a tall, slender woman and a man who was at least six-five, she couldn't help but place her hand over her nose and mouth as the man raised his arms to cheer the runners, his body odor so foul she had to move away. Trying to make her way through the crowd, she was pushed and shoved. It was like being in a mosh pit at a punk rock concert. One overenthusiastic spectator jumped up and almost landed on top of her, causing her to bump into a young man, maybe in his early twenties with ink-black hair. He glared at her, and for some reason, Katherine felt a chill run down her spine. Though she was unsure why, he frightened her. She mumbled a quick apology and forced her way to the group closest to the finish line, where all the hoopla took place, away from the dark-eyed man.

Suddenly, what sounded like a loud explosion filled the air. *Fireworks.* Katherine smiled to herself. It sounded like someone had started celebrating. She eyed the throngs of people, searching for the source of the loud bang, but was unable to locate the revelers. Katherine continued to try and find where the sounds were coming from. She turned her head in the opposite direction and saw a large crowd gathered around several runners slumped on the ground, blood streaming from them. Katherine's own blood pumped as she shoved her way over to the scene. Before she could determine precisely what was happening, she heard a second blast close to where she stood. The mass of people surrounding her looked as shocked as she did. Quickly, the uninjured sprang into action. Those unhurt ripped their shirts off to use as makeshift tourniquets for the wounded, who were writhing in the middle of the street. Screams and sirens played a cacophony in the background as Katherine pushed through the crowd, searching for Adam, trying to recall his full bib number. He'd ranked low during the required qualifications and begun the race around 11:15, in the last wave. He wore a yellow bib, but Katherine still couldn't recall his exact number, just that it was around 26,000. The runners had emergency contacts on their bibs if they fell ill during the race. She felt in her jeans pocket for her cell phone. *Surely he would call if he were injured,* she thought, as fear rooted her, immovable, amid the catastrophe surrounding her.

Hundreds of voices were now screaming and shouting out the names of their loved ones. Katherine didn't call out Adam's name. It felt as if a rock were lodged in her throat; she couldn't make a sound. Confused and uncertain about how much time had passed, Katherine forced herself to run in the opposite direction, away from the giant white clouds of billowing smoke.

There were cries and shrieks of pain. Calls for help. Men and women in bright yellow vests that read POLICE or PHYSICIAN. People wearing white vests with the Red Cross sign raced through the streets, passing Katherine, stopping to help the multitude of injured. Katherine caught sight of a sneaker with the bloodied foot still snugly inside, minus the leg, and waves of nausea rose up within her. Falling to her knees, heaving, she emptied the contents of her stomach in the street, closing her eyes as if it could erase the image of the sneaker and the severed foot. Taking a deep breath, she used the hem of her shirt to wipe her mouth, then forced herself to stand, pushing her way through the scene of destruction.

She and Adam had arranged to find each other at the family meeting area after he'd completed the race, in case they didn't connect near the finish line. She realized she had been running in the opposite direction. Turning around, Katherine felt hot tears roll down her cheeks and smelled the smoke and blood. There was so much blood. She did not like the sight of blood. The smell of blood. Yet it surrounded her. People were bleeding, crying, and searching for their loved ones everywhere she went. She touched her forehead, pulled her hand away, and saw it, too, was covered in blood. She'd been injured by whatever had blown Boylston Street into this bloody mass of hysteria.

Moving forward, she passed Trinity Church and located the family meeting area. Red Cross workers, emergency medical technicians, police officers, and volunteers scurried beneath the white tent.

"You're bleeding," a Red Cross worker told her, guiding her to an area where medical supplies were tossed haphazardly on a long plastic table. "Here," the man said, as he soaked a gauze pad with liquid and placed it on her wound. Katherine winced. "You have a piece of metal stuck in your forehead," he said. "I can remove it, or you can wait and go to one of the hospitals, but it could take a while. They're overwhelmed with injuries, and this doesn't seem to need stitches."

She nodded. "Just do whatever you need to." The last place she wanted to go was a hospital. Finding Adam was her top priority now.

He nodded back and said, "This'll sting a bit. You may want to see a doctor if you have any infection, but I think we've got this." He smoothly removed the piece of metal. "Keep it clean with peroxide, use an antibiotic cream, and remember to see your doctor if you have any issues." With that, he moved aside to assess another victim.

Victim. Where had that word come from? *Victim of what?* Katherine wondered as she held the gauze to her forehead, pressing firmly against the wound to control the bleeding. Pushing the thought aside, she focused on finding Adam.

Dazed, she walked among others who were stunned, just like herself. No one else seemed to know exactly what had happened. She heard someone say, "Weapons of mass destruction," but mentally ruled that out. Possibly a gas line at one of the many restaurants that flanked either side of Boylston Street had leaked. There could be no other rational explanation.

"Adam!" she called out, seeing a splash of rust-colored hair. She shoved her way through throngs of people, and disappointment coursed through her veins when she realized the tall red-haired man wasn't Adam. Unsure what to do next, she decided that she should just stick to their original plan—wait here, and hope that Adam would soon join her. She found a place to stand where she could observe people coming and going.

She continued to check her phone in case Adam called, but nothing so far. She knew that he had checked his bag containing his cell phone before the race had started. The runners were supposed to pick up their personal items at the end of the race, but had Adam been able to retrieve his belongings? Did he have his phone? Unsure of anything other than the mass confusion around her, Katherine left the crowded family meet-up tent. Determined to find Adam, she retraced her steps back to the finish line. So many people were gathered around, some shouting, some crying, others appearing to be in a daze. Sirens continued to blare; the closer she got to the finish line, the louder they became. The mass hysteria reminded her of the attack on the Twin Towers in New York on September 11th. Was this another attack on the country? Desperate to find out, she scanned the crowd for a police officer. Seeing a blue-uniformed Boston officer speaking to a small group, she hurried over to hear what he said.

"If you haven't located your friends and family, I suggest heading to the family tent. We're setting up more locations as

I speak. We hope to have more news soon and share it with the families waiting to find out where their loved ones are," he instructed.

Everyone began shouting out questions at once. The officer held his hand in the air. A Red Cross volunteer with a megaphone spoke to the crowd. "I know you all are concerned for your friends and family. We are doing our best to provide you with names of those injured and unaccounted for as soon as we have them. We'll meet at the family meeting tent as soon as we have more information to share."

Most of the crowd dispersed, heading to the tent. Katherine followed them. Checking her phone again to see if she'd received a call from Adam, she wasn't surprised when it showed no missed calls. She checked the settings to ensure the volume was as high as it could go, then quickly changed Adam's ringtone to the loudest, most annoying sound her phone offered. She was grateful she still had plenty of battery life left.

Walking back to the family meeting area, she was startled when her phone rang. It wasn't the tone she'd just changed for Adam. Sliding her finger across the screen, she answered.

"Hello?"

Chapter One

Katherine logged onto the Friendlink fan page for readers of her bestselling young adult series, "Girls with Unusual Powers." She wanted to see if her current work-in-progress, *Second Sight*, had generated any responses yet from her readers, who had seen the teasers on her website. She used the name *Bigfan216*, the numbers signifying the date she'd sold her first manuscript. Her identity had never been made public as far as she knew, so she felt safe enough using the numbers as part of her online handle.

This was her favorite time of the evening after a long day spent creating the series that had catapulted her pseudonym into bestseller status. K.C. Winston was a name she'd created for herself at the Burgess Hill Girls' School in Spain many years ago, when her parents no longer wanted her in the way of their world travels. Only twelve, she had been so frightened traveling alone, then spending almost five years of her life with girls who tormented her because she had a Southern drawl, teasing her to the point that her only refuge was at night when they slept. She wrote stories about strong girls with superpowers who were never made fun of or picked on. Girls she wanted to be, girls from Texas, girls from Louisiana who spoke as she did, and no one poked fun at them. She hid her spiral notebooks beneath her mattress, just like she had at home. She was always fearful they would be found while she attended class.

Katherine had been lucky. No one, not even nosy headmistress Griffith, had known of her secret stories. She knew many other girls complained to their parents about the headmistress sneaking in to look at their private possessions when they went home during holiday breaks. Katherine rarely went home during the breaks, so she knew for a fact the old woman did indeed prowl through their belongings. But she kept quiet for fear the mean headmistress would focus her wrath on her.

To Katherine, her years in Spain were a bad memory, but her entire childhood was dreadful. She'd spent her formative years with parents who ignored her and then the five years before college with classmates who bullied her. It had taken years of reading self-help books and online therapy to accept that she was lovable and kind. Katherine was grateful that part of her life was behind her, and her current lifestyle was not for the faint of heart. Extreme to most, it'd been her normal for more than seven years.

All those years ago, she'd waited for word of Adam during the chaos at the Boston Marathon. Sadly, he'd been one of the three killed by the homemade bombs. It was senseless— several people lost limbs, and lives were changed forever. She remembered when her phone rang and a police officer asked her to come to Massachusetts General Hospital. She had identified Adam's body, contacted his family members, and then, in a daze of grief and shock, she'd caught a taxi to take her to her apartment.

At home, she'd packed a few essentials and hit the road. She hadn't even attended Adam's funeral. It was all too much. She'd spent several days driving through states she'd never been to, not caring that she'd left her job at *The Boston Globe* and her apartment without a word. She owned the apartment and didn't need the job, though it was unlike her to act so irrationally. Eventually Katherine had needed to stop. She didn't care where, just that she had to find a safe place where no one would get hurt, where she could heal.

That place was Blowing Rock, North Carolina. Here, she'd finally had an emotional breakdown. She checked into a motel and just cried for three days. On the fourth day, emotionally exhausted, she decided Blowing Rock was as good a place as any to stay and try to start a new life. She'd contacted a real estate agent, told them exactly what she wanted, would accept nothing less, and that the price wasn't an issue. For once in her adult life, she was thankful to her parents for leaving her a fortune that would continue for as long as their company, Winston Refineries, located in Texas and Louisiana, continued to process the millions and millions of barrels of oil as it had for four generations before her. She could live in luxury and never want for anything. Katherine found her haven two days later—or so she thought. Once she'd unpacked her few possessions and opened her laptop to check her email, her face turned a ghostly white. It was him—the guy with the dark hair and eyes.

Dzhokhar Tsarnaev.

He and his older brother Tamerlan Tsarnaev had planted the bombs, injuring hundreds and killing three. How could she have known it was him that she'd glimpsed that day? At the time, she'd only wanted to find Adam. But now his face would haunt her forever.

The estate she now called home sat atop a small, private mountain overlooking the Blue Ridge Mountains. It had six bedrooms, five full baths, and a luxurious master suite with amenities fit for royalty. Her kitchen was massive, with a giant rock fireplace in the casual dining area. There also was a formal dining room with a ridiculously ugly table that would seat at least twenty or more, if desired. She'd immediately fallen in love with her new home, even the furniture it came with—minus the hideous dining room table. She'd made the house her home. The solid oak floors were buffed to a warm golden shade. She added colorful throw rugs throughout the downstairs and in the kitchen, where she spent most of her time. The large kitchen windows gave her a fabulous view of the vast mountain range. She'd purposely left all the downstairs windows unadorned, as she needed to see the view, the trees, the curve of the roads, and the outside world. She'd painted the kitchen cabinets a creamy antique white and added touches of green, with her various plants and herbs scattered on the many windowsills throughout her enormous kitchen. In the dining room and living area, she'd added personal touches here and there. A favorite blanket she'd had since childhood was tossed over the plush gray sofa.

Gardenia-scented candles she'd ordered from a local candlemaker filled the downstairs with the intoxicating scent when she lit them. On her desk was an eyeglass holder shaped like a dachshund, a gift from her editor at the *Globe*. She kept her computer glasses there when she wasn't working. She had no photos of her family or of Adam scattered around, as she'd put that part of her life behind her.

She loved her large home, which could've housed a big family. It was befitting a wealthy entrepreneur or even a president. It was private, the security system equal to that of the White House, or so she'd been told by the realtor when she'd purchased the mansion. She didn't believe her for a minute and had her new system installed immediately after she moved in.

Now her only family was Sam and Sophie, her two adopted German shepherds. They were siblings, abandoned by their mother, according to a post she'd run across during her nighttime chats on Friendlink. She'd taken down the number to call, and, sight unseen, she'd had the two pups delivered to her doorstep. That was four years ago. The brother and sister were better than a security system; plus they loved her unconditionally. Katherine returned their love tenfold. Wishing she'd had them when she'd first moved into the large home for both protection and companionship, she was grateful she'd read that ad, and now she couldn't imagine her life without them. She'd had nightmares for months after the bombing, and they continued to haunt her occasionally. But their intensity had lessened not long after Sam and Sophie entered her life.

When she bought her house, also sight unseen, she'd had the real estate agent outfit her new home with essential supplies that would last for at least a few weeks. The refrigerator was stocked with everything from Perrier mineral water to a dozen meal kits. Local wines were shipped in from the Biltmore Estate. Cheeses and jams were a lifesaver. When her supplies ran low, she prepared for her first visit to a locally owned grocery, the Apple Blossom Gourmet Market, another tidbit of information the realtor provided. She'd been down to three cans of lobster bisque soup and a few crackers. Craving something more substantial, Katherine decided it was time for a trip to the market. She could meet some locals and see where this new life journey had led her.

She'd made a list and checked her wallet to ensure she had enough cash on hand, as she didn't want to use a credit card with her birth name engraved on it for all to see. As she prepared to leave, she reached for the doorknob. Katherine turned the knob, and broke out in a cold sweat. Her heart rate increased, and it was hard to breathe. With the sound of blood rushing through her ears, her vision changed, narrowing as if she were looking through a pinhole, and then everything around her faded to black. When she came to, she was slumped on the floor and didn't know how long she had been out.

She was frightened by the experience, but that had been just the beginning. The feeling of impending doom and the rapid change in her ability to breathe became an almost daily event. Now Katherine understood the trigger. Each time she prepared to leave her home, intense fear prevented her from stepping over the threshold. She would get lightheaded, her arms and legs tingling. She'd been sure it was a heart problem. She'd scoured the Internet, searching for her symptoms. After hours of research, she concluded she was having anxiety attacks.

She'd tried joining an online therapy group but found that when others discussed their symptoms, she'd start to have them herself. Katherine tried talking with a therapist via Skype, but discontinued the sessions when he insisted that she had to face her fears and walk out of the house. She just wasn't ready for that. She'd tried yoga, hoping it would help her relax, but the attacks were so debilitating that she didn't have the physical strength to perform even the most basic yoga moves. Meditation helped relax her somewhat when she wasn't in the throes of panic. But she had no way to calm herself during an attack, and nothing helped. She resigned herself to living her life inside until she could control the attacks. They became less frequent once she made this decision. *Stay away from the damned door* became a mental mantra. She didn't venture out of the house since. Her ten-year-old Nissan remained in the garage to this day, untouched. And she'd never bothered to maintain it; she couldn't imagine herself using it. She should've had the car towed to a junkyard years ago.

For seven years, she'd lived as normally as anyone could, given her situation. She'd managed to purchase almost everything she needed on the Internet. She obtained a fake ID under a fake name: Kristine Cynthia Wingate. Because she used her initials on her books, only somewhat of a pseudonym, she'd convinced her accountant to set up a checking account in that name, though he was aware of her true identity. Kristine Wingate was the name any locals who delivered goods directly to her house knew her by. She used the fake name for the post office, UPS, and FedEx.

She could order her groceries at the Apple Blossom Gourmet Market and have them delivered within two hours. All of her clothes were ordered online. Sam and Sophie's needs were taken care of courtesy of Doc Baker, whom Katherine considered an old-time country vet, since he still made house calls. He never once questioned her lifestyle or why she never brought the dogs in to the clinic. His focus was always on the dogs, though Katherine suspected he knew she had issues.

One of the few people she had contact with, Doc Baker would text her his expected arrival time, so she knew when she heard a car that it was him. Not that Sam and Sophie didn't warn her with their excitement as they ran in circles around the house. They were so smart that she often thought they were humans disguised as dogs. They were smarter than many of the people she'd known throughout her life, which, sadly, weren't that many.

When she'd lived in Texas with her mother and father, they'd rarely had visitors other than her father's occasional business colleagues, including his assistant Helen, whom Katherine remembered because her mother didn't like her, and she made that clear to Katherine's father every time Helen came to their home. Most of the time, Katherine's parents had traveled the world using the seemingly unlimited fortune left to her father by his family.

Katherine remembered a series of nannies and housekeepers who took care of her. Audrey, her favorite housekeeper, had a daughter close to Katherine's age, and she brought her to work with her often enough that they became good friends. Katherine and Tracie played together and pretended they were sisters. She'd been around five or six then. Audrey would tell them they were close as two peas in a pod. Then Katherine was sent away to that horrid school in Spain. Tracie had been her only friend. She often wondered what had become of her and had tried to locate her, but her efforts proved fruitless, without having a surname to work with.

She had hated boarding school with a passion; the only positive from that time in Katherine's life were the stories she'd written and the success she'd achieved after spending all those years alone with her spiral notebooks. Sometimes she wished her parents had lived long enough to see what she'd made of herself. Audrey had been at their funeral, but without Tracie. Audrey and Katherine had spoken only briefly. Audrey had told her how proud she was, and that Katherine's parents would've been, as well, had they survived.

Katherine didn't believe that. She suspected they wouldn't have cared one way or another, because they were so self-absorbed. Their lives ended suddenly in a tragic accident. Katherine remembered getting the phone call from Audrey. Her parents were on safari in South Africa when a pride of lions attacked them and their guide. She was told her parents hadn't suffered during the attack, but to this day, she didn't believe that, given the way they'd died. Of course they had suffered. Only one person in their group had survived, and her understanding was that they were maimed so horribly, they barely looked human. Katherine didn't know who the other person on the tour was, and was never told anything else about this survivor, so Katherine had eventually put it out of her mind. She didn't like to think about her parents' ending. She had so many emotions, yet she put them in separate spaces and only occasionally did she allow herself to feel them. Katherine had experienced plenty of tragedies in her life. Some she'd never spoken of and never would. That was the past. Done and over with; she would not go there, though the images often plagued her when sleep wouldn't come.

A month after her parents' deaths, their attorney contacted her. Every single thing they'd owned was now hers. Cars, homes, investments, the Winston Refineries, all of it—lock, stock, and oil barrels. She wanted absolutely nothing from them, but knowing her father had hundreds of employees, she couldn't let the business collapse. She hired an attorney of her own to oversee everything. Lisa Pratt-Stevens knew the law upside down and backward, and Katherine trusted her. Lisa also knew publishing laws, and when Katherine was offered a contract for a second book, she asked Lisa to represent her. So far, she'd been a dream in promoting her writing career. She'd also placed a team of oil experts in Texas and Louisiana. The Winston Refineries were making millions daily. It was so much money that it boggled Katherine's mind.

Focusing on the present, she now directed her attention to the comments on her Friendlink fan page. Skimming through the few posts, she saw that the group was pretty quiet tonight.

Blondebookbabe: I heard the series was ending after the next book.

WHS524: I'm sure they're just rumors. I heard a movie was in the works. Want to bet who's right? I'm always right, girlies. I know more than you think.

HotandCool: You're a jerk, Walter. I say neither of you are right. As long as the books continue to sell, they'll be published.

Blondebookbabe: I think the author should have a book signing; meet us fans before calling it quits.

Bigfan216: I agree, HotandCool. Like why would the money dudes stop selling like the hottest books in the world?

WHS524: I know I would be at a book signing. In Texas or Louisiana, right, Bigfan216?

Bigfan216: WTF, Walter? Why would anyone in their right mind go to those garbage states? Wanna fill us in?

WHS524: Wouldn't you like to know? Well, the

weather is warm year-round, and I'm in Louisiana.
That's just my thoughts, okay, girlies?

Katherine was not comfortable with Walter's comments.
His reference to Texas and Louisiana alarmed her. Was it just
a coincidence that he named the two states where Winston
Refineries were located? Was he a fan, or some weirdo get-
ting his kicks off trying to scare her? She couldn't let her
Friendlink fans scare her.

Katherine reminded herself that her online handle said she
was only sixteen. A sophomore in high school. She couldn't
tell them she knew there would be more books in the future
because she'd recently signed another contract for four more
books. Which would be published as fast as she turned them
out. Lucky for her fans, she had absolutely nothing else in
her life besides Sam and Sophie. The series could continue
until the characters were married with their own children.
She read on.

WHS524: I agree with Blondebookbabe. K.C. Winston
needs to meet the fans. Didn't J.K. Rowling? And what's
with the initials? Don't they have real names?
Bigfan216: Who cares what the author's name is? I,
for one, couldn't care less.
HotandCool: Agree, Bigfan216. It's probably a team of
people, anyway. Has to be cuz no one can write that fast.

If they only knew how fast she cranked out the stories, it
would whet their appetites for more. And then she'd have to
write even faster.

The Friendlink fan page Katherine had created required
approval before anyone could join. Aware that people might
not be who they claimed to be, she had a list of criteria to be
met before she accepted their request to join the fan club.

They had to know at least two characters' names in the series and their special powers, and they had to have a second social media account with the same name they'd used to request to join her fan page. She knew it was silly. It wasn't a foolproof system, and it wouldn't be that difficult for anyone to join, but this attempt at security actually comforted her.

When Katherine created the Friendlink group, she'd posted her book covers, arranged in a collage, and added a photo of herself in the lower left corner of the fan page. She'd had the photo taken during her years at the *Boston Globe* when her hair was cut very short, and she'd been in her "blondes have more fun" stage. The photo was much too old and looked nothing like her now, which was perfect, since she did not want anyone to recognize her. Her publisher used the same photo on the books, and although they were wary when Katherine said she wouldn't do any media or events to promote the books, once the series proved successful, they gladly accommodated Katherine's special stipulations.

Her online persona was just as carefully created. Searching the web, Katherine had found a cutesy stock photo of a girl who looked around fifteen or sixteen, the average age of her readers, according to the demographics. The girl's face was turned slightly away from the camera, so it wasn't exactly a full-face shot, but enough to match the description she'd created for herself. Short blond hair, a heart-shaped face. Eye color could be blue, maybe hazel, as it was difficult to tell. Average-looking. Nothing like herself, as her hair was long and dark now, with streaks of silver throughout. Her light green eyes were her best feature. Katherine was tall, her features angular and sharp, courtesy of her father. The opposite of her online photo. When choosing this photo for her online persona, she made sure there were no funky-looking shirts, tattoos, piercings, or anything that could identify the girl as a stock image—at least Katherine hoped that was the case.

She'd created a simple profile that wouldn't be questioned. She'd added an Instagram account with the same profile picture and information, in case anyone chose to search the phony name she'd used, Darby Marie Whitton. According to her profile, Darby lived in Utah, went to public high school, and loved books. Generic enough, and no one had ever asked her for details. And why would they? She made sure her settings were private. She disabled the messenger, so if anyone tried to contact her privately, they would be out of luck. As moderator of the page, she decided who could join, though she had a different handle she used when monitoring: *TIC927.* It stood for "talk is cheap," and the 927 represented her old apartment number.

She scanned through a few more comments and found none of them interesting. About to click out of the page, she saw a new request for permission to join the group.

"Looks like we've got a newbie," she said out loud. Sophie lay curled up by her feet, Sam in his bed beside her desk, and both dogs gave a slight growl in answer. She swore they understood her.

She ran through the required info. Apparently klcLUV/007 had read her books. Katherine sent a link to the email address they provided. Once they opened the link, they would have to confirm they received her email and were then free to share their opinions of the books. Good or bad. Katherine truly did want to know if there were aspects of her work that needed improvement. Most of the chats seemed to be about the characters, though many times the members also chatted about her identity, the topic of this evening's discussion.

Waiting to see if klcLUV/007 joined the current chat, Katherine wasn't surprised when she saw the new user's picture pop up a few seconds later, after being accepted into the group. Her photo was the usual teen selfie. Pouty lips, chin tilted upward, eyes suggestive. Katherine thought this young girl was unusually pretty, though she wore too much makeup. She had green eyes and gorgeous copper-colored hair that fanned across her left shoulder. She reminded Katherine of someone, but she couldn't put a name to who it was.

> *klcLUV/007: Hi! I'm Karrie. Great to meet other K.C. Winston fans!!!*
> *WHS524: klcLUV/007, you just broke the rules. No names. Didn't you read the requirements?*

Katherine was curious to see where this conversation was headed. It was requested that they use a handle, but not required.

> *klcLUV/007: Oops, sorry! I read them. Can I stay? I love the girls in the series so much. I kinda feel like they're my friends! Puh-lease???*

Katherine smiled, because she felt that way, too, even though the characters were products of her own imagination.

> *WHS524: Not my decision. Have to wait and see if the moderator tosses you. You have to follow the rules or you'll be in hot water.*
> *Blondebookbabe: Let her stay. We don't care! The more, the merrier.*
> *Bigfan216: I second that! Welcome, klcLUV/007.*
> *klcLUV/007: Awesome, thanks! Does anyone know when the next book comes out? I looked on Amazon but didn't find anything!*

This new girl bubbled with enthusiasm. Katherine wondered if she was younger than she claimed. Katherine knew the art department had finished the cover design last week, and the bookstores should have it on their sites by the end of the week. Today being Wednesday, the fans didn't have long to wait before they could preorder her latest, which would be released the first Tuesday of next month, October.

>   ***HotandCool: Next month.***

Katherine had to hand it to HotandCool. She always knew when her books were released.

>   ***klcLUV/007: No way! That's too long to wait! I guess I'll reread*** **Charmed and Dangerous** ***again,***

she wrote, referencing the current release in the series.

>   ***Blondebookbabe: One of my favs! I love how Adriana gets even with that bitch, Elle!***
>   ***WHS524: Hey, watch your language, Blondebookbabe.***
>   ***Blondebookbabe: Kiss off! We can say whatever we want. Freedom of speech, buddy!***
>   ***klcLUV/007: LOL.***

Katherine didn't feel the need to step in as moderator just yet. They were all teenagers, at least according to their profiles. Let them speak freely. She truly did not want to censor them. Their words hardly warranted a reprimand. Katherine didn't recall the profile for WHS524, so she clicked a few keys and brought it up. If he'd been truthful, he was a middle-aged adult who lived in Baton Rouge, Louisiana, worked as a nurse, and knew her books inside and out. He definitely didn't fit the demographics of her average reader. She'd watch his comments. If he got too bossy, she'd kick him off the page. Easy-peasy.

>   ***WHS524: Keep your filth to yourself or else.***

Katherine perked up. While the "or else" wasn't quite a threat, she didn't think it was necessary.

Bigfan216: Let's cool it. This is a free speech zone for us to dream in. We're as badass as the girls. Don't want to get thrown off!

Purposely using "badass" to see if WHS524 would comment, Katherine waited, then saw he'd logged off. Good. She didn't need to intervene. The others saw he'd left the page, too.

Blondebookbabe: What a jerk! Maybe we should turn him into the moderator who ISN'T doing their job! Get rid of him. Probably a perv anyway!!!
HotandCool: I say keep him so we can mess with him!
klcLUV/007: HotandCool, you've got guts!
Blondebookbabe, I hope you aren't tossed off for cussing!
Bigfan216: She won't be. Cussing isn't a big deal anymore. I always say the f-word; it's lost its shock value. Sometimes, I say it in front of my foster parents, and they don't seem to care!!!
klcLUV/007: My dad grounds me if I say "damn"!

Good for her father, Katherine silently agreed. While she didn't want to encourage bad language, she hoped she'd elevated her level of coolness. She didn't use bad language unless she stubbed a toe or something, and then it was mild. Swearing was not her jam, but when she was Darby, she figured she probably would say the f-word in front of her parents.

Another *ping* sounded from her laptop. Another new member alert. She went through the usual steps processing another teenage girl's request. As expected, the new user joined the group a few seconds later by introducing themselves.

> *SKRfan4evr: Hey, fans!*
> *klcLUV/007: You're a soccer fan? Me too.*
> *SKRfan4evr: Yep, and a GWUP fan, big time! Can't wait for the next book to come out!*

GWUP. Katherine approved of the acronym. It was faster than typing "Girls with Unusual Powers." It was amazing that she'd created these characters that entertained so many people. Writing had made her happy for as long as she could remember—in a sense, it had saved her life—and it was gratifying to see how her writing made others happy, too.

> *HotandCool: Welcome, soccer girl! A new book is out next month.*

Katherine monitored the page a bit longer. Seeing that the girls were just chatting about the books, she logged off. She needed to feed Sam and Sophie and let them out. Someday she hoped to take them for long walks on her property. It had over a hundred acres and mountain streams filled with trout, and she dreamed of bringing the tasty fish home and eating what her land provided. Every once in a while, she tried to venture outdoors, but then a panic attack would hit her head on, forcing her to remain inside to live the solitary life she'd grown accustomed to.

Though she had lived alone all these years, Katherine sometimes felt like she was being watched, that there was someone or something outside her house, lurking in the dark. It might be an animal—most likely it was—but she felt the presence of something, and it spooked her. She never told this to Doc or the delivery people. They already thought she was odd. No sense letting them think she was crazy, too.

Not having contact with people other than Doc Baker, the mail carrier, and the FedEx and UPS employees was sad, yet they treated her kindly. She knew they wouldn't waste their time spying on her. Years ago, she'd explained her condition to the FedEx guys and girls and her mail carrier, who then told her UPS delivery folks. They'd accepted it and continued to deliver all she needed, placing her packages inside the doors she always kept unlocked. Often the delivery people would leave a little gift for her. A flowerpot for her herbs or packets of seedlings. Occasionally her mail carrier dropped off a bottle of local wine, always with a note attached. She so appreciated these small gestures of kindness. On holidays, she always made sure to have gifts for them and included a big bag of baked goods.

Katherine knew there was talk about her in town, especially among those who frequented the Apple Blossom Market. It was probably just normal small-town gossip, but it hurt when she read all the rumors posted on the Blowing Rock community website. The "crazy woman on the mountain," they called her. Honestly, she didn't blame them. Her life was weird, even though she'd learned to live quite comfortably. She understood the curiosity, the rumors. She'd probably do the same if she were in their place.

On her website, maintained by her publisher, there were hundreds of questions about the mysterious author. Gayle, her editor, told her not to look at the website. Of course that was impossible and unreasonable. So many times, Katherine was tempted to answer their questions. Gayle said the mystery surrounding her helped sell more books and helped to keep her employed. Katherine couldn't attest to this one way or another, yet it didn't prevent her from fantasizing about book tours and meeting those who read her books in person. *Someday*, she told herself.

Sam and Sophie followed her to the kitchen. She opened the French doors so they could romp outside while she prepared their food for the evening. She fed the big dogs organic kibble, adding duck, chicken, and organic eggs to the mix. A local farm Doc had recommended delivered the frozen ducks and chicken once a week. Both dogs weighed around seventy-five pounds and had hearty appetites. Providing them with proper nutrition came at a price, though this mattered little to her. It would've been difficult for her to maintain their top-notch diets had she not had a fortune left to her.

Once she'd started earning enough to sustain her large home and the needs of the dogs and herself, she refused to touch the millions of dollars that continued to flow in from the refineries in Texas and Louisiana. Her attorney, Lisa Pratt-Stevens, handled all business-related issues associated with the family estate and knew where to invest the profits. Katherine wanted no part of her inheritance at this stage of life. When the time came, she'd donate every last cent to charity or maybe Doc's clinic.

Sam and Sophie bounded back inside, tongues hanging out of their mouths. "Drink your water," Katherine said, and pointed to their bowls. The pair almost always waited for her instructions. They lapped up the water, then focused on the hefty portions of food in their bowls. Chomping, then licking, every morsel from their dishes, they stared at her, knowing they'd now get their evening treat. Katherine gave them each a natural beef strip, watching as they carried them over by the French doors she'd left open. The breeze cooled her as she stood before the doors, the fresh mountain air swirling, daring her to step outside to experience what she'd been unable to enjoy, always fearing the darkness that came over her.

Maybe, she thought as she watched Sam and Sophie gnawing on the treats, *just one tiny step*. The open doors led to a large deck with a staircase leading to the second floor. Katherine stood in the evening shadows. The sky was fading to a dark blue, with pink and peachy colors that couldn't be replicated. The stars would be out tonight. The season was beginning to change. She watched as the fiery red ball disappeared behind the rolling mountains. *Stunning*, she thought as she stared at nature's beauty. Wanting so badly to learn the trails, the animals, and what kind of trees were on her property, she slowly made her way closer so that she stood at the edge of the wood flooring, her feet mere inches from the deck. Her heart rate had already increased, and her hands trembled. She quickly stepped inside, away from the doors, and her heart returned to its normal rhythm after a few minutes.

Not yet. It was too frightening. Remembering the crowds as she had raced through the chaos of the Boston Marathon bombings, she knew it was at the root of her illness. Her online therapist had concluded this, too, and had encouraged her to start running marathons herself. Katherine no longer consulted her after this. She thought it was cruel to even suggest it. She'd read dozens of books on anxiety, panic attacks, and stories of those who'd fought and won the battle. She knew it could be done, knew she had to push through her fear . . . yet couldn't. It was so frightening to feel that way. It was easier to stay inside, where she was comfortable and under control.

Her thoughts made her nervous. She returned to the kitchen and made a cup of tea, taking it to the living room. She sat on the gray plush sofa, placed her tea on the side table, and motioned for Sam and Sophie to join her. They jumped up onto the sofa, each settling into their usual spot, one on either side of her. "So this is it?" she said. She knew they didn't understand her words, but also knew that they felt her emotions. Sam placed a giant paw on her lap, tilting his head as if in question. Sophie whined, moving even closer to her. She wrapped an arm around each furry neck. "What would I do without you two?"

Two soft grumbles were her answer.

"My two kiddies." She fluffed them both between the ears. "I say it's time we called it a night. I've got a brand-new book waiting for me." She finished her tea, then took her mug to the kitchen, washed it with hot soapy water, rinsed it three times, and finally put it upside down on the drainboard. If she allowed herself, she'd rinse the damn cup five times, then still worry that she hadn't rinsed off all the dish detergent. The beginnings of OCD, something she'd started a few months ago. Katherine could let this go; she knew she could. It was only a damn cup.

Enough was enough.

Chapter Two

After a hot shower, Katherine settled down with the book she wanted to read. Both dogs slept at the foot of her massive bed. She didn't care if this was normal or not. She wanted them close to her, and they never bothered her when she slept. Engrossed in the story, she jerked her attention away from her book when both Sam and Sophie suddenly leapt off the bed. Sam's bark was loud, continuous, and ear-piercing. He bolted out of the bedroom, Sophie trailing him. Katherine tossed the book aside and followed the shepherds downstairs.

"Hey, you two, calm down," she called out as she walked across the living room into the kitchen. Their deep, frantic barking continued. "Quiet!" she commanded, raising her voice. Neither dog stopped, their deep guttural growls alarming her.

Wanting to make sure she'd armed the security system, Katherine checked the control panel in the kitchen. It read ARMED.

"Okay, nothing there," she said to the dogs. They were now panting, running back and forth from the kitchen to the living room, and still growling.

It was probably a rabbit or a deer, Katherine told herself. Possibly even a bear. She'd seen all kinds of wild animals on her property through the windows, though never a bear, and they had never bothered the dogs. Having had no problem with wildlife for seven years, why now? Was it the mating season? She should know this.

She flipped a switch, flooding the circumference of the house with bright light. Peering through the French doors, she didn't see an animal of any kind, didn't hear any wild pigs snorting, no buck bellowing. The dogs continued to emit a low growl, teeth displayed, drool dripping from their mouths.

"Sam, Sophie, down!" Katherine used her hand to indicate *down*, and both dogs sat, but she could see it was hard for them. She refilled their water bowls. "Drink your water."

They reluctantly obeyed. They never acted this way. She checked the control panel again, ran upstairs to her bedroom, grabbed her cell phone, and then went back to the kitchen. Both dogs had settled, but their pupils were dilated, a glassy look she'd never seen before. Had they gotten into something when she'd let them out earlier? Wouldn't they have had symptoms earlier? Alarmed enough by their actions, she accessed the outside surveillance cameras through her phone. She would be able to see if anything or anyone were still out there. Between the seven cameras, one at each entrance, she saw nothing unusual. Glancing at the time, she decided it wasn't too late to send Doc Baker a text. Unsure of what was happening with her best friends, she wanted to ensure they were okay. She texted:

Dogs are a bit hysterical. I'm concerned. K.

Seconds later, her cell phone rang.

"Hey, kiddo, what's up with those two ornery pooches?" Doc asked.

"I'm not exactly sure." She explained how they'd jumped out of bed and their wild barking.

"Can you FaceTime me and let me have a look at them?"

The wonders of technology never ceased to amaze her. Without them, she'd probably be institutionalized.

"Sure," she said. "Let me call you back." She hit the camera icon on her phone, and a few seconds later, Doc Baker's face filled her screen. "Hi, Doc. Sorry to be such a pain in the butt, but I've just never seen this behavior from either dog before. Here, have a look." She reversed the camera's view so he could see both dogs.

"Bring it a bit closer to their eyes, kiddo," he said.

She held the phone close to Sam, then Sophie.

"You had any troubles at your place? Them big pupils make me think they might feel threatened or scared."

"I didn't think German shepherds scared that easily."

"As a rule, they're pretty darned courageous. I'm just guessing, but from what you say, and those pupils, I'd say they're afraid. Now, I can't be sure without actually seeing them in the flesh, or fur in their case, but I'm pretty good at this kinda thing. So let's diagnose the pooches as scaredy cats . . . dogs." He chuckled.

"I trust you, so I'll just . . ." Katherine looked at both animals. "I don't know, keep a close eye on them."

"Give 'em a treat and a good rub. That'll calm 'em down. I'll stop by in the morning, check them over, have a look around, see if I spot anything unusual."

"I'd appreciate it," she said. "Thanks, Doc. I'll see you in the morning."

"You bet."

Katherine observed both dogs. They were uneasy, to say the least. She took two beef sticks and gave one to each, but they didn't seem to be as excited as they normally were when she gave them this special treat. "Hey, it's okay," she said, running her hand along their backs, between their ears. Sam whined while Sophie carried her beef stick to the bottom of the staircase, where she gobbled it up in a few bites.

Somewhat calmed, Katherine wondered what had caused

them to behave so oddly. She'd never seen them act fearful. Though she didn't go outside with them, she always kept the French doors open so she could watch out for them. Was it time she forced herself to go outside and watch them? The mere thought frightened her so much that her heart started racing. "Not now," she said to herself. Sometimes talking helped calm her down. It didn't matter that she spoke to the dogs, didn't matter what words came out of her mouth; for whatever reason, it took her focus off the physical sensations she felt when stressed. Other times she would go so far as to pinch herself so hard it brought tears to her eyes. She'd bruised herself more than she cared to admit.

Checking the control panel in the kitchen yet again to en-sure it was on, she shut the outside lights off. Most likely the dogs had heard a wild animal in distress or a bear close by. Being in the Great Smoky Mountains, bears were common-place, despite her never spotting one. Either way, she was ex-hausted and hoped Doc Baker could figure things out in the morning. "Come on, you two—let's go back upstairs."

Having finished their treats, the dogs guzzled the rest of the water in their bowls before following her upstairs. Katherine found it hard to relax, even though both dogs were now calm, resting at the foot of her bed. She tried to pick up where she'd left off in her book but couldn't concentrate, reading the same paragraph over and over. Tossing the book aside, she took her cell phone from the nightstand and clicked on the app for the security cameras. One by one, she viewed the videos that were automatically sent to a website every hour for backup. She saw nothing out of place. With a hundred plus acres, the surveillance cameras didn't cover her entire property. Sam and Sophie rarely, if ever, ran too far from the house, not that she watched their every move. She clicked out of the app, satisfied no wild animals were close to her property line.

Restless, Katherine knew sleep was out of the question.

She still kept a spiral notebook, though she didn't have to hide it under the mattress now. Taking the red notebook from her nightstand and flipping through the pages, she read through a rough outline for the book she would start next. Disciplined, she could finish a rough draft in a month. Another week or two for an edit, then she was on to the next story. Satisfied with the outline, she glanced at the time and saw that it was after midnight.

She grabbed her phone, opened the Friendlink app, and went to her fan page. Maybe she'd find someone there to talk to. A message immediately popped up.

klcLUV/007: Hi! Can't sleep either?

Katherine smiled and typed back:
Nope. Have a lot of homework tonight.
klcLUV/007: My dad makes me do homework the second I walk through the door!
Bigfan216: Wow! That's not right! Why?

Katherine waited several seconds for an answer. Maybe klcLUV/007 had decided it was none of her business.

klcLUV/007: I dunno, he's always been this way since my mom has been gone.
Bigfan216: Parents divorced?

Breaking her own rules by asking personal questions, she found she couldn't help herself. She was curious.

klcLUV/007: No.
Bigfan216: Sorry, not my biz!
klcLUV/007: It's okay. I lost my mom a while ago. I still miss her. Hope you don't think I'm a big baby! I do miss her, though.

She knew exactly how losing a parent at a young age felt. No matter how absent her parents had been, she still felt their loss. They had been very different people, but you didn't get to choose your parents, and she had tried to mourn them in her own way.

> *Bigfan216: I'm so sorry. I don't think you're a baby at all. Both of my parents are gone.*

Too much info? Probably, yet for whatever reason, she truly felt bad for this girl.

> *klcLUV/007: OMG, I am so so sorry. It sucks, huh?*
>
> *Bigfan216: It was a long time ago. I don't like to think about them much. Does that make me a horrible person?!?!*
>
> *klcLUV/007: Absolutely not! Between us, I wish my dad had died instead of my mom. Does that make me a horrible person too?!?! I wasn't even allowed to go to her funeral!!!*
>
> *Bigfan216: Wow, that's not right. Is your dad a jerk?*
>
> *klcLUV/007: Beyond, especially now.*
>
> *Bigfan216: How so?*
>
> *klcLUV/007: Money. He's got big ideas and thinks he's about to hit the jackpot. He's weird that way.*
>
> *Bigfan216: So he has a lot of $$$?*
>
> *klcLUV/007: He says he's got an inheritance or some bull. I'm not sure I believe him!!!*
>
> *Bigfan216: Send $$$ my way if he does! LOL*
>
> *klcLUV/007: Maybe. LOL*
>
> *Bigfan216: Not serious!*
>
> *klcLUV/007: I kinda wish you were! Serious, I mean.*

Katherine wasn't sure what line she was about to cross. Too wired to worry about it, she decided Darby would straight out ask the question.

Bigfan216: What do you mean by serious?
*klcLUV/007: I'm getting sleepy. I talk too much. I'll
TTYL.*
Bigfan216: Wait, don't go!
*klcLUV/007: Sorry, I'm just looking for new friends. I
love all the books for real, though I was hoping I could make
a friend, ya know? One I could call, like if I needed to.*
*Bigfan216: Okay, I'm cool with that. I'm here a lot. We
can be friends.*
klcLUV/007: I mean outside of here, the fan page.

She mentally kicked herself for getting too involved in this
chat. She was a thirty-seven-year-old woman, and now she
was concerned about this young girl who, it appeared, needed
a friend. She knew how it felt; it's what inspired her writing
all those years ago when she was alone, possibly not unlike
klcLUV/007.

Bigfan216: Depends.
klcLUV/007: ???
Bigfan216: Where we live!
klcLUV/007: Duh, that makes sense.

She would check her profile thoroughly later and see what,
if anything, she could find out about this girl.

Bigfan216: No worries.
klcLUV/007: Where do you live?
Bigfan216: Utah.

Lying didn't come easy for Katherine, but she could not reveal her location or true identity.

klcLUV/007: Wow! Far away from me! I'm in Texas.
Bigfan216: For sure. We can email.
klcLUV/007: Send pics!

She expected this at some point and had an iron-clad excuse prepared as to why she couldn't send photos, or "pics," to her new "friend."

> *Bigfan216: camera on my crappy laptop is broken!*
> *klcLUV/007: really? Don't you have a cell phone?*
> *Bigfan216: No $$$ for one. Foster parents can't afford it.*
> *klcLUV/007: Sorry. I didn't know you were in foster care. Is it terrible?*
> *Bigfan216: Not so bad. They're friendly, just broke!*

Lies seemingly rolled from her easily. She didn't like this, but she had no one to blame but herself for stepping outside the boundaries she'd created when she formed this page. Though, in her defense, she'd never said that you couldn't reveal your name or where you lived. It was only suggested that they only use their handles when they were on the page, as WHS524 had reminded them all earlier.

> *klcLUV/007: I can send you $$$? I have $$$ saved!*
> *Bigfan216: No, but thanks. I have a part-time job. I'm saving up for the new iPhone that just came out.*
> *klcLUV/007: Same here. I work at a hair salon on Saturdays. I want to open my own salon! Going to start cosmetology classes as soon as I graduate.*
> *Bigfan216: Awesome!*
> *klcLUV/007: What about you?*
> *Bigfan216: Maybe a veterinarian? No $$$, but there's always school loans!*

Where had that come from? Possibly her earlier dealings with Doc Baker?

> *klcLUV/007: Wow! A doctor. You must be super smart. Any pets?*

Bigfan216: LOL, still trying to figure that out! I have two dogs.

She didn't see any harm in telling her she had two dogs. She didn't have to reveal what breed of dog or their names.

klcLUV/007: Dad won't let me have a pet.
Bigfan216: What a jerk!
klcLUV/007: Right! He's not a nice guy. Really. If you only knew.
Bigfan216: What are you saying?
klcLUV/007: Just that he's super mean to me, more since Mom died.

Fearing this young girl might be in a bad situation that technically was none of her business, Katherine decided she would keep up with her on Friendlink. One never knew what went on behind closed doors. She'd experienced it herself, though never any physical abuse. But she'd been mentally and emotionally abused as a child. Katherine often wondered if that was worse.

She wanted to end the conversation and tell klcLUV/007 she was tired. It was after one in the morning. But she held back, because she needed to ensure the girl wasn't in actual danger. How she planned to do this, she hadn't a clue.

Bigfan216: Are you, like, safe?
klcLUV/007: I think so! He's strict as hell. He only gets mad when I don't follow his rules.
Bigfan216: Does he hurt you?

It took so long for her to respond that Katherine thought she wouldn't answer her question at all.

klcLUV/007: Sometimes.
Bigfan216: He hits you?

klcLUV/007: It's not that bad. He's just a jerk
sometimes.
   Bigfan216: Jerk or not, it's against the law!

Katherine waited for a reply. Nothing. Five minutes later, she saw klcLUV/007—Karrie—had logged off. Fearing Karrie's father had somehow read the comments about him and taken his anger out on her, Katherine quickly scanned klcLUV/007's profile information. She hoped she'd broken the rules and included her phone number. But there was only an email address. Before she changed her mind, Katherine typed an email to Karrie.

> To: klc16@gmail.com
> From: DMW@yahoomail.com
> It's me, Bigfan216. Darby. Are you okay? I think I scared you off. Sorry. Just concerned.
> XOXO,
> Darby

It had been an eventful night. Katherine was about to close her laptop when her computer pinged, letting her know she'd received a new email. She logged back into her email account and saw she had a reply from Karrie.

> To: DMW@yahoomail.com
> From: klc16@gmail.com
> I'm okay. No worries.
> TTYL,
> Karrie

Katherine wrote back immediately.

To: klc16@gmail.com
From: DMW@yahoomail.com
I am worried! Are you sure you're not in immediate
danger? I can call the police for you.
XOXO,
Darby

She knew she probably came across as an adult in her
emails. It didn't matter. If the girl was in trouble, she could at
least alert the authorities. Waiting for a reply, she chewed her
nails, a bad habit she should've outgrown by now. Her fingertips were always sore, as she bit her nails down to the
quick and sometimes picked at her cuticles until they bled.
Fifteen minutes passed. Sure that Karrie wouldn't reply to
her email, Katherine logged off and shut her laptop down.
Her day hadn't been this exhausting in a long time.

She lay in bed, troubled. Uneasy, she turned off the lamp,
trying to fall asleep. A million thoughts raced through her
head. With daylight approaching, she drifted off, only to be
awakened by Sam and Sophie's barking.

Chapter Three

"I'll be right there," Katherine called out, hearing someone knocking on the kitchen door. That must be why the dogs were barking. She pulled on a pair of jeans she'd tossed on the chair last night along with a gray T-shirt. After hurriedly dressing, she ran downstairs, both dogs on her heels.

Doc Baker tapped on the drape-less French doors.

"Sorry. I was up most of the night," Katherine explained, opening the door. She really should consider blinds or some other type of window covering. *I couldn't hide if I wanted to,* Katherine thought as she stood aside. "Come on in." Sam and Sophie danced around the vet, tails wagging so fast they created a breeze. "Looks like they're happy to see you," Katherine said.

Doc Baker was probably in his late sixties and was in excellent physical condition. He was tall with broad shoulders, a full head of silver hair, and bright blue eyes that lit up when he smiled. Time had been good to him.

He stooped down and held one hand out for the dogs, offering them a treat. When they gobbled it up, he used his free hand to get a hold of Sam. Doc reached into his shirt pocket for a penlight and quickly examined Sam's eyes. Once satisfied, he removed another treat from his pocket, and held it out to Sophie. Always eager for treats from Doc Baker, she approached him, enabling him to check out her eyes, too. His examination complete, he took out two more treats and tossed them high in the air. "Good pups." He always referred to them as *pups*, even though they were four years old.

"So, what do you think?" Katherine asked him.

Shaking his head side to side, he said, "Their pupils are normal, no glassiness in the eyes. I'll stand by what I said last night. Something probably scared them."

Katherine nodded. "I've never seen them act that way before. Reminded me of a wild animal."

"Could be that's what scared them. You said they were sleeping, then went a bit cuckoo?"

She nodded.

"They hear sounds humans can't. I'd hazard a guess and say they heard a wild animal. Maybe it hurt their ears, and they reacted. I will look around the property and see what, if anything, is out there. Tracks, carnage. I'll be back shortly. You've got a lot of land to cover, but I'll search closest to the house. You said they'd been out back earlier? Their usual jaunt out those doors?" He nodded toward the French doors. He'd spent time outside with the pair many times before, so knew their habits.

"I always let them out through these doors and can usually see them from the kitchen and the office windows." The fact that she didn't know their exact outdoor routine once they were out of her sight hung in the air.

Doc Baker nodded his head. "We'll talk when I'm back."

"I'll make breakfast," Katherine said, smiling. She was grateful for someone other than herself to prepare a meal for. Adam was the last man she'd cooked for.

"I'll take ya up on that offer," Doc said before heading out.

Katherine spent the next half hour preparing brioche French

toast, crispy bacon, and fluffy scrambled eggs. Lastly, she made a whole pot of coffee, knowing Doc Baker was a coffee connoisseur just like her. She wasn't a huge breakfast lover, but she did enjoy the smell of frying bacon, and the coffee sent a pleasant aroma throughout her kitchen.

Doc Baker tapped on the door, then came inside, both dogs tagging behind him. "I didn't find a thing—no tracks, no evidence of a wild animal. Nothing human, either."

Startled, Katherine put down the pot of coffee she held. "What do you mean 'human'?"

"Just what I said. There's nothing out there. No tire tracks where the dogs romp around, no footprints."

"That's reassuring," she told him, even though it didn't do much to settle her nerves. That persistent feeling of someone watching her still bothered her, but she didn't think it warranted mentioning. Just one more thing to add to her list of issues.

She handed him a mug of coffee and nodded toward the kitchen's large island. "Have a seat." She handed over a plate piled high with eggs, several slices of bacon, and a stack of French toast.

"If I ate like this every day, I think I'd be in trouble. Looks delicious." He dug into his food, stopping to wash it down with coffee. When he finished, he placed a hand on his stomach. "This'll do me until dinner."

Katherine grinned. "Glad you enjoyed it."

He took his empty plate to the sink, rinsed it off, then put it on the drainboard. She'd rewash and rinse his dishes later.

"So, K"—Doc always called her that—"tell me what's going on with this staying-in-the-house business. I've known you for four years, and you've never brought the dogs into my clinic. I always bring them myself."

Her face turned ten shades of red. She thought he knew the extent of her disorder. Apparently, he didn't.

He held both palms out. "I know the medical terms, kiddo. As a friend, I'd like to offer my help. I've got a buddy in Asheville. He was my roommate in college, and we've been friends ever since. He practices psychiatry. Kind of like me, he makes house calls. You wanna talk to him?"

Visions of a doctor trying to persuade Katherine to leave her home were too much. Instantly her throat was dry, and she could barely swallow. She just shook her head.

"You probably don't need to hear this, but I was a medical doctor before I became a veterinarian. Found I liked animals a lot more than humans." He watched her carefully. "Here." He pulled out a barstool. "Calm down. I'll get you some water."

Wanting him to leave, she now regretted her spur-of-the-moment invitation. She did as instructed and took a sip of water, despite how difficult it was to swallow. Embarrassed, she looked away when he made eye contact.

"K, I'd better scoot. Though promise me you'll think about this?"

Finally focusing her gaze on his, she nodded. "It's not a choice," she whispered as he turned away.

He nodded before leaving through the open doors.

But it was *a choice*, she thought after he'd left. She chose to stay away from the outside world, finding comfort in the cocoon she'd created for herself, one she felt relatively happy with. Technology made her life livable. She had everything she needed, minus a relationship. After her experience with Adam, having a man in her life wasn't a top priority, though she often wondered if her life would've been different had Adam survived the bombing. They'd discussed marriage and in general terms if they wanted children, topics couples discussed as the relationship progressed. Theirs hadn't been a long relationship, though it'd been intense in a good way.

Focusing on Sam and Sophie, Katherine gave each a good

scratch between the ears. She was unsure if she should leave the kitchen doors open, giving them free rein to run in and out as normal. Thinking better of it, she shut the doors with her foot, continuing to give her dogs attention.

"You two have to stay with me today," she said, before returning to the kitchen. She washed Doc Baker's plate, cup, and flatware five times and still felt she needed to repeat the process. But she stopped herself before she reached for the plate yet again. This was insane. She vowed she wouldn't allow this excessive dishwashing to become another uncontrollable habit. She was sure that she could do this on her own; she didn't need a physician to tell her it was abnormal.

After tidying the kitchen, she went to her office, which was also the dining room. She supposed she could have used one of the bedrooms as an office, but they remained empty to this day. Having her office here, she could see straight through to the kitchen and the living room. Because one of the dining room walls had floor-to-ceiling windows, she positioned her desk so she had a view of the incredible Blue Ridge Mountains. Fall was her favorite season. She would gaze at the mountains with all of their jewel-toned colors. She often spent hours staring out the windows. It kept her from feeling claustrophobic. She felt fine looking outside, even opening the doors. She just could not bring herself to put one foot out the door. Every time she tried, it was always the same ending. Living alone, she couldn't risk another blackout. She had to remain alert at all times, because for years, she felt like she was being watched. *Crazy*, she thought. "Enough, Katherine," she said out loud.

Booting up her laptop, she clicked on her calendar, a practice she'd yet to give up, knowing exactly what plans she had for today—paying bills. Most days were the same as the ones before. Katherine paid her electricity bill, her cell-phone bill, and the company that monitored her security system. All of this came at a price, and she knew she'd gone a bit overboard on the security system. But it kept her safe, and that's all that mattered.

Her thoughts drifted back to the night before. She closed out the calendar and opened her email, wondering if Karrie had responded to her last message. Scanning through dozens of emails advertising everything from sunscreen to organic beans, she deleted them. There was nothing from Karrie, so she opened her Friendlink fan page to see if she was online. She was probably in class, though most kids had cell phones, and Katherine knew they were allowed to bring them to school. Suddenly a message from another user popped up.

> *HotandCool: Hey girl, what's up?*
> *Bigfan216: School.*
> *HotandCool: Utah starts early!*

Katherine had forgotten about the time difference.

> *Bigfan216: Getting ready, I mean. Makeup, hair, takes 4evr!*
> *HotandCool: I gotcha.*

While Katherine appreciated the conversation, she wished Karrie would log on. More than a bit concerned after last night, she could only hope the poor girl's emails hadn't been discovered by her father. If she was being truthful about his abuse, who knew what could have happened. Why Katherine had involved herself in her fan's issues last night was beyond her, other than sheer loneliness. She typed another message.

> *Bigfan216: Super long hair, it takes a lot of time!*

She realized her mistake, but before she could delete her comment, she saw the gray dots indicating HotandCool was responding.

> *HotandCool: Pic shows hair very short!*
> *Bigfan216: It's from a couple of years ago. Acne is too bad now; no pics!*

Karrie logged on.

> *HotandCool: hi!*
> *klcLUV/007: hi back!*
> *Bigfan216: hey, friend!*

Katherine added "friend," wanting to remind Karrie of their conversation last night.

> *klcLUV/007: hey, y'all at school?*

She wasn't going to respond to that question. She'd screwed up already talking about her long hair.

> *HotandCool: Study hall!*
> *klcLUV/007: I'm home, I feel crappy.*
> *Bigfan216: Like crappy how? You got a cold or something?*
> *klcLUV/007: cramps.*
> *HotandCool: sorry, not good.*
> *Bigfan216: ugh, that sucks.*
> *klcLUV/007: part of being female. Guys couldn't handle it! :>)*
> *SKRfan4evr: What's up? I'm in English class. booorrring!*
> *HotandCool: klcLUV/007 has her period. Cramps. She gets to skip school.*
> *SKRfan4evr: Cool, at least ur not pregnant!*
> *klcLUV/007: Not hardly!!!*
> *HotandCool: I think klcLUV/007 is a V-I-R-G-I-N!!!!*
> *Bigfan216: Not our biz.*

> **WHS524:** *You're all disgusting. This is a book discussion page only—no personal issues allowed. I'm reporting all of you to the moderator. You all act like whores.*
> **HotandCool:** *Hey, screw off, old man. Yeah, I read your profile. WTF are YOU doing here?*

Katherine considered switching to her other profile used for moderating but didn't think she'd use it just yet. These were kids expressing themselves in their own way. She agreed with HotandCool. Why *was* an older man on her fan page? While she appreciated readers of all ages worldwide, he was bossy. She decided then that she wasn't very fond of WHS524, but she'd let him slide for now.

> **WHS524:** *You're all disgusting. I'll make sure every one of you is removed from this page! You just wait.*
> **SKRfan4evr:** *whatcha gonna do, old man? Delete us??? Hunt us down and eat us alive?*
> **Bigfan216:** *I say we forget this conversation!!! He's just tryin' to piss us off.*
> **klcLUV/007:** *I agree with Darby, uh, Bigfan216. Sorry!*

So much for using handles.

> **Bigfan216:** *No worries, but let's stick to using handles. Who knows what that creep is gonna do?*
> **WHS524:** *That's enough. You wait, all of you!*

He logged off then. Unsure if she should take his words as a threat, Katherine decided she would block him if he continued his insults.

Katherine wanted to steer the conversation away from that creep and lighten the mood.

> *Bigfan216: Frig him. He's outta here! I wanna talk about BOOKS!*
> *klcLUV/007: I'm reading* **Frankenstein** *again!*
> *Bigfan216: Creepy!*
> *SKRfan4evr: Saw that old movie once! Never read the book.*
> *Blondebookbabe: Hey chickies!! What's happenin'???*
> *HotandCool: We're talking about books!*
> *klcLUV//16: I'm reading* **Frankenstein,** *BOO!*
> *Blondebookbabe: Awesome. I read that last year. Saw the movie too.*
> *Bigfan216: Don't like horror books or movies.*

That was true. It was probably the only time she'd been completely honest since forming the page a few years ago. For some reason, she felt comfortable among these girls. She'd had fans come and go, but this group seemed tight, like they'd cover one another's backs if need be—a real-life group of Girls with Unusual Powers.

> *SKRfan4evr: I'll scope it out next library visit. I'll kill myself if we don't get the next GWUP soon!!!*
> *klcLUV/007: Don't say that! We'd miss you here.*
> *SKRfan4evr: Duh, it's a figure of speech.*
> *klcLUV/007: You never know. Suicides happen.*
> *SKRfan4evr: Frig that! I'm not suicidal. I'm "dying" for the next book in the series. Geez!!!*
> *klcLUV/007: Sorry, I lost someone I cared about that way. I'm PARANOID!!!!*

Katherine felt terrible for Karrie, but a discussion about suicide wasn't something she thought appropriate, at least not on this forum. It should be discussed at school or with their parents. They were young girls—at least, she hoped they were. Possibly some were vulnerable, so she felt the topic needed to go in another direction.

> *Bigfan216: Sorry, this topic is too morbid for me. What about boys?!?!?*
> *HotandCool: My fav! Except for GWUP!*
> *Blondebookbabe: Me too. I've met the hottest senior! OMG, he's to die for. Oops! Sorry about that.*
> *SKRfan4evr: how hot is hottest?!*
> *Blondebookbabe: all the way hot!*

Katherine couldn't help but laugh. These girls were fun; she'd bet they were a little wild. She liked them, and it didn't matter that they were only names on her computer screen. She felt like they were her friends. She would make sure to check in several times daily. Katherine worried about Karrie; with her mother gone and having lost a friend to suicide, she truly did need someone to confide in. Deciding the current subject matter was better left to teenagers, she logged off and would check in later.

What a sad life, Katherine thought after she'd closed the app. Depending on the Internet for everything wasn't the life she'd planned, yet here she was, alone in a mansion. Of course she knew things could change if she tried working through her fears. She remembered reading a book about it: *Feel the Fear and Just Go for It*. Maybe it was time to take all the advice she'd gathered throughout the years and put it to use. She needed to learn Sam and Sophie's stomping grounds, literally. After last night, it made sense. Katherine couldn't imagine her life without them. They'd helped her in so many ways. She owed it to them to protect them as best she could.

With that thought in mind, she closed the laptop and hurried upstairs to her room. Inside her closet, she found a pair of sneakers that had to be at least a decade old, though they looked fairly new. White Nikes. She remembered buying them in Boston. She'd kept them in her locker at the gym. She would work out almost daily, feeling a rush of endorphins afterward. If only she could do that now. With all the property she owned, it would take a lot of running to familiarize herself with her land, and she'd for sure wear out her sneakers. Just thinking about it made her feel jumpy and on edge, though oddly enough, she had no anxiety. Before she lost this sudden surge of confidence, she slid her feet into her sneakers, and, as she tied them, Sam and Sophie sniffed them. "I do have shoes, ya know," she teased the dogs. They were used to her Ugg slippers, which she always ordered from the website. She'd forgotten what a good-fitting pair of sneakers felt like. Sam and Sophie trailed alongside her to the kitchen, where the scent of bacon and coffee lingered. After Katherine opened the French doors, both dogs raced outside, as was their routine.

Did she really believe she could walk outside?

She stood in front of the open doors, a cool mountain breeze enticing her, tempting her. It was nearing the end of September, and the trees were starting to show off their vibrant colors. She so desperately wanted to go outside, walk along her property line, jump in piles of leaves, roast marshmallows, and do what normal people did. Without further thought, she took a small step out onto the deck, farther than she'd ever been.

Waiting for the onslaught of physical sensations to hit her, Katherine only felt a mild tightening in her throat. She was conscious of her heartbeat, but didn't feel the usual rapid pounding in her chest. She daringly took another step farther out, when all the familiar symptoms of an anxiety attack suddenly forced her back inside. Closing the doors, she slid to the floor, frightened. She began to sweat, her hands trembling. She wrapped her arms around her knees, trying to still them. The room spun like one of those old metal merry-go-rounds she and Tracie used to play on at the park when they were little girls. Shutting her eyes, she focused on the feel of the hardwood floor beneath her, the chill in the air. After a few minutes, she opened her eyes, and the room stopped spinning. Taking a deep breath and slowly exhaling seemed to calm her, so she repeated the process. After a few minutes, she was steady enough, forcing herself to stand, then peered out the doors, looking for her dogs. They were nowhere in sight, but she could hear them barking. They weren't far away, just out of her sight. She opened the doors farther for them.

She spied Doc Baker's dishes on the drainboard, but instead of rewashing them, she walked away. She had no urge to rewash them. At least for now. "Good," Katherine said, needing to hear a human voice and not caring if it was her own. As she was preparing to make a cup of tea, both dogs bolted through the open doors, the click of their nails on the hardwood sounding louder than normal. "Hey, you two." She turned, then stopped when she saw Sam's jaw clenched around a ball of fur.

Chapter Four

"Sam, drop it!" Katherine demanded. The shepherd unclenched his jaw, releasing his powerful grip on the furry item in his mouth. "Good boy."

Katherine stooped down and saw that Sam's trophy was just an old, ragged stuffed animal. Probably someone lost it at some point. She had no clue how it wound up on her property. Relieved, she picked it off the floor to toss into the garbage, then stopped. Something about the threadbare animal struck a memory. Examining it, she realized it was a tattered stuffed lamb. It looked old; the glass eyes were yellow, and the eyebrows were done in X-style stitching, giving the lamb an odd look. Its feet were a faded red cloth material, the left ear torn. As fast as she'd picked the animal off the floor, she tossed it into the kitchen sink, the blank yellow eyes staring back at her, the dirty brown fur beckoning her to look closer.

She felt her heart start to race, her throat closing. "It can't be," she whispered. She repeated the process, inhaling then exhaling, as she'd done a few minutes earlier.

Duckie.

She must have been around four or five when her father and his assistant, Helen, returned from Australia with a stuffed lamb. They'd given it to her as a souvenir, a rare gift. Katherine treasured this present from her dad, naming the lamb "Duckie," her new best friend. When she'd been sent to Spain, her mother snatched the lamb from her luggage, reminding her that she was twelve, practically an adult, and adding that she didn't need anything from "that woman."

Distraught, Katherine had surreptitiously searched the house until she found the stuffed animal and put it back in her bag. With Duckie at her side in Spain, she wrote even more stories of brave girls who didn't need a stuffed lamb to cuddle at night. Duckie had been her only friend.

Back in the present, Katherine found herself glued to the floor. She had to force herself to walk over to the sink, intent on picking up the raggedy stuffed animal. Taking Doc Baker's fork from the drainboard, she lifted the stuffed animal out of the sink using the tines. Both dogs growled. Katherine carried the plush animal to the kitchen island, placing it on a dish towel. "This can't be what I think it is," she said to herself as she began to inspect the toy. The empty, yellow eyes were the same, but that didn't amount to much. Probably thousands of these had been made. The tear on the ear bothered her. Hadn't Duckie's ear been torn? She experienced a flash of memory—when Katherine had been quite young, her mother slammed the car door before Katherine could get Duckie inside. Katherine had yanked on the lamb, and a piece of the fabric ear tore off.

How could this be hers? But the longer she inspected the toy animal, the more convinced she was that it had once belonged to her. She had no memory of bringing her childhood toy with her when she left Boston. Though, in all fairness, in the days following Adam's death, the bombings and all the mass hysteria, private and public, it was possible she'd tossed Duckie into her car with the rest of her belongings. She was relieved in knowing that in all likelihood, that's what had happened, and then possibly Sam or Sophie had dragged Duckie out of a closet or wherever she'd stored it all those years ago. And now the dogs were returning it to her after finding the ball of fluff during their jaunt outside.

Katherine had always thought of Duckie as a female. Deciding she'd keep Duckie on her bed as she'd done as a child, Katherine felt it needed a good scrubbing first. It was much too old for the delicate cycle in her washing machine. She filled one side of the sink with hot water and a splash of dish detergent with just enough bleach to whiten and hopefully disinfect the material. Who knew what kind of germs old Duckie had picked up?

Both dogs sat on their haunches, watching as she used an old dishcloth on the lamb. She dipped the cloth in and out of the water, scrubbed the matted fur, then wiped the fur with a clean cloth. Half an hour later, Duckie looked decent enough. She sprayed a bit of disinfectant on the fur as a precaution, just in case. Protection from what, she didn't know, but at least this action wasn't prompted by her latest phobia. Placing her childhood toy on a chair she kept by the open French doors, Katherine decided to leave the lamb there until Duckie was completely dry. She wouldn't let the dogs out just yet.

"Let's get to work," she said to them, knowing they would follow her to her desk, where each had a comfortable napping spot. She wanted to check the Friendlink fan page to see if Karrie was logged on. As soon as she connected to the Internet, her cell phone rang. She didn't get many calls. She took the cell from her jeans pocket and said, "Hello?"

"It's just me," Doc Baker said. "Hope I didn't interfere with your writing?"

"Not at all," she replied, curious as to why he was calling, since he had just been there a couple of hours ago. Maybe he'd left something behind.

"Remember that friend I told you about?"

Taking a deep breath, she said, "Yes."

"He's in the hospital."

She didn't want to appear unsympathetic, but how was this connected to her? "I'm sorry to hear that. Is it serious?"

"The old coot, I swear, he's worse than a newborn calf. Fell off his motorcycle and broke three ribs and his ankle."

Seated at her desk, still eyeing the computer screen in case Karrie logged on, Katherine wished Doc would get to the point. "Poor guy," was all she could come up with.

"Yep," he said. "Seamus Lee Newlon, a helluva guy."

"Doc, what does this have to do with me?" Admittedly, she was slightly curious, since this was completely out of character for Doc. When they normally spoke on the phone, it was always about the dogs.

"Seamus has a son, Tyler. He's a psychiatrist, too."

Katherine felt the blood drain from her face. How dare he once again bring up her illness without her permission? "The way I live is of my choosing," she said, her voice sounding more terse than she intended. But it was her choice. If she decided she could no longer cope with her lifestyle, she would change. Maybe. Could she? She just didn't see the point of trying now. Sure, if she were being honest, she'd love to leave her house without fear and walk around her property, but Katherine had no desire to travel any farther than her own land. Yet it wasn't anyone's business.

"This ain't about your . . . agoraphobia, K. Tyler, Seamus's son, has a friend who needs a place to keep a couple of horses. I thought of you."

Horses? Was he kidding? *Where* in the world would she keep horses, and *why?*

"You're serious, aren't you?"

"I wouldn't be asking if I weren't," he said. "Your stables are in good condition; the paddock is large enough for six horses. It would only be for a short time."

Floored at the request, Katherine was truly at a loss for words. "I have stables?"

"That's why I'm asking," Doc said.

Feeling foolish, she had to explain. "Doc, I didn't know there were stables here." When she'd bought the property, her main concern had been privacy. She didn't even think to ask about anything else, and she never did explore the land.

"Oh, kiddo, I didn't know."

Katherine was embarrassed, and maybe that's what prompted her to say, "If you say I have stables, then of course, I have stables. Tell your friend he can use them for as long as he needs to." She wasn't keen on the idea of a stranger on her property, but Doc had always been good to her, and she hated to say no to him.

"Thanks, K. You're a lifesaver. The guy is only here for a short time. I'll tell him as soon as I hang up. We'll probably be there in a couple of hours. You do know this is a move in the right direction?"

She knew exactly what he was referring to. Maybe it was; maybe it wasn't. She'd see how it played out, allowing a stranger to use stables she didn't even know she had. "I suppose."

"I'll text you when we're at the turnoff," he said.

This being their usual routine, she agreed and then ended the call. She was clueless as to why he'd brought up his friend's accident and his friend's son. What did that have to do with the man who needed to stable his horses? Unable to make sense of his call other than the need to stable the horses, she hoped he'd fill her in, maybe add more details when he arrived.

Returning to her computer screen, she saw four girls were chatting on the fan page. Karrie included.

> **Bigfan216: You feel better?**
> **klcLUV/007: Much. U in class?**

Katherine glanced at the time on her screen. Dang, again she hadn't factored that in. You couldn't pull anything over on this small group of fans. She liked that about them. Now if she could keep up with *her* fake persona, she'd be okay.

> *Bigfan216: Library.*
> *SKRfan4evr: Cool. Sneaking, huh?*
> *Bigfan216: No, it's allowed. Not everyone has a computer!*

That came out of the blue. She hoped it was true in some schools.

> *klcLUV/007: Same here. We can use it at school for homework if we need to.*

Score one point for a lucky lie. Not being honest with this set of fans bothered her. Had she made a mistake by allowing herself get too involved with them? Normally she would visit the page in the evenings. It gave her something to look forward to. Now she felt concerned for Karrie and decided it was her duty as moderator to keep watch over her. Not that she'd be able to do much other than phone the authorities, if needed, but who knew if Karrie's stories were even true? She could be telling lies as easily as Katherine was. Katherine would try to pay closer attention to Karrie's comments, log on as the moderator, and scroll through the comments made when she wasn't online.

> *Blondebookbabe: Not here, they monitor you. Probably think we're all looking at porn! LO*
> *klcLUV/007: Gross.*
> *Bigfan216: Your dad off your case now?*

She couldn't help asking. Coming from a "friend," maybe it wouldn't seem too nosy.

> *klcLUV/007: Not really.*
> *Blondebookbabe: He must be a real jerk!*
> *Bigfan216: Parents are weird sometimes!*

A truthful statement for a change. Katherine had barely known her dad, as she'd spent little time with him. Even when he wasn't traveling the world, he stayed in his study at home, with the doors always locked. Katherine thought of Audrey, the favored housekeeper and Tracie's mother. Audrey told her to *never* knock on her father's office door and *never* enter his study without his permission. Even if it was a matter of life and death. She remembered those words and what she'd experienced when she'd disobeyed them. Katherine often wondered if she had imagined what she'd seen. She'd been told she was prone to an overactive imagination as a child, and to this day, she wasn't sure what was real and what was a figment of her imagination.

Her thoughts were interrupted when she saw WHS524 had logged on and focused her attention on him. If he even hinted at anything remotely inappropriate, she would kick him off. HotandCool would probably put him in his place before she could block him. She seemed to be the most aggressive of the group, though Blondebookbabe could hold her own, too. This small group of girls was tough, like the characters she'd created, minus the special powers she'd given them.

> *HotandCool: What about ur foster dad? Is he a jerk or what?*

Katherine was grateful for the question, because it reminded her to stick to the persona she'd created. Darby supposedly lived with foster parents.

> *Bigfan216: He's really cool, and my foster mom too!*

She would be the girl with nice parents, but not too nice. Darby was still a teenager, and all teenagers butted heads with their parents sometimes. WHS524 hadn't offered an opinion. Maybe the man was a pervert. He might not even be a man. He could be whoever he wanted to be here, just like her. Maybe she should give him the benefit of doubt. It could be that he was like her. Lonely, with no real life to speak of.

klcLUV/007: You're lucky, Darby.

Again, she wished Karrie would stop using her phony name; it reminded Katherine of her lies. But she'd have to continue. These girls would be blown away if they learned of her true identity.

HotandCool: Darby, huh? Let's blow the handles, use our real names, just our first names. I'm Lola.
Blondebookbabe: Ashleigh.
SKRfan4evr: Melissa here.
WHS524: Walter.

Katherine knew it was up to her to acknowledge Walter and give him a chance to redeem himself.

Bigfan216: That's my foster dad's name!

Lies poured from her like water from a spigot.

HotandCool: So Walter, why aren't you at work? You always seem to be on here.

A legitimate question. Katherine guessed he worked the night shift, if he was really a nurse. He wasn't online early in the morning, at least when she'd been here, nor was he on late at night. She wasn't a hundred percent sure, but most likely, he worked during the hours they slept. She decided to change her online routine to keep a closer eye on things.

> **WHS524: I have a job. Just mind your business.**
> **HotandCool: Okay, Nurse Walter.**
> **Blondebookbabe: LOL, Lola!**
> **Bigfan216: Y'all be nice!**
> **klcLUV/007: Yeah, poor Walter has to work!**
> **WHS524: Wait until you're an adult. You spoiled rotten brats won't be laughing then.**

Walter *was* a jerk.

> **HotandCool: Duh! You're a creep, WALTER!**
> **Blondebookbabe: Agree. Walter, why are you here?**

A question Katherine wondered, as well.

> **WHS524: I am a reader and a fan. Isn't that what this page is FOR???**

Katherine heard her cell phone ping—it was a text message from Doc Baker.

> **Bigfan216: Gotta go! TTYL friends!**

Sam and Sophie must've heard Doc's old battered Ford truck, because they jumped out from their napping spots and were running around in circles, apparently waiting for her instructions. "Go," she said, knowing both shepherds knew exactly what the word meant. They ran to the kitchen, waiting for her to open the door. She clicked out of the app, shut her computer down, and opened the doors for Sam and Sophie. In the kitchen, she made a pot of coffee for Doc Baker for the second time that day. She wasn't sure what her other guests drank, but she'd ask when they arrived.

It occurred to her that she'd never had guests other than Doc Baker. Even he wasn't a guest in the true sense of the word. He took care of Sam and Sophie. However, Katherine did consider him a friend, especially in her isolated world. Not a single soul besides him had ever entered her home. Her groceries and her online orders were always left by the door, and usually her delivery people would set bags and boxes as close to the door as they could without actually entering. That way, she didn't have to go outside to the deck to bring her purchases into the house. Maybe Doc Baker was right. This could be the beginning of a positive change for her. Having control of her life for so long, it would be difficult to adjust to anything different, but at least she was giving the idea some thought. Surprisingly, she didn't feel the usual beginnings of panic that normally hit her when she thought of going out into the world.

Katherine busied herself in the kitchen, scrubbing the sink after Duckie's bath and wiping down the counters, though not excessively. She refused to let hyper cleanliness become a problem. With that in mind, she folded the cloth she'd used and placed it next to the dish detergent.

She heard Doc's truck pulling in, along with another vehicle. She didn't want to appear anxious, so she took a deep breath and then exhaled, hoping it would keep her calm while a stranger was inside her home. She could hear Sam and Sophie barking outside.

"K," Doc Baker called out.

"In here! I've just made a fresh pot of coffee." She'd ordered yet another fancy coffee maker a couple of weeks ago, and this was the first time she'd used it. This was coffee maker number four. She'd donate one to the delivery people. Or two.

Doc Baker came inside and sat down on a barstool. "Smells

good, kiddo. I wanted to check with you before I asked those two inside for a quick introduction. You good with that?" His blue eyes were dark with concern.

Two? The guy with the horses and who else? Must be Doc's friend's son, Katherine reasoned. She took another deep breath and then said, "Sure, ask them to come inside."

Uncertain if they'd been informed of her illness, she'd do her best to appear as normal as anyone else. Her hair was still in a long braid from yesterday, but Katherine raked her hand over the top of her head to smooth down any flyaway hairs. Glad she still wore the Nikes, she walked with Doc Baker to the open doors, standing beside him.

Leaning against the deck were two men, both around her age. Her heart rate increased and her face flushed when they stepped inside.

One man appeared average in height and weight, nothing remarkable about him other than his long sandy blond hair and his skin leathered from too much time in the sun. He stepped forward and held out his hand and introduced himself. "Carson Murphy."

Katherine shook his hand. The words *strong* and *capable* came to mind, as his hands were callused and rough.

"Friends call me Car," the man added, grinning.

She released his hand. "Carson, *Car,* I'm K." She used Doc's nickname for her. If these two didn't know her pseudonym, she'd stick to the nickname for now. Katherine returned Car's grin with a shy smile.

"I can't thank you enough for the use of your stables," Car said. "I won't be here too long. I'll be out of your hair in just a few days."

It had been so long since she'd looked at a real live man close to her own age that she felt bashful. Worse, the still-silent man beside him was movie-star handsome. His hair was black as a raven's wing, and he had light blue eyes. He was the complete opposite of his friend. He was very tall and very broad in the right places. Katherine took a deep breath again. She couldn't believe two real live men were standing in her doorway.

"Tyler Newlon," the other man said, offering his hand and smiling at her as if he knew her intimately. He must be the psychiatrist. Wanting to appear normal, she shot him a slight smile. "Pleased to meet you," Tyler said as she extended her hand to his. His hand was large yet smooth, unlike his friend's. His fingers were cool as they touched hers. She liked the feel of his hand in hers. Momentarily surprised at her reaction, she quickly withdrew her hand, cramming both hands in her jeans pockets. She nodded, giving herself a couple of seconds to recover.

"You, too," she finally replied. "I've made a pot of coffee." Katherine turned toward the kitchen. "I'd like to hear all about your horses, if you'd care to tell me."

Sam and Sophie chose that moment to barrel through the doors, panting, their tongues hanging out of their mouths. Slobbering, they circled Doc Baker like he was a piece of meat.

"Take a drink," Katherine said to the dogs. They obeyed.

"Good dogs. You train them yourself?" asked Car.

Katherine took four mugs from the cabinet, filling them with coffee. The action was unfamiliar, since she normally only used two mugs. One for her, one for Doc Baker.

"I did. I've had them since they were pups. They're brother and sister," she told him, surprised at how relaxed she was.

She placed three mugs of coffee, a bowl of sugar, and cream on the kitchen island. "Please, help yourselves," she said, thankful she'd remembered her social manners.

Carson reached for a cup, sipping the coffee without adding cream or sugar. Tyler and Doc drank their coffee black, as well. It pleased her that these men drank black coffee, for some odd reason. It came across as very manly to her, though she would never put a voice to these silly thoughts.

"I guess you ought to explain why you need the stables," Doc Baker told Carson.

"Of course, yes. I'm a horse farmer in North Florida. Tyler and me, well, we've been buddies for as long as I can remember. We met in college, just like our fathers. I sold these two horses last week to a fella here in Blowing Rock. He's building new stables, but they're not quite finished. He needs four or five days at most. I hope this isn't too long or too much trouble. I'm going to hang out with Tyler for a few days, and so I'll take care of the horses. Hopefully you won't even know they're here."

"It's fine. I don't mind having them here," Katherine said. Had Doc told him she hadn't even realized she had stables? She hoped not. It was embarrassing. Maybe this would motivate her to change her lifestyle. It seemed like all she could think about was needing motivation to get her out of the house.

Sophie chose that moment to race out of the kitchen, only to quickly return with Duckie hanging from her mouth. The shepherd dropped the plush old lamb next to Doc Baker, her paw pressing on Duckie. It was her way of wielding power over toys and, sometimes, treats.

"What do we have here?" Doc asked, looking at Sophie's trophy.

"Sophie, let me have that." Katherine yanked Duckie from beneath the dog's paw and placed the plush animal on the counter behind her. "An old childhood toy of mine," she explained. "They brought this to me earlier. They must've found it on one of their jaunts outside. I cleaned the old thing up a bit, though I have no idea how it wound up outside." She smiled a truly genuine smile. It felt good to have a conversation with people face-to-face.

"I didn't see it when I looked earlier. Bet they had it buried out there," Doc Baker stated.

"Probably," Katherine said—though wouldn't it then have

been covered in dirt? It didn't matter, but she still couldn't help being curious about how her old pal found its way out of the house. Maybe it was a hint in some weird way, telling her she needed to go outside and join the world again. *Or someone watching me put it there for me to find. Impossible. Stop it, Katherine!* she scolded herself.

She waited for the panic to start, but when she felt nothing, she took it as a sign that perhaps she could overcome all of the irrational things preventing her from living a normal life.

Carson drained the rest of his coffee and said, "I'd best get those horses stabled before they go stir crazy cooped up in the trailer."

"Yep, let's get them in their temporary home," Doc Baker said. "Tyler, you wanna give K Carson's contact info while I help him with the horses?"

"Sure thing," Tyler said.

Doc and Carson thanked Katherine again, then left to take care of the horses. Sam and Sophie bolted out the door, following Doc Baker outside.

Katherine's heart thumped so loud, she was sure it could be heard. It wasn't out of fear. Could it be even slightly possible that she was excited to be alone with a very handsome man? *Maybe?*

Tyler removed a pen from his shirt pocket and a business card. He jotted something down on the back of the card, then gave it to her. She accepted the card.

"Just in case there's a problem with the horses, here is Carson's info," Tyler said, then added, "My personal cell number is on the back."

"Sure." She didn't know what else to say.

"Doc told me you stay inside," Tyler said, his tone completely normal.

It wasn't Doc's place to say that, though she knew he wanted her to get help. What better way than to bring a shrink to her house? She wanted to be angry at Doc, yet couldn't, as she knew how concerned he was for her. She nodded. "I do." Feeling a dreaded warmth spreading throughout her body, Katherine turned away for a moment. She didn't want him to see her shame.

"Anytime you want to talk about it, call me. I want to help, but only when you're ready."

"I'll think about it, but I won't promise anything," she said, her voice hoarse. She cleared her throat. "I don't like to talk about this."

"I can tell, but talking is healing." He smiled at her. She felt butterflies in her stomach and a flutter in her heart. She nodded in agreement, wishing he'd leave. But another part wished she had the courage to take him up on his offer to help her.

"I've helped people in your situation before, with a lot of success," he continued.

That's encouraging, she thought. "I promise to give your offer serious thought. I know the way I live isn't normal, but I'm relatively happy." Even though she'd structured her life around her agoraphobia—a word she normally did her best *not* to think of or verbalize—there would be a time she would *have* to leave her house. Unsure of when that would be or what would force her from her safe space, she acknowledged this was a small step toward change.

"When you're ready," he said. "I make house calls."

Oddly enough, she wasn't experiencing any panicky feelings now. Just thinking about a world beyond her mountain sanctuary could send her into a full-blown panic attack. But there was nothing now. She took a calming breath, releasing it slowly. "Doc Baker told me about your father, too."

Tyler chuckled. "That old coot was on his Harley on his way to a house call when he . . . bit the dust."

Katherine watched Tyler's stark blue eyes shine with humor. "I'm sorry. Doc told me about it, though he didn't say he was going to make a house call. I hope he's okay—and his patient, too."

"Dad will be just fine. He's a tough old dude, like Doc. His patients are under my friend's care until he's back on his feet."

Out of the blue, Katherine wondered if Tyler was a good kisser. *Where did that thought come from?* Even though she hadn't verbalized it, she felt brazen even thinking it, and felt her cheeks start to burn.

"Would you want to have dinner sometime?" Tyler asked.

She stared at him, shocked by his question.

"I'm sorry. Forget I said that. I don't know what's come over me. A beautiful woman is rare around here," he said, looking outside, where they could hear the horses neighing as Doc and Car hustled them to the stables.

"I'd love to," Katherine said, "if you let me make dinner."

Several seconds passed before he replied, "Really?" He was clearly surprised that she'd accepted his invitation.

"Really. I enjoy cooking. It will give me something to look forward to," she said. He grinned at her, sending her heart racing wildly for reasons other than the prospect of making dinner. Was she so out of touch that she'd fallen for the first attractive guy that entered her home?

"Tomorrow?" he asked.

"Perfect," Katherine told him.

He was making this too easy. Was it because of her condition? Had he asked so he could play psychiatrist? He seemed too eager, she decided. Struck with newfound boldness, she asked, "Will I be serving Tyler or Dr. Newlon?"

Laughing, he replied, "Good question. I'd like to have dinner with you to get to know you better. I'm always Tyler and a doctor. I know where you're headed with this; I won't be psychoanalyzing you, if that's what you're worried about."

Katherine guessed that he was used to this. She nodded. "I am."

"I understand if you change your mind," he said.

A bit too quickly, she added, "No, not at all. I just had to make sure." Offering a shy smile, she continued. "I enjoy playing around in the kitchen."

He laughed. It was contagious. She began to laugh with him. "Cooking. Not what we're both thinking." It was unbelievable that she was speaking to a complete stranger like she really knew him. It blindsided her. Maybe they would become friends.

"How does seven tomorrow evening sound?" he asked.

That was normally time she spent with her Friendlink fans, but she thought dinner with him sounded way more exciting. "Perfect."

"Tomorrow, then," he said, lightly brushing her cheek with his fingertips.

"Seven o'clock," she whispered, because she was as close to speechless as she'd ever been.

Chapter Five

Katherine didn't know how long she stood in the kitchen, her hand still on her cheek where Tyler had touched her. How could this be? One minute she felt like she would die from a panic attack . . . and now she didn't. Had Doc spiked her coffee? Of course he hadn't, though she couldn't begin to understand the sudden change in her behavior. She couldn't focus on this yet. It was crazy.

Before she could work herself into a panic attack, she went to her office and sat down in her desk chair. She booted up her computer. She needed to check on the girls and see what they were up to.

Sam and Sophie lay curled up in their usual spots. The busy afternoon running outside with Doc and the horses had worn them out. They both slept soundly, an occasional soft *woof* coming from Sam. He must be having a doggy dream.

When Katherine pulled up the Friendlink page, she saw Blondebookbabe and HotandCool were chatting.

Bigfan216: Hey! What's up?
Blondebookbabe: Shootin' the crap, Darby.

There went the handles again. For now, she'd ignore using their first names.

> *Bigfan216: Cool.*
> *HotandCool: Karrie hasn't been on all afternoon.*
> *Bigfan216: Is she still sick?*
> *Blondebookbabe: Who cares?*
> *HotandCool: Me! She seems cool.*
> *Bigfan216: I like her too.*
> *Blondebookbabe: I don't like that old fart, Walter.*
> *Looked at his profile. A nurse. What a creep!!! Maybe he feels up his patients??? LOL*
> *HotandCool: Gag! We should search hospitals, find him, and get him fired!*
> *Bigfan216: No, that's just wrong!!! He needs $$$ for books!*

Katherine could not allow that to happen. While she agreed Walter wasn't the nicest fan, it would be cruel to jeopardize his job. A change of topic was what they needed.

> *Bigfan216: I got invited to homecoming today!*

Making dinner tomorrow night for Tyler Newlon was much bigger than homecoming, though these girls would never know that.

> *Blondebookbabe: Lucky! Is he hot?*
> *HotandCool: An ATW date?*

Katherine knew "ATW" meant "all the way."

> *Bigfan216: No! This is our first date!*
> *HotandCool: So?*
> *Bigfan216: Not my style.*

Blondebookbabe: It's def mine! LOL
HotandCool: We should meet @ ThanksG break!

That would be a disaster for Katherine but fun for them.

Bigfan216: No $$$: >)
klcLUV/007: Hi!
Bigfan216: Feeling better?
klcLUV/007: Kinda.
Blondebookbabe: Ever heard of ibuprofen???
HotandCool: I ripped off pain meds from Mom last time I had cramps! They are awesome!!!!! Got a buzz, big time.
Bigfan216: Don't say that. Who knows who's watching? Pain pills aren't cool.
HotandCool: What do u call cool? Weed?

Taking a deep breath, Katherine knew she had to get the girls under control. She switched to her moderator handle.

TIC927: Folks, let's cut out the drug talk. I'll have to report this if you continue. Remember, this is a fan page. Use your handles!

She switched back to Darby's handle.

Bigfan216: I told you!
klcLUV/007: Not good! Maybe we should just IM instead. As a group?
Blondebookbabe: No way. The moderator wins if we do.
HotandCool: For sure.
Bigfan216: Right!

The email account Katherine had created for Darby pinged. Minimizing Friendlink, she opened the email and read:

To: DMW@yahoomail.com
From: klc16@gmail.com
klcLUV/007 isn't always me! I am Karrie, the real Karrie.
Please help me!

She quickly wrote back:

To: klc16@gmail.com
From: DMW@yahoomail.com
I don't understand. Is this a joke? Not funny.
Darby

Katherine pulled the Friendlink page back up. Karrie was still in the chat.

> **Bigfan216: Karrie, what the hell is going on????**
> **klcLUV/007: What???**
> **Bigfan216: The email????**
> **HotandCool: WTF???**
> **Blondebookbabe: I second WTF???**
> **Bigfan216: Your email???? You said you need help????**
> **HotandCool: What kind of help?**
> **Bigfan216: This isn't funny. Is it your dad?**

Karrie logged off. *Damn.* Was Karrie playing games with them? With her? If so, she wasn't the least bit amused. Obviously, she had misjudged Karrie. Again, you could be whomever you wanted online. She herself was doing it now. Though her reasons for doing it were justifiable; she had to maintain her privacy, for obvious reasons.

> **HotandCool: Told you she was weird!**
> **Blondebookbabe: She could've lost her connection, duh!!!**

Bigfan216: Probably! The Internet sucks sometimes.
BRB!

Katherine didn't think of that. That could be true. She'd send her another email.

To: klc16@gmail.com
From: DMW@yahoomail.com
Karrie,
If you truly need help, why don't you call 911?
Darby

Then she returned to the forum and wrote:

Bigfan216: I gotta get to work. TTYL
Blondebookbabe: Have fun!
HotandCool: Later.

If Katherine were a gambling woman, she'd bet Karrie was an attention seeker. Possibly she thought Darby was gullible, since she'd been friendly to her. Katherine planned to spend more time watching the fan page and the email she'd set up. She would do what she could with the limited information she had if she sensed the young girl was in danger.

Focusing her attention back on Tyler Newlon, she hoped this wasn't just a case of being attracted to the first man her age she'd been around since Adam. It wasn't her style, but maybe she'd been out of the dating game for so long she no longer had a style.

Prepping tomorrow night's dinner was at the top of her list. She had dozens of cookbooks in her kitchen. She stood and stretched, and then Sam and Sophie followed her to the kitchen. "I bet you two want a treat?" she asked, laughing at how fast their tails wagged when she said "treat." They were so smart. She couldn't imagine life without them.

"Sit," she told them, handing them each a bully stick. "Good kids." If someone were to overhear her conversations with the dogs she thought of as her "kids," they'd think she was even more off her rocker.

She thumbed through a couple of cookbooks. Not knowing if Tyler was a meat-and-potatoes guy, she opted for something in between, deciding a simple roasted chicken would suffice. Returning to her office, she went to the Apple Blossom Gourmet Market's website and ordered what she would need for dinner. She'd make an apple pie for dessert. Katherine had gone overboard last week when she ordered apples, as there were none better to her than a North Carolina apple.

As soon as she finished her order, she opened her Darby email account to see if Karrie had responded. There was nothing, which made her even more suspicious of the girl. If Karrie had the ability to go online and send an email, couldn't she just as easily email her local police department? It made no sense to her. Feeling foolish, Katherine felt she shouldn't have responded so quickly to Karrie's emails and comments. From now on, she would be more careful in screening future fans who wanted to be a part of her community.

The dogs started barking, letting her know they wanted to go out. She'd closed the doors earlier, not wanting to leave them open until she discovered what had caused them to go berserk. The fact that there were potentially bears outside was another reason to keep the doors closed. She'd never thought too much about it, which she now realized was sheer stupidity on her part.

Opening the doors, she said, "Go on." She watched them race out of sight. "The horses," she said to herself, closing the door. That must be where the dogs were headed. As long as the horses were stabled safely, Katherine didn't see anything wrong with Sam and Sophie hanging out at the stables. She wished she knew their exact location; she should've asked Doc Baker to snap a photo. Not that it would matter, given her inability to take a casual walk to go find the stables, regardless of whether she had a picture. They could be miles away, for all she knew. But she had heard Doc shouting when they let the horses out of the trailer, so they couldn't be that far from the house.

With that thought in mind, she returned to her desk, her view of the mountains as stunning as always. As it was nearing the end of September, the dogwoods were starting to turn their deep shade of red. In a few weeks, the countless varieties of maple, hickory, and oak trees would set the mountain ablaze with bright colors, as though Mother Nature were opening a box of crayons, mixing reds, oranges, browns, reds, and burgundies. Katherine knew the beauty kept her sane, and she looked forward to the autumnal changes. Yet each year, she tried to combat the lingering thought that those colors also signaled the passing of time, another year gone by. How long could she continue to live this way? A solitary life with no hope of change.

"Bull," she said, slamming her hand on her desk. There was all the hope in the world. All she had to do was make it happen. After years of researching panic attacks, she knew they wouldn't kill her. All was well and good when she wasn't in the midst of one. She still held the power to live a normal life. All she had to do was decide to start. And she would. Tomorrow after dinner, she would accept Tyler's offer to help her overcome the colossal fear that controlled her life.

She heard the dogs barking. Her grocery order must've arrived. Rather than have them leave the bags outside the door, she would step out and bring the bags in herself. Her heart pounded in her chest as she headed to the door; her throat felt like it was closing. Forcing herself to take a deep breath, to focus on the technique she'd learned and practiced multiple times, she touched the doorknob and gasped for air. She felt as though a vice were cutting off her air supply. She reached the kitchen and found a small brown paper bag she kept in a drawer. Breathing into it to prevent herself from hyperventilating, she sat down on a barstool for a few minutes, waiting for the dizziness to pass. Katherine heard the delivery person leave. If she didn't bring her groceries inside, they would spoil. Without hesitating, she walked over to the door, closed her eyes, and yanked the door open, stooping for the bags and then dragging them inside. Potatoes, lettuce, and tomatoes spilled out of the bags and onto the floor. She left them there until she felt calm enough to put them away.

A few minutes passed before she could stand once more and pick up the food. Her hands shook as she dumped the produce into a clean dish, filled it with tap water, and left it in the sink to soak. She put the chicken inside the refrigerator, along with the eggs that, by some miracle, were still in the carton, none cracked.

Maybe she'd jumped the gun by accepting Tyler's invitation to dinner. What if she had a panic attack in front of him? She would die of humiliation, even knowing he'd probably had dozens of patients whack out in front of him. Katherine didn't want to be one of them. Not sure what to do, she washed the tomatoes, scrubbed the potatoes, and put them in the produce drawer. She washed the lettuce, laying each leaf on a paper towel and carefully patting it dry. She put the lettuce into a plastic bag and then in the veggie drawer when she finished. The task was mundane; it occupied her and kept her focused.

Sam's loud bark reminded her she'd closed the door on the dogs. "Hang on," she called out, knowing their barking would stop when they heard her voice. Without thinking, she turned the doorknob, swinging it aside so they could enter. Since she was puttering in the kitchen, she'd leave it open. Wild animals be damned.

Normally she would begin work on her next novel at this time of day, but not today. She didn't feel the urge to dive into the lives of the fictional girls she created. Instead, she would make the apple pie crust for tomorrow's dessert. Even if she backed out of the dinner, she could still eat the pie. The thought made her smile. "Okay, Katherine, you can do this." She spoke to herself, though Sophie acknowledged her with a loud *woof*.

"A family has to stick together." Katherine reached down and fluffed both dogs between their ears.

Realizing it was close to time for the dogs' evening meal, Katherine decided to tend to them first. She took out duck livers, free-range chicken legs, a cup of their kibble, and two eggs from the refrigerator. She kept their food separate from hers in special containers. They'd been on this raw diet since she had them, and Doc approved, so she didn't see any reason to stop. They were healthy, and their multicolored coats shined. She always added omega oil to the food in the morning, knowing this was especially good for them. "Okay, sit," she instructed, holding out both large bowls. "Good kiddos," she said, placing their bowls before them.

She washed up, then started making the pie crust, which was simple—a bit of flour and salt with shortening. Katherine sometimes used unsalted butter instead. She'd taught herself to bake during her many years alone and was quite good at it. When the pastry crumbled, after rolling it out, she made two discs, covered them in plastic wrap, and put them in the refrigerator for later. Whether she went through with making dinner for Tyler or not, she would have a damn good apple pie.

She cleaned her mess, then returned to her office. Still concerned about Karrie, she checked her email to see if she'd answered her.

Logging on, she saw she had two emails from Karrie.

To: DMW@yahoomail.com
From: klc#007@gmail.com
I know who you are. Selfish bitch.

Stunned, she read the second email.

To: DMW@yahoomail.com
From: klc#007@gmail.com
Please be careful, Darby! He says he knows your family. He's
changed my email address, I'm not sure why.
TTYL
Karrie

Neither email made sense. She checked the time. They'd
been sent hours apart. Only one bore Karrie's signature, if
you could even call spelling out one's name on the bottom of
an email a signature, though she always added TTYL. Suspicious, Katherine read through them again and clicked on the
blue arrow to expand the details. There was nothing other
than their email addresses and the timestamps.

Katherine concluded that someone on her fan page knew
she was K.C. Winston. That had to be why she received the
sinister-sounding emails. It wasn't a huge problem. All she
had to do was deny it, writing, "I wish," or something equally
juvenile.

She clicked out of the email, logging onto her Friendlink
fan page. The usual members were online. She scanned the
page for a reference to her being someone else, but there was
nothing. But she did see that Karrie was online.

>*Bigfan216: Hi, Karrie. Any new warnings???*
>*klcLUV/007: What are you talking about???*
>*Bigfan216: Puh—leeeze!*
>*klcLUV/007: I don't know what you want. Why are you
>saying these things to me?*

HotandCool: What's with you two? Having a lovers
spat??? LOL
   SKRfan4evr: Y'all are gay?
   klcLUV/007: No way!
   Blondebookbabe: I think you're lying!!!
   Bigfan216: We aren't gay! Do you ever think about
something besides sex???
   HotandCool: You've hit a nerve, SKRfan4evr!!!!
   Bigfan216: No nerve hit, just pissed.
   klcLUV/007: I did not do what you accused me of! Call
me. 281-555-8702!!! Please!
   Bigfan216: I don't have a cell.
   SKRfan4evr: Right. Everybody has a freaking cell
phone!

Katherine didn't dare call her on her own cell, but what if
she had one of those disposable phones? She knew the Apple
Blossom Market sold them, because she'd seen them on their
website. Unsure why a so-called gourmet market sold disposable phones, she decided she'd order a couple and hoped it
wasn't too late to have them delivered that evening. She could
only imagine the gossip this would add to Blowing Rock's
community webpage. Quickly, before she changed her mind,
she minimized Friendlink, pulled up her account at the market, and placed an order for two phones. She added laundry
detergent, Advil, and tampons. Might as well give them
something to talk about, so she added a bottle of cheap wine
and a box of chocolates. A few seconds later, her order was
confirmed, with delivery in ninety minutes. When she had a
safe cell number to share, she would send Karrie an email
with her number to call. In the meantime, she posted:

   Bigfan216: I'll see if my foster dad will let me use his.
I'll call if he does. Later.

Logging off before the girls could get nastier, she had to admit she was even more curious about Karrie and the emails she claimed she'd sent and those she hadn't. It could be that she was nothing more than a drama queen. Or some bored person who had nothing better to do. Numerous scenarios came to mind, none of which would explain the cry for help or who knew that Darby was, in fact, K.C. Winston.

Katherine returned to the fan page, using her moderator handle so no one would bother her. Checking Karrie's profile again, Katherine noticed she'd added her last name and the same cell phone number she'd given her earlier. Had Karrie wanted Darby to have this information? It wasn't required. Honestly, Katherine thought giving out too much information was a bad idea. She read the profile carefully. Karrie Collins. Lived in Dallas, Texas, with her father, though that wasn't on the updated profile. Had Karrie's mother passed away? Katherine had lots of questions that she didn't have answers for. She'd have to be careful about speaking if she decided to call her. Katherine still had a Southern accent, which didn't exactly fit her story of living in Utah. She could tell Karrie she'd lived in the South and moved when she started high school. More lies. She had become quite proficient at lying. Not a skill she was proud of.

Closing the app, she pulled up her Google account and typed in the search engine: *Karrie Collins, Dallas, Texas.* There were hundreds of hits, as she'd expected. It was a pretty common name, and spelling the name with a K rather than a C wasn't unheard of. As she scrolled through the dozens of names, she stopped when she saw an obituary in *The Dallas Morning News.* She clicked on the link, then read through the obituary:

> Tracie Denise Collins, age 34, born August 7, 1984, left this earth on February 8, 2005, to join Our Heavenly Father. She is survived by her hus-

band, Jameson Ray Thurman, age 30, and daughter, age 12, Karrie Lynn Collins, and mother, Audrey Ann Collins. Services are to be held at Restland Chapel in Dallas.

Tracie.

Katherine's heart began its usual pounding, a surefire precursor to a panic attack. Hands trembling, her vision diminishing to a mere pinpoint of light, she took a deep breath. Her head fell forward, sending her laptop crashing to the floor.

Chapter Six

Katherine wasn't sure how much time had passed when she came to. Both dogs were all over her, Sam's paws digging into her shoulders, his breath warm on her face. Sophie nudged her arm with her nose. Katherine gently pushed the dogs aside, leaning her head down to get the blood flowing to her brain.

Had she fainted? Shifting into an upright position, the light-headedness easing, she stood, carefully keeping one hand on her desk to steady herself as she bent down to pick up her computer. The webpage she'd been reading was still up. She glanced at the time in the upper right corner of her screen. Barely five minutes had passed. Though she was hesitant to read through the obituary again, she knew she had to.

The names were too close to those in her memory for this to be a coincidence. Her hands shook once more, and she squeezed them together, trying to still them. Reading the obit once more, she acknowledged the possibilities. The odds were so high that anyone who knew of her situation would agree something strange was happening. This was not a coincidence. Nor was it a coincidence that Karrie had just added her last name to her profile. Wishing she had a friend who wasn't on her fan page or who hid their identity behind a computer, Katherine needed to share this with someone she trusted. The only person she knew she could trust was Doc Baker. Without hesitating, she took her phone out of her pocket, its usual home when she wasn't charging it, and texted him.

Can you come over? It's important. Dogs are fine.

Was she overreacting? Probably. No, she wasn't. This was too much to be just a coincidence.

You okay, kiddo? Doc texted back.

No, she wasn't, though she didn't want to text those exact words to him.

A problem I need to discuss.

Hearing the market delivery vehicle pull up, both dogs began to bark, running to the doors she'd left open earlier. She followed them, waiting behind the door while the delivery boy put her bags outside. "Good dogs," she heard him say. It must be Royce, their favorite friend from the market. Katherine knew he was the owner's son, and her dogs seemed to like him, since he usually had a treat for them. Hopefully he didn't share her shopping list with the community events webpage. Most likely his mother was the culprit, as she was a huge gossip hound, according to Doc Baker.

When Katherine heard Royce's car pull away, she brought the bags into the kitchen and removed the two disposable cell phones. She wanted it done before Doc Baker arrived, fearing he'd question her about them. For now, she didn't want him to know she'd gone this far. Feeling calmer, she would fill Doc in on the basic details and hear his thoughts before deciding whether to phone Karrie. She stuffed the rest of her order and the disposable cell phones inside the pantry.

For the third time in one day, she heard Doc's old Ford truck wind its way up the drive. His office was nearby; he'd told her that when they first met. Sam and Sophie did their usual pouncing out the door to greet their true best friend.

Following the dogs inside, he called out, "K, it's me."

"In here," she said. On a whim, she took a good bottle of

wine from the refrigerator and two glasses from the cupboard.

"No coffee? This must be heavy duty," Doc said, sitting at the bar.

"You okay with a glass of Chablis?"

"I'd love a couple of glasses, but one will do. I gotta drive home."

"Of course." Katherine hadn't considered that, as she could get smashed and never have to worry about driving home. Not that she got drunk very often but, sadly, she could whenever she chose to.

"I know what I'm about to tell you is going to sound crazy," she told him, while uncorking the bottle of wine. If he'd thought her crazy before, what she was about to tell him would convince him he was right. In all fairness, Doc had never even insinuated anything about her mental status other than this morning, when he asked her if she would consider talking to his friend.

"Listen, kiddo—I've heard crazy and crazy. Not much surprises me these days," he said.

Katherine poured half a glass for him and one for herself. She sat beside him and took a sip of wine before she began her story. "Promise me what I'm about to tell you will remain between us?"

He nodded. "I'm not one for carrying tales, K."

She knew that but needed it said anyway. "I trust you. I wouldn't have called you if I didn't. You know my pseudonym, right?"

Grinning, he said, "My granddaughter has read every one of your books, so to answer your question, yes, of course, I do."

Katherine raked a hand through her tangled mass of hair. "I didn't know you had a granddaughter." She didn't know if he was married, single, divorced, or widowed.

"She's fifteen, going on thirty."

He didn't offer more details of his family life, so she didn't pry. "It seems many girls are like that these days." That knowledge came from her research and from her interactions on the fan page. She hoped Doc's granddaughter didn't cuss as most girls online did.

"So, why'd you drag me away from suturing a cat's ear?" Doc asked.

Katherine laughed. "I didn't mean to take you away from work, though since I did, I'd better explain why." She took another sip of wine and said, "My parents weren't around much when I was young. They traveled the world together and had little time for a small child. I had plenty of nannies and housekeepers to care for me, plus a private tutor." She traced her finger along the stem of her wineglass. "My family was very wealthy," Katherine told him. "They left their fortune and their business to me. I used some of the money to purchase this place."

Doc laughed. "I wouldn't dare ask what this set you back, but go on," he encouraged.

"Six point four million," she said. "A lot for just one person, but I had my reasons for wanting land and privacy."

"I won't ask what those six point four million reasons were," he said, chuckling.

"Thank you," she said, then continued. "I was sent to boarding school in Spain when I was twelve. It was awful, as I'd never been to a real school. Up until then, I'd had a private tutor at home. Needless to say, after graduating, I left Spain and all the bad memories behind. Went to college in Boston, got my master's degree, and a job. I worked at *The Boston Globe* for a few years." And then there was Adam. She would keep that time of her life to herself. Doc didn't need to know, as it wasn't relevant to her current situation.

"I'm impressed," he said.

She could tell. "Thanks. I enjoyed my work. I still do, despite my fears. Without my work, I'd be one screwed-up woman. More screwed up, anyway," Katherine added, a wry grin lifting the corner of her mouth.

"What can I do to help?"

She nodded. "My family had a housekeeper in Dallas, and she had a little girl around my age. I can't remember her exact age, five or six, but her name was Tracie. She was my best friend until I was sent away to boarding school. I never saw her after that. I often wondered what became of her. I even tried searching for her when I was working, but, oddly enough, I didn't know her last name, so it was useless to continue my search. Fast forward. I have a Friendlink fan page; your granddaughter may know about it. People come and go. There is always a rush of new fans after a book is released, but I'm rambling." She took a sip of wine. "I act as the moderator, but I also have an account set up for . . . I guess you could call it my alter ego. This alter ego is a teenager who visits the fan page daily.

"A young girl joined the fan page recently. She seemed eager to make a friend. I felt bad for her, and we chatted. I was trying to be nice. Some girls are downright mean; others remind me I'm glad I never had children. I gave the girl my phony email address, because she implied her dad was not the nicest man in the world. She said he hit her occasionally.

"She emailed, asking if I would help her. I responded by telling her I'd call the police, but then I began to wonder—if she could email my alter ego, why couldn't she email the police, a teacher, or maybe a neighbor? So then I get another email. This one said, 'I know who you are, selfish bitch,' and another said, 'Be careful Darby, he knows you.' "

"Darby's the alter ego?" Doc asked.

Katherine nodded. "What doesn't make sense is that two people are seemingly sending the emails from the same address. After the last email, I checked the girl's online profile and saw she had added her last name and phone number. It matched the number she'd shared during a chat. My old reporter instinct kicked in, so I Googled her name. Her name is common, though spelled slightly unusually. I found an obituary for Tracie Denise Collins, survived by Karrie Lynn Collins of Dallas, Texas. Maybe I'm losing it, but I think this Tracie is—rather was—my friend. And now she's dead."

"I'm sorry, K. Though both are common enough names," Doc said.

"I know, but here's the kicker—the obit said Tracie was also survived by her mother, Audrey. That was Tracie's mother's name. So is this girl on my fan page in trouble? Should I reach out to the authorities with this information? Was her mom the little girl I knew when I was a kid? All of this seems way too far-fetched, but the strange messages make me wonder if this is just a teenager being a teenager, or if Karrie's connection is legitimate. When I read that obit, I panicked."

"What's your gut tell you?"

Her instincts had once been excellent, fine-tuned as a violin. But after spending almost a decade alone, Katherine hadn't any need to use her natural skills. "Nothing. That's just it. I could be making more of this than necessary, or it's possible Karrie is in real trouble. Though why reach out to a total stranger on a fan page? Or does she know my pseudonym? My real name. That's what concerns me. Supposedly someone knows who I am and sends me those weird emails. I don't know if I should take this girl seriously, call the police, or what. I needed to share this with someone who could advise me. I'm not sure what, if anything, I should do."

"Could you contact your publisher and see if they've received any similar emails on that website you have? It's probably nothing more than a prank. Some bored kids may have done some online research on their favorite author. If not, contact the authorities or her school. Does she list where she goes to school on your fan page?"

"No," Katherine said. "Though I can email Gayle. She's

my editor. My publisher maintains the website. They'd tell me if anything was awry. I can ask if any similar emails have been sent to the website, though my identity is pretty secure. I don't see how one could find me, or a connection to my past, as I've been extra careful not to reveal anything about myself personally or my pseudonym."

"Good idea, though I don't know how that works. You'll want to stop whatever they hope to accomplish if it's a kook. Some folks have bad intentions, K. You gotta watch out for them."

She was very familiar with crazies with bad intentions. She almost let it slip that she'd been in Boston on the day of the bombings but caught herself. "It's not as though I'm in the public eye," she said. "I'm pretty sure no one around here other than you know what I do for a living. Any correspondence I receive from my publisher is by email. I don't ask for copies of my books, as I have no need for them."

"You're quite the mystery, according to Bethany, my granddaughter."

She smiled. So the granddaughter had a name. "You'll have to keep me a secret, Doc."

"Yep, just as I've been doing all these years, kiddo. I take my medical oath seriously, even as a vet. I respect my pet patient's owner's privacy, as well."

"I know, and I am so grateful. I couldn't deal with the publicity if the locals learned the weird mountain woman was K.C. Winston."

"Stop that kind of talk. Who cares what people think?"

"Thanks, Doc. You're one of the good guys," she said.

He laughed. "Glad you think so."

She finished her glass of wine. "It's true. So what are your thoughts? Am I overreacting?"

He sighed and finished the last of his wine, shaking his head. "There's not a physical threat, at least one you know of. Whoever is doing this wants to stir up trouble, maybe scare you a little. I'd leave it alone for now. Though I'd call that publisher of yours and tell them what's happening."

"You're right. That makes sense," Katherine said. "I'll wait and see if this turns out, as you said, to just be some kook wanting to scare me."

"I'm glad I could help. Now, I need to get home and get a bit of shut-eye. Four in the morning comes early when you're my age." He stood up and took his glass, placing it in the sink. Both dogs, lying on the throw rugs scattered about the kitchen, jumped up when they saw Doc stand.

"Sit," Katherine said. The dogs sat, but she knew they were waiting for her to tell them to "go" so they could follow Doc out to his truck and romp about one last time before calling it a night.

"You need me, K, just call. It's just me at the house," Doc Baker said.

She wouldn't have asked if he hadn't spoken of it. But he had, and she was glad. "Doc, are you alone? You know, alone as in single? Widowed?"

"And why would a pretty gal like you want to know?" he asked, his eyes alight with humor.

"Because we've never discussed your . . . personal life. I know it's none of my business. Sorry to be so nosy."

"I'm divorced, more than ten years. The happiest day of my life."

Katherine couldn't help but laugh. "Good. I mean, not good that you're divorced, good that you're happy."

"We're still friends and should have stayed that way. But then I wouldn't have Stephanie, my daughter, Bethany's mom. So that pretty much sums up my life."

"Thanks for sharing that. I often wondered but didn't want to pry."

"Steph is probably about your age. She's thirty-six. Teaches high school in town. Great kid."

"Then she must take after her father. I'm thirty-seven, so

yes, we're close in age." Katherine thought of the obituary. Tracie would've been thirty-six had she lived. She'd died two years ago. Poor Karrie. If it was all true, she sympathized with her.

"Okay, I gotta scoot. You know my number, K." Doc gave a half wave and left through the open doors, with Sam and Sophie waiting impatiently to follow.

"Go on," Katherine said to the dogs. She stood in the doorway, the cool air refreshing. Soon, she wouldn't be able to leave the doors open. Autumn days could get chilly in the mountains, and the nights were downright cold.

Back in the kitchen, she rinsed out the wineglasses and returned the bottle of wine to the refrigerator, reminding herself to take the phones and other items she'd purchased out of the pantry. Katherine removed one of the phones from its heavy plastic wrap and read the instructions while waiting for the dogs to come back inside. She jotted down the phone number and charged the phone with the cord provided. If she felt she needed to contact the authorities or Karrie herself, she'd now have a phone with a number that didn't have a North Carolina area code.

Katherine heard Sam and Sophie bolt through the door, their nails clicking on the wood floor. They would always go straight to the kitchen for their nightly treat. "Sit," she said, then handed each a beef stick.

Leaving them to chow down, she locked the doors, returning to the kitchen to ensure the alarm was on. If they had another visit from a wild animal tonight, the alarm would activate and catch it on the surveillance cameras.

Once upstairs, she showered and went through her usual nightly routine. When the dogs were settled on the bed, she slid beneath the sheets, fluffed the pillows behind her, then booted up her laptop. She logged onto the fan page, hoping to catch Karrie online.

Bigfan216: Hi!
Blondebookbabe: What's going on?
Bigfan216: Just finished homework! Ugh!
Blondebookbabe: I did mine in detention today!!!
Bigfan216: LOL, what'd you do?
Blondebookbabe: Told my science teacher to F off!

Katherine could not believe the language these girls used and seemed so comfortable with, even though she'd seen them use profanity regularly.

Bigfan216: Cool! Anybody else been online?
Blondebookbabe: Not yet, Lola is out with her parents.
Who knows about the others?

Katherine remembered Lola's handle was HotandCool. She was so vain, but maybe she *was* hot and cool.

Bigfan216: You know her?
Blondebookbabe: Kinda.
Bigfan216: How's that?
Blondebookbabe: Groupie fans. Katy Perry, Taylor Swift. One Direction.
Bigfan216: They ever join the chats?
Blondebookbabe: Nope!

Katherine could see this conversation was going nowhere. Karrie wasn't online, so she decided she'd sign off.

Bigfan216: I'm gonna chill with a book! TTYL!

She clicked out of the page and went to her alter-ego email account. There was an email from Karrie waiting.

From: klc#007@gmail.com
To: DMW@yahoomail.com
Darby,
Are you able to use your dad's phone? Please call me. It's a matter of life and death.
Karrie

To: klc#007@gmail.com
From: DMW@yahoomail.com
I don't believe you.
Darby

Katherine decided Karrie was a little drama queen. Life and death? She seriously doubted it. If this were a life-and-death situation, wouldn't she call, email, or text someone she actually knew? A person close by that could help her. She should take Doc's advice. Karrie was most likely a little on the kooky side, looking for attention. Her email pinged.

To: DMW@yahoomail.com
From: klc#007@gmail.com
Darby,
Please, believe me. Just call.
Karrie

Should she call this girl just to put the matter to rest? Nothing Karrie said made sense, though she could ask if Tracie was her mother and Audrey her grandmother. She didn't see any harm in that. Hurrying downstairs, Katherine found the disposable cell phone, then went back upstairs.

Both dogs were sound asleep at the foot of the bed. She used her moderator handle to log onto the fan page and skimmed through their chats, searching for Karrie's number. She typed out the number in her Notes app on her cell phone, then clicked out of Friendlink.

Before she called Karrie, she would send Gayle an email. Better yet, she'd text her, knowing Gayle always had her cell phone with her. Quickly explaining the situation in as few words as possible, she sent the text. Katherine saw the gray dots, indicating Gayle was writing back to her. *Nothing out of the ordinary here*, was her response. Katherine was relieved these emails were narrowed down now to just Karrie. She knew there were ways to track an internet provider's address and locate the server, but she didn't have that skill. She fired off another email.

To: klc#007@gmail.com
From: DMW@yahoomail.com
Karrie,
If you're in danger, can't you dial 911???
Darby

She would wait and see if Karrie answered, then decide if she should call her. A few minutes later, her email pinged again.

To: DMW@yahoomail.com
From: klc#007@gmail.com
Darby,
No, I can't. It would cause more trouble for me. Just call!
Karrie

Though Katherine had no children of her own and hadn't been around that many, she couldn't help but feel a sense of responsibility toward Karrie. A phone call couldn't hurt. Maybe she could put this to rest once and for all. Before she changed her mind, she dialed the number Karrie had given her.

"Darby, is this you?" Karrie asked, her voice not more than a whisper. Katherine could detect a deep Southern accent, one similar to hers.

"Yes," Katherine said, trying to disguise her voice.

"Listen, I can't talk long. My dad is raging. I found this notebook." She lowered her voice even further. "They're about our favorite author. Dad keeps saying he's going to ruin whoever K.C. Winston is. I don't know how he got the notebook, but it's like the first book. He says he wrote it, and someone stole it from him. I thought you could help me figure this out."

"Okay," Katherine said, as her heart began to race.

"You know a lot about the books," Karrie said, "and you were nice to me when I joined the fan page."

Katherine wasn't sure how to react, so she asked, "What kind of notebook? Like a journal or something?" She hoped she sounded like a sixteen-year-old, but her thoughts were those of the adult woman she really was.

"No! I swear this spiral is like the first book in the series! I don't believe Dad wrote it like he said. He's been acting weird since my grandmother came to visit."

Was Audrey her grandmother? Should she risk revealing her true identity and ask Karrie?

"Weird, like how?" Doing her best to sound sixteen, Katherine used the word *like* as they seemed to do, even though it annoyed the hell out of her.

"I found the notebook while I was looking for one of Mom's sweaters. It was stuffed in a bag in the back of the closet."

Katherine had all of her notebooks. There was no way Karrie's dad could have one of her old notebooks. It was impossible.

"Could he, like, have copied them or something?" she asked in her Darby voice.

"I never thought of that. It wasn't his handwriting, but he might've. I guess he could've disguised his handwriting, though I'm not sure why he'd do that."

Neither was she. This couldn't be a coincidence. Karrie really could be Tracie's daughter.

"So what is it you want me to do?" Katherine asked.

"I don't know. I just needed to tell someone."

"You want to keep this secret just between us?"

"Yes, the other girls would laugh at me," Karrie said.

"I'll keep it a secret. Listen, I gotta go. My dad needs his phone back. Talk later." Katherine ended the call.

Taking a deep breath, then releasing it slowly, Katherine's gut instinct kicked in. She needed to find out who Karrie's father was . . . before he found her.

Chapter Seven

Katherine thought it best to privatize her fan page for a while, allowing only the girls she'd been chatting with to stay. She remained unsure about Walter, the male nurse. Maybe she would block him. Something about him seemed a bit off. Could it be possible he was Karrie's father? She would go online, look at his posts, and try to read between the lines.

While she appreciated all of her readers, Walter was the only male ever to join the fan page. Her books were about teenage girls, and each had a special power. Lark could move objects telekinetically. Adrianna had psychic powers that enabled her to know things before they happened. Harmony possessed strength far beyond normal, and Jayden produced sounds that could be deadly. Katherine's years at the Burgess Hill School had elevated her imagination far beyond that of other girls her age. Her characters represented powers she herself had wished for. Right now, she could use Adrianna's psychic abilities.

Katherine could think of no explanation for Karrie's father claiming he wrote her books, and no way was it humanly possible for him to have possession of one of her notebooks. She'd kept each one in a large plastic bin in her closet. Just for the hell of it, she went to the closet, pulled the storage container out, and scanned the stack of spirals. All of her notebooks were exactly where she'd left them.

Why did Karrie fear her father? She had admitted that he hit her sometimes. Karrie reaching out online to "Darby," of all people, made no sense. Did Karrie know of their possible connection in real life? Katherine wanted to think this was nothing more than a childish prank, yet there were too many coincidences for this to be a joke. No one knew she'd moved to North Carolina. Not even her former colleagues at the *Globe*, nor the couples she and Adam had socialized with. She'd left her life in Boston behind. She'd never contacted anyone.

Wait.

It had been so long ago that she'd almost forgotten. She'd sold her apartment a few months after moving here. All of the transactions had been made through emails and banks. When her apartment was sold, the money was wired to the business account of K.C. Winston, Inc. If someone wanted to find her, and they were technologically gifted, they could have located her. If they were truly hell-bent on destroying her, maybe they could do just that.

Deciding this was a starting point, she could possibly trace the transaction. As far as research went, she was decent enough, though not so knowledgeable that she knew exactly how to go about this. Katherine would hire an expert and find who was involved in selling her old place and everyone who'd communicated with the real estate agent. Maybe a certain name would ring a bell, offer an explanation, help her discover who in her past would have reason to . . . *what*? She didn't know. Send a teenage girl to her fan page to screw with her and tell a few lies about being the author of her novels? It couldn't be that stupid or simple. And why now?

In her office, she searched online for a computer forensic expert. There were hundreds. Katherine clicked off. If she were going to hire a professional, she needed to meet them face to face.

Unsure how to go about it, she decided that she would ask Doc. He'd lived in North Carolina his entire life. He knew a lot of the local business owners. Tomorrow she'd ask him if he knew a professional to assist her and keep it private. But then she had to stop depending solely on him.

Before she changed her mind, she pulled up the Friendlink fan page again and changed the settings. She could manage posts and limited activity to only five current members. Especially WHS524—Walter. The more she thought about him, the more suspicious he became. He'd joined recently and was extremely bossy with the others. She wanted to keep an eye on him. She scanned through his comments since he'd joined. She didn't read anything other than his rude threats, which seemed fairly tame. He could be just a bossy old coot with no life.

Tired, Katherine shut down her computer, her thoughts racing everywhere. The past two days had been full, and she was tired. After she went through her nighttime routine, she crawled beneath the warm blankets with both dogs and dreamed of a life with Tyler.

Chapter Eight

Surprisingly, Katherine had slept like a baby for the first time in years. She usually woke up several times during the night. She had been busy the past two days, which was probably her reason for getting such a good night's rest.

Katherine looked forward to dinner with Tyler that night. It was strange to think she had accepted an invitation from a man, invited him into her personal space, and even more so that she'd only just met him and knew absolutely nothing about him, other than he was a doctor, and Doc liked him.

Stretching, she got out of bed, took a quick shower, and dressed in jeans and a sweatshirt. She slipped on her Uggs while Sam and Sophie danced around, eager to go outside.

"Come on, let's go," she called. Downstairs, she opened the kitchen door, both dogs racing to be the first one out. While the dogs burned off their pent-up energy, she made coffee. Filling the dogs' dishes with their usual mix of kibble, chicken, liver, and a blend of organ meat, she added a raw egg and omega oil to the mix, placing their dishes on the vinyl mats. Ten minutes later, the two dogs came bouncing through the doors, straight to their food.

"Guess I don't need to tell you two it's time for breakfast," Katherine said. Sitting at the bar, she sipped her coffee, anticipation sending a warm glow throughout her body. A renewed appreciation for life filled her. She knew it had something to do with that evening's dinner. It had been too long since she'd had contact with a man, especially one as handsome as Tyler. She finished her coffee and rinsed her cup, placing it on the drainboard. She took the pie crust she'd made yesterday out of the refrigerator and gathered several apples along with a lemon to ensure the apples wouldn't turn brown as she peeled them. When she had sliced enough apples for a pie, she mixed together flour, sugar, cinnamon, nutmeg, orange zest, and a dash of ground cloves. Once the pie crust was at room temperature, she would fill it with the sliced apples, sugar mixture, and some chopped dried apples, and then drizzle some apple butter over the filling before adding the top crust. Then she would bake it until it was golden brown and some of the filling started bubbling through the slits in the top crust.

Her thoughts returned to last night's phone conversation with Karrie. The poor girl had sounded distressed. If it were an act, then she considered Karrie to be one heck of an actress. A smidgen of her gut instinct was beginning to kick in. This was more than a simple prank. Before she changed her mind, she sent Doc a text.

Call me when you have a minute. Not an emergency. K.

Katherine grabbed her laptop and logged in online to see if Karrie had sent any new emails or posted on the fan page. She checked her Darby email account. Nothing. Switching over to Friendlink, she didn't see any of the girls or Walter online. She glanced at the time. Just after seven in the morning. The girls were probably at school. Later, she would check in and see if Karrie was online.

Returning to the kitchen, she was about to unwrap her pie crust when her phone rang.

"What's up, K?" Doc Baker asked. "You okay?"

"I'm fine. I have yet another favor to ask. I need to find

someone who can trace a real estate transaction. I know this sounds crazy—heck, everything sounds crazy coming from me these days. Tell me if I'm overstepping any boundaries. Do you know who does this kind of work? I'm not sure who to contact."

She heard him sigh. "Kid, that's gonna take some thought. Let me make a few calls. I'll get back to you on this as quickly as I can. I have to help George and Sandy with a newborn calf right now, but I'll see what I can do."

"Thanks, Doc. I don't know what I'd do without you. I'll repay you some way," Katherine said, adding, "What's your favorite cake?"

"Bribing me with sweets! That'll work, kiddo. I like a good old-fashioned chocolate cake with heaps of icing."

"Perfect. I'll get started." But no, she couldn't. "Does tomorrow work for the cake? You'll hear about it soon enough, so I might as well tell you myself. Tyler invited me to have dinner. Here. Tonight." Saying it aloud made her anxious, though in a good way.

"Hot damn! I knew you two would pair up. I'm proud of you, K. Tyler's as good a fella as you'll ever find," he said, and chuckled.

"It's just dinner, and I'll admit I'm more than a little rusty at this." She thought of Adam and felt a wave of sadness. If he were alive, he would be so disappointed in her, not living life to the fullest. "He offered to help me. I may accept." Once the words were out, even if they were just to Doc, it incentivized her to work on her issues.

"He's one of the best in his field, though if you ever meet Seamus, don't say I told you, 'cause he'll talk your leg off trying to convince you otherwise. I'll check with a few business contacts about your question. And I'll look forward to that cake," he told her, before ending the call.

Doc Baker would be her first choice if she could've hand-picked a father. She was quite fond of him and was pretty sure he cared about her, too. Maybe one day she could meet his family. Smiling, she looked forward to the rest of the day, making dinner and getting to know Tyler.

She preheated the oven and took a pie plate from the cupboard. She unwrapped the pie crust, splaying it across the plate with the edges hanging over. Using a knife, she cut off the excess crust and then used her fingers to pinch the edges. Katherine wanted the pie to look as good as it tasted. She'd made this particular apple pie recipe dozens of times, so she wasn't too concerned. Adding the apples, then the second layer of crust, she used a butter knife to pierce the crust, trying to create a star design. "Not my best, but close enough," she said out loud. Placing the pie in the oven, she set the timer.

With time on her hands, she returned to her desk, logging onto Friendlink. Lola, aka HotandCool, was online.

> *Bigfan216: What's up? U in class?*
> *HotandCool: No, in bathroom cutting class!*
> *Bigfan216: Don't get caught!*
> *HotandCool: No biggie if I do.*
> *Bigfan216: What class do you hate that much???*
> *HotandCool: All of them!*

Katherine understood Lola's dislike for high school. Hopefully, she wasn't being picked on or made fun of. Kids could be so cruel. It seemed girls were even crueler than boys. She herself had been forced to attend many coed events during her years at the Burgess Hill School, which often partnered with Wellington's School for Young Men for social events. Those had been some of her most miserable times, especially when she was called out for her lack of participation. It didn't matter if it were a coed dance, which she'd despised more than anything, or weekend movie nights with both schools gathered in the boys' gymnasium. She'd been alone. None of the boys were interested in her. She was taller than most of them and knew this had intimidated them.

The girls had made fun of her every opportunity they had. Especially for her accent. She never went home. Had no family come to visit. She'd been a total outcast. Yes, she completely understood Lola's hatred for school. Even now, just thinking of all she'd endured made her cringe. The day she'd graduated, she booked a flight to Boston and took nothing with her except her spiral notebooks. Her parents provided all the money she needed for college, and anything else, as long as they didn't have to deal with her. She'd never looked back.

> *Bigfan216: I hate school too.*
> *HotandCool: I can't wait till TG break!*
> *Bigfan216: For sure! Any plans?*
> *HotandCool: Sleepin' late!*

Katherine was an early riser now, though she hadn't liked getting up at six in the morning, either, at that age. Going to the hall for breakfast with all the mean girls when she was in high school had been torture. No one liked the early start. Katherine knew many of the girls back then had taken their anger out on her. For almost five years, she'd tolerated them, which had angered them even more. The day she left Burgess Hill had been the best day of her life.

She glanced at the time on the screen. The scent of cinnamon and apple beckoned her to the kitchen. It was time to take the dessert out of the oven. She didn't want it to burn.

> *Bigfan216: I gotta go, I'll ttyl.*
> *HotandCool: See ya!*

She left her computer on so she could hear the *ping* when a new email arrived. She used two bright yellow potholders and removed the pie from the oven. Both dogs sniffed, their noses dampening.

"Not for pooches," she told the pair. "Though maybe we can find an extra treat for you this morning." Sam and Sophie barked. She placed the pie on a wire rack to cool, then took two beef sticks from their special canister. "Sit," she instructed. When they obeyed, she gave them their treat. "Good pooches." Their behavior still amazed her.

She took the chicken for dinner out of the fridge, and after she cleaned it, she snipped a few sprigs of rosemary and thyme, tucking the herbs beneath the bumpy skin. She salted and peppered the skin, then put the chicken back in the refrigerator to marinate.

She was unsure if she should dress up for the date, so she went upstairs to her bedroom to see what she had to wear. She didn't own many clothes. There was no need. Katherine spent her days in jeans and T-shirts. It wasn't as though she needed to dress up for work or to socialize. She pulled hanger after hanger aside, finally settling on a pair of black jeans she'd bought a few months ago. She decided on a simple red cashmere sweater and black booties she still had from her days in Boston, doubtful Tyler would care what she had on her feet. With that out of the way, she entered the bathroom, looking at herself in the mirror. Her hair reached down to her waist and would've been to her knees if she hadn't started trimming it herself. Opening drawer after drawer, searching for a tube of lipstick and maybe some mascara, she found she had nothing. She hadn't needed it. Now she wanted to feel pretty, feminine. She didn't think she could purchase makeup in such a short amount of time, but she raced downstairs to her computer. Apple Blossom had a cosmetics section; she'd seen it online before, though she had always skipped past that page. Glancing at the clock, she realized she had enough time to make an order. They had a two-hour delivery window, and they'd never been late in all these years she'd used their service.

Before she changed her mind, she ordered a tube of Revlon's Super Lustrous lipstick in the color Bare Affair, which made her grin. She also chose a blush in shade Berry Merry. She wondered who chose the names for this stuff. A brown eyeliner pencil and a tube of Maybelline mascara, still sold in the same pink and green tube she remembered, rounded things out. Before she went crazy, she thought she'd best add a few other items she would need anyway: garbage bags, food-storage bags, dishwasher detergent, and an extra bottle of dish soap. Remembering she'd promised Doc Baker a chocolate cake, she ordered cocoa and an extra bag of confectioners' sugar. She would use all of it sooner or later. She placed her order, and a window popped up, saying her items would be delivered in forty-five minutes. It must have been a slow morning.

Katherine thought *her* morning unusual, since she hadn't experienced the first sign of anxiety, not one symptom. She looked at the clock again. Could she go outside to the deck? For just a minute or two? She awaited the fast heartbeat to kick in, the dry mouth. Nothing.

"Okay. Maybe I *can* make progress."

Chapter Nine

Both dogs were lounging on the deck, the autumn sun shining brightly, the temperature comfortable. They didn't like the cold. Katherine took this as a sign. Without bothering to put her shoes on, she walked over to the door and, without thinking, she stepped outside onto the deck. Her heart was racing just a little. Her hands weren't *too* shaky. She tried swallowing, and there was no problem—another step. Katherine started counting out loud. "One, two, three . . ."

When she reached thirty-two seconds, she stepped back inside, both dogs following. If she were to rate her sense of panic on a scale from one to ten, she'd give it a four. Amazed by her progress, she wanted to tell someone, but there wasn't anybody. "Sam and Sophie, I am going to run with you. Soon." She spoke to them as though they understood. She didn't know why she'd been able to step outside just now, but she would accept this as a victory—one step at a time. Wasn't that the Alcoholics Anonymous mantra?

Katherine heard a *ping* from her computer. She'd forgotten all about Karrie's problems for a few minutes. She opened her email. Nothing from Karrie, just an ad for socks. "Last thing I need," she said, and deleted the email. But she left the computer on, with the volume turned up as loud as it would go.

She couldn't stop wondering how she had managed to walk out to the deck and feel okay. Could it be that her mind was focused on something other than her usual fear when attempting to go outside? She was not a psychiatrist—though lucky for her, Tyler was, and he would be there tonight. She wanted to tell him of her recent victory. Would he encourage her to push herself beyond her comfort zone? If all the books she'd read were true, then yes. With each success, there would come more if she allowed herself to endure the fear. Easier said than done. She knew therapies and medications could treat her disorder but didn't want to go that route. Focusing on the possibility of a normal future, she decided to personally accept the delivery from Apple Blossom's delivery guy rather than have them place her bags outside the door.

She went upstairs to put her sneakers on. Downstairs, the dogs started their usual barking when they heard a car entering the drive leading to the house. Taking a deep breath, then slowly exhaling, seemed to calm her. When she heard a car door close, she took another breath, blowing it out before stepping onto the deck. Katherine felt lightheaded, but not so much that she couldn't function. A young man, in his early twenties maybe, with sandy brown hair, carried two paper bags up the stairs. Katherine took another deep breath, releasing it slowly, focusing on this person who must be Royce. Both dogs circled him when he reached the top of the steps. He seemed as surprised to see her as she was to see him.

"Hi," he said, about to drop the bags.

"No," Katherine said, her voice strong, assured. "I'll take them."

He handed the bags over to her. She took the paper handles, her knuckles whitening as she gripped them. She was about to go back inside when the man spoke. "Nice to finally put a face to the name."

Nodding, she stepped inside, then turned to look at him.

"Thank you," she said, glad she was such a generous tipper to offset any awkwardness.

The dogs followed Royce down the steps. Katherine stopped for a minute, still holding the bags. "I can't believe this," she said out loud to herself. Shaky but able to tolerate it, she took both bags into the kitchen. Giddy at this major accomplishment, she still felt the urge to tell someone about her progress. If she felt comfortable enough, she would tell Tyler Newlon that night.

She put the few items away and thought about the evening ahead. It'd been so long since she'd had a date . . . coming up on a decade. Would she still know how to have a normal conversation with a man? Most of her conversations were those she created for her characters and on the Friendlink page. Of course she talked to Doc, but it was usually about her dogs. She stayed current on world events, though she knew very little about the city of Blowing Rock, only what she read online. Never having traveled downtown since her arrival, she would check out the local artisans online and purchased many of her household items from them. The pots she grew her herbs in and the handmade rugs scattered throughout the house had all been made locally. She'd purchased much of her wall art from nearby artists via the Internet. She'd personally thank each vendor someday.

After her small attempt at making a change, she now had more hope than ever for treating her agoraphobia. She would ask Tyler to begin treatment as soon as possible, though Katherine had to admit she was leery about Tyler digging too deep. For as long as she could remember, she'd had weird dreams; she couldn't put an exact word to them other than *dark*. Maybe there was something she wanted, needed to remember, yet couldn't. Whatever the cause, she did not want a psychiatrist picking her brain apart like a wild animal picking at a carcass.

Her cell phone rang, bringing her thoughts back to the present.

"Hello! Think I found a gal to help you," Doc Baker said. "She's retired CIA. Has connections everywhere."

Dumbfounded, Katherine asked, "As in Central Intelligence Agency?"

"Yes, the one and only, as far as I know. She'll need your computer, and of course, she'll want to meet with you," he explained.

"Would I be presumptuous to ask how you know her?"

"Yep," he said, "you would."

That was Doc, succinct as ever. "Then I won't. How do I contact her?"

"I'm going to bring her to your house, that's how."

He must've told this woman about her condition, which was starting to embarrass her. "I appreciate this, Doc. If it weren't important, I wouldn't ask."

"You're good with me, kid. I do what I can."

"I know, Doc. Thanks. For all that you're doing for me. So, when do I get to meet this CIA—former CIA—agent?"

"Tomorrow afternoon, when I come to pick up my cake," he said, adding, "By the way, her name is Ilene Silva."

She couldn't help but laugh. "I'll add an extra layer for both of you." Katherine felt sure Doc was more than friends with this Ilene Silva; she'd heard the change in his voice when he said her name. At least she hoped that were the case, for Doc's sake.

"Sounds good. Now get yourself all gussied up for your date tonight. We'll talk later."

Katherine couldn't remember the last time she'd heard the term "gussied up." If he only knew how she'd hurried to order some cosmetics just for this purpose, he would have had one heck of a laugh. She returned to the kitchen and gathered up the cosmetics, taking them upstairs. It wouldn't hurt to experiment. It'd been a long time since she'd applied make-up. She took the makeup from its plastic packaging, laying each item on the counter. "Here goes," she said to her reflection in the mirror. She used the small brush provided in the blush compact and added a peachy color to her cheekbones. Leaning close to the mirror, she lined her eyelids with the brown liner, then used a Q-tip to smudge the line so it wouldn't appear so stark, a trick she remembered from back in the day, when this was part of her normal routine. She coated her already dark lashes with mascara, then added the lipstick. She took a step back to look at herself.

"Not bad," she said, then twisted her hair into a version of a chignon. This was not the frightened woman who couldn't step outside without fear. This was the version of herself that she used to be. Yes, she had silver streaks in her hair and saw a few fine lines around the corners of her eyes, but she hadn't aged that much, given the stress she'd been through. "Self-inflicted," she said to the image in the mirror. Feeling more confident by the minute, she left the makeup on, though she'd shower, wash her hair, and redo the makeup later this evening before Tyler arrived.

Back downstairs, she checked her email again to see if she'd received anything from Karrie. Nothing. Texas was an hour behind North Carolina, so if Karrie were at school, she'd probably be having lunch now. The girls logged onto Friend-link numerous times throughout the school day, yet when she switched to the fan page, not a single girl was online. Hot-andCool was skipping classes today. Odd that she wasn't on. She could be in class now, and her earlier talk of skipping was just that. Talk. Katherine found this odd, but hoped the girls were in a classroom where they belonged. Still, they all had cell phones and used them *during* class. She clicked out of the page. She'd check back later, before she started preparing dinner for Tyler.

She kept the computer on. The volume was still set to

max, so she would hear if she received an email. Katherine didn't want to miss any emails from Karrie. She was worried about her, and she admitted to herself that she was also a little bit frightened by her. She crossed her fingers, hoping that Karrie was being overly dramatic about her relationship with her father. Having had a distant relationship—if you could even call it that—with her own father, Katherine understood better than most how a parent's neglect could destroy one's self-esteem. If Karrie were being honest about the physical abuse, she was destined for severe emotional harm and a future filled with a lack of trust. She might be unable to maintain a healthy relationship with men or women when she was older. Katherine knew this from the years of therapy she'd had after her parents were killed. At the time, she'd felt guilty that she hadn't felt their loss more, and didn't grieve as most would have after losing their parents in such a tragic way. Now she knew she had been in shock for a long time after losing them. Also, she recalled how attentive her father's assistant was at that time. Katherine remembered how she'd wailed like a banshee at the funeral. She remembered being so embarrassed, tucking her chin to her chest to avoid eye contact.

Katherine hadn't thought about that period of her life in a long time. Maybe it was another subject she needed to share with Tyler. Regardless, she felt she needed to keep in contact with Karrie. If it turned out she'd been exaggerating, then "Darby" would call her a dirty name, which would be the end of it. But what if her suspicions turned out to be true? What if Tracie was Karrie's mother? And Audrey her grandmother? Then why would Karrie's father call Katherine a bitch? She had no idea who he was, and she hoped he didn't know her true identity. Sighing, she forced herself to put all that out of her mind so she could enjoy the date tonight.

Katherine returned to the kitchen to prep for dinner. Sam and Sophie were curled up on their favorite rugs, each lifting their head when they saw her, then plopping back into their original positions. She'd left the door open, so they must be tired, hanging out there when their plush beds were much more comfortable than a kitchen rug.

"You two are tuckered out, huh?"

Sophie gave a soft growl and closed her eyes. Sam resumed sleeping, his snoring causing Katherine to grin. It was unusual for them to be this tired at this time of day, so she guessed their outside adventures had been more exhausting than usual.

Katherine gathered the supplies she would need for her creamed potatoes from the pantry. She also took out green peas from the freezer, courtesy of Doc's trip to their local farmer's market last week, and placed them in a small bowl to thaw. She hoped Tyler didn't expect anything too fancy. Later, she might dazzle him with an elaborate meal if this turned into something more than a doctor-client relationship. Katherine put the reins on her wild thoughts. Nothing would work out if she didn't overcome her irrational fear of leaving her house. But she had made some progress today, and wasn't that a step in the right direction? She took the potatoes, washed and peeled several, then dropped them into a pot of water. She added a lid so that she only needed to hit the digital panel on her stove when it was time.

She glanced at the clock on her cell phone and saw it was about time for school to let out. She went to her computer and logged onto the Friendlink fan page. No one was there, not even Walter. Had she accidentally blocked them when she'd changed the settings? Clicking into her moderator's handle, she rechecked her settings. Just as she'd expected, there were no blocks for the five members she'd kept. Had Karrie tried to contact her by phone? She would have her number from their call last night.

Hurrying upstairs for the disposable phone she'd used, she saw no calls. She crammed the burner phone in her pocket just in case. Katherine could not get this girl out of her head. Unable to pinpoint exactly why, she forced herself to instead think of the evening ahead. Her heart raced a little, her throat tight, a sure precursor of a panic attack. After a few deep breaths, she felt calmer and in control of her body and mind.

"I can do this," she said out loud, returning to the kitchen. Both dogs perked up when they saw her. Grabbing their treat container, she led them to the French doors. "Go," she commanded. They ran outside to their happy place.

Waiting by the door with their treats and feeling especially brave, she stepped out onto the deck. Her heartbeat increased, and her mouth felt dry. She fought against the uncomfortable physical sensations. Using her breathing technique, she took a deep gulp of cool mountain air. After another breath, she felt almost nothing. Walking to the edge of the large deck, she saw both dogs digging. "No!" she called, dreading the mess they'd track in. They would probably both need to be bathed.

Katherine stood on the deck watching Sam and Sophie, amazed she could do this with such ease. The dogs stopped digging, turned toward her, and headed back to the house. They weren't used to seeing her outside. It must be strange for them, too. Even stranger was Katherine's lack of fear. Her hands trembled slightly, and she felt lightheaded, but she could handle these symptoms. As she turned to head back inside, both dogs followed her to the kitchen. "You two are going to get fat if I keep this up," she said, giving each a chunk of dried liver. The dogs took the treats to their favorite spot in the kitchen, their munching sounds filling the quiet.

Amazed at her new ability to handle herself, Katherine pushed aside negative thoughts. This evening would be the best she'd had in almost a decade.

Chapter Ten

Katherine took one last glance in the bathroom mirror before heading downstairs. She'd washed and dried her long hair, deciding to wear it loose. She didn't want to appear as though she were trying too hard. The makeup enhanced her features but didn't exactly change them. Her red sweater was stylish, but not too overdone, even though it was cashmere. The black jeans and shoes she'd selected completed the outfit. Most women planning an evening alone with a handsome doctor would ensure they looked their best. That's what she'd done when she'd first met Adam, and she didn't think that aspect of dating had changed.

Returning to the kitchen, she checked the chicken in the oven and saw it was browning nicely. The potatoes were simmering on the stove. Saving the peas for last, as they only took a few minutes to prepare, she took a loaf of French bread from the pantry and wrapped it in foil so it would be ready to put in the oven when Tyler arrived. She took the disposable cell phone out of her pocket and checked the time. There were no new calls, so she left it on the center island.

Katherine left the French doors open for Sam and Sophie so they could run outside when they heard Tyler's vehicle. It was chilly inside. Rarely did she light a fire in the kitchen's fireplace, but she thought it would be appropriate. She checked for a draft to ensure the damper was open and placed a Dura-flame log on the grate. She closed the damper, added several newspapers she saved just for this purpose, then piled the kindling horizontally in a small stack. When she finished, she lit the newspaper, waited for the kindling to emit an orange-red glow, then added a large log that should burn throughout the evening.

Next to the fireplace, she cleared off a small round table she used as a catch-all for everything from junk mail to reusable shopping bags from Apple Blossom. The table was old and had come with the house, along with two matching chairs. The real estate agent had told her it was real ma-hogany and walnut and should be cared for with a special polish, which she didn't have. She had never used the table for a meal, so tonight would be her first time.

Because her office was in the dining room, and the dining table was so long, she wouldn't even consider inviting a guest to share a meal there. She'd wanted to get rid of the ridicu-lous dining table and chairs for years but had no motivation. Katherine decided that she would finally donate the flamboy-ant furniture to a local church. Doc could advise her how to do it, as he had with most things lately.

Katherine used Lemon Pledge to buff the antique table to a high shine, since she didn't have a tablecloth to cover the fine wood. She took a step back, admiring the shimmer of the dif-ferent wood grains, enhanced by the flames from the fire-place. She then polished the chairs and pushed each beneath the table. To set the table, she used dinner plates made by a North Carolinian artisan. The dishes were all a deep forest green, mottled with many lighter shades of green. Each piece was handcrafted and unique. Katherine had found them rus-tic when she'd ordered them years ago, though she rarely used them anymore. Having no cloth napkins, she used her everyday paper napkins. She wished she had the guts to add candles, though she knew that was too much. This was only a first date. It may not lead to a second date. She was getting way ahead of herself. They could hate each other, for all she knew. They'd barely spent any real time together. It could be that those few minutes together yesterday were nothing more than a fleeting physical attraction. Katherine felt sure they had nothing in common other than the obvious—he was a doctor, and she needed his expertise.

The oven timer buzzed, the temperature automatically lowering for the bread she would add as soon as Tyler arrived. She thought modern technology was awesome, even though it'd taken her a while to learn the oven's many features. She took the chicken out, spooned the drippings into a small saucepan for a gravy, then covered the chicken with foil, allowing the natural juices to permeate. If the smell was any indicator of the taste, tonight's meal would be scrumptious.

Katherine checked the time. If Tyler were punctual, he'd be here in twenty minutes. Enough time for her to make the chicken gravy. She took the saucepan with the drippings and added flour, salt, and a dash of white pepper. She whisked the ingredients together until they thickened, then set the burner to simmer. Taking the peas from the sink, she emptied them into another small pot and added a smidgen of butter and a dash of salt.

She had two bottles of the Biltmore Estate's best Chardonnay chilling in the refrigerator. She seriously doubted they'd drink both, but she wanted to be prepared. Should she offer him a glass of wine before dinner? Or something stronger? If he wanted anything else, all she had on hand was a bottle of Grey Goose vodka, given to her last Christmas by her UPS carrier. She found it on a bottom shelf in her pantry and put it in the freezer to chill. A sudden thought occurred to her: she hadn't made an appetizer. Rolling her eyes, she took out a block of Monterey Jack cheese and cut it into cubes. She found a jar of her favorite Greek kalamata olives and a box of wheat crackers in the pantry. Arranging it all on a dinner plate, she placed it in the center of the island.

She washed and dried her hands and sat on a barstool, suddenly feeling anxious now that it was time for Tyler to arrive. She took deep breaths, in and out, and closed her eyes, knowing she had the power to stop the flow of anxiety. A couple of minutes later, she felt calm as she released the built-up anxiety.

Shrill barking from both dogs out on the deck told her Tyler was indeed prompt. She glanced at the time. 6:59. Katherine appreciated it, as she'd always been very punctual herself. Taking one more deep breath, she smoothed her hair away from her face and smiled.

There came the sound of a car door closing, and then a few seconds later, she heard footsteps. A light tap sounded on the open door. "Anybody home?"

Katherine went to greet Tyler at the door. "Hi, please come on inside. It's a bit cold out this evening," she said, hoping she didn't sound as nervous as she felt.

"Thanks," he said, handing her a small bouquet.

Surprised, she accepted the bouquet of cream-colored flowers. "These are beautiful," she said, and meant it. They were blush-colored dahlias and creamy white mums, wrapped with a thick, dark green ribbon. "Thank you." She closed the door behind him to keep the chilly air out.

"My pleasure. I wasn't sure what to bring."

She smiled. "You didn't have to do this, but I do love dahlias."

"Good. I'm glad you like them." A smile lit up Tyler's already sparkling blue eyes.

They stood there silently for a few seconds before Katherine found her social manners. "Would you like something to drink? I have Chardonnay, vodka, and a variety of sodas." She headed to the kitchen. "Hope you don't mind hanging out in the kitchen while I finish dinner." Katherine filled a large drinking glass with water, placing the small bouquet inside. Arranging the flowers, she placed them on the windowsill.

"Not at all. Isn't the kitchen the heart of a home? And a glass of Chardonnay sounds perfect."

Katherine removed two wineglasses from the cupboard, her Rabbit corkscrew, and the chilled bottle of wine from the refrigerator.

He was about to sit down when she took the wine from the refrigerator. "Do you mind?" he asked, taking the corkscrew.

Grinning, she shook her head. "It's all yours."

He made fast work of opening the wine and filling their glasses. She watched him, admiring how at ease he was in her kitchen. His movements were graceful for a man of his size, though Katherine thought that might have something to do with the fact he was a doctor. Wasn't gentleness in his field to be expected? It was probably her imagination, but his movements were positively exquisite, very self-assured. As she watched him, something about his easy motions soothed her. It had been so long since she'd been close to a man her age that she felt like a teenager, a little too giddy and excited. Her heart raced—in a good way, for once. Tyler held out the glass of wine, and she took it, their hands briefly touching, sending a shiver of warmth throughout her body. Tyler lifted his glass. Katherine watched his hands move succinctly, precisely.

He held his glass, lightly clinking it against hers. "Cheers."

She raised her own glass. "Cheers." Taking a sip of wine, she felt totally out of her depth but remembered that if she felt overwhelmed, she could do the breathing exercises that seemed to relieve her anxiety.

Katherine removed the paper towel she'd placed over the appetizer plate. "Please, help yourself," she offered. She had two small plates and napkins beside the plate of cheese and crackers. "It should hold you over," she added, a grin on her face.

"Don't mind if I do."

The ear-piercing sound of Katherine's disposable cell phone halted her response. She grabbed the phone, looked at the caller ID, then ended the call. She didn't recognize the number; it wasn't Karrie's. But who else had the number? Karrie was the only person she'd called using the phone.

"You okay?" Tyler asked.

Taking a deep breath, she nodded. "I'm fine. Just a wrong number." She felt his gaze on her. "It's nothing, really," she continued. "Probably a prank call."

She knew she was digging deeper into unnecessary lies. She stuck the phone in her front pocket, leaving her personal cell phone in her back pocket. She went over to the stove and turned the burner on for the peas. "This won't take long," she babbled, as she tried to gather her thoughts. Now wasn't the time for Karrie to call her—or whoever it was. Maybe it was the father? Possibly he'd taken Karrie's phone away from her, then used his own to make the call. A million possibilities filtered through Katherine's head as she tried to get control of herself before she had a full-blown panic attack.

Tyler sat back down, munching on a piece of cheese. "I can wait however long it takes."

Katherine dropped the spoon into the pot. In a hushed voice, she asked, "What do you mean?"

Tyler nodded at the stove. "The peas."

Shaking her head, she said, "Oh, yes, of course."

"Were you thinking of something else?" he asked, his azure eyes lighting up his handsome face.

Katherine felt a knot of heat in the pit of her stomach. "No. I'm sorry. It's a work thing," she explained, hoping he didn't ask her to expand, because she wasn't sure if he knew she was an author. Had Doc told him? If he had, surely he would have mentioned it to her. Or maybe he had, and she'd completely forgotten. Either way, she didn't see any harm in telling Tyler her occupation if the topic came up again.

"Are you okay?" Tyler asked, his voice changing to that of Dr. Newlon. At least, that's how she perceived it to be.

She took a deep breath, then slowly released it. She turned her back to him while she tended to the peas. She scooped the spoon out, tossed it in the sink, then took another spoon from the drawer next to the stovetop. "That's a very loaded question."

"How so?"

She gave a wry laugh. "It would take forever to explain." She turned away from the stove to face him once more.

Reaching for another chunk of cheese, he said, "I've got all the time in the world."

"Is that what you tell your patients?" She had to ask, because she didn't want to have dinner with Dr. Newlon. Katherine needed him to be Tyler tonight, just for a while.

"No, most of my patients have appointments and come to my office," he reminded her. "Why don't you tell me what's bothering you? Ever since your phone rang, you seem disturbed."

He was very spot-on. "I'll make a deal with you," she said.

Tyler chuckled, the sound music to her ears. Though cliché, it was true.

"I'm game. What are you offering?"

Determined to reserve her problems for later, she spoke confidently, even though she felt rattled. "After dinner, we can talk about my . . . issues."

"I agree, but only if you're comfortable. I'm not here as a doctor, Katherine. I want to be honest with you. You're a very attractive woman and, I'll admit, I'm more than a bit smitten with you."

Once again, he grinned, causing her stomach to tighten with long pent-up frustrations that had lain dormant far too long. She wondered how it was possible to be "smitten" when they barely knew each other. If she were being honest, she would say the feelings were mutual, and in the scheme of life, it didn't really matter how long they'd known each other.

"That's a relief," she told him. It was all she could come up with. Her emotions were dancing like jumping beans.

"That I'm not here as a doctor, or that I'm smitten with you?" he asked in a teasing tone.

She turned back to the stove so he couldn't see her smiling. "Both."

"And would I be jumping the gun if I asked if being smitten is mutual?"

Oh boy, he was not one for being subtle. "I think you're very nice. Doc Baker said you're an excellent doctor, so I guess I am a little smitten, too. Now I need to finish this." She motioned to the pots on the stove. "Otherwise, that cheese is all we'll have for dinner," she teased in a humorous tone, hoping it would take focus off the fact she'd acknowledged she was just as smitten with him.

"Then what can I do to help speed up the process?" he asked, standing up and walking across the kitchen to where she stood. Having him this close made her dizzy, though also in a good way. "I love the fire and the table. I didn't notice them at first," he said when he saw her handiwork around the corner. He'd been unable to see that area earlier, since the large room was L-shaped and the fireplace area was more of a small sitting room. She'd use it as her new dining room now. It would be cozy in the winter. She could bring her laptop with her and work.

"I don't come in here very often. I'm ashamed to say tonight is the first time I've used this room for a meal."

"It looks inviting."

"I can take you on a house tour after dinner if you like," she offered. "I don't use all the rooms. It's a bit of a waste, but I like my privacy."

"So I hear," Tyler said.

She wanted to ask who he'd heard that from but didn't. If he wanted her to know, he would have said their name. It didn't matter anyway. She wasn't going to allow gossip to ruin the first dinner party she was having in the privacy of her own home. "I use the formal dining room as my home office. The view is amazing, especially this time of year."

"When I was coming up the drive, I saw the wall of windows. I hope that's your office, because the mountain view must be stunning. In another month or so, the trees will be at their peak. One of the reasons I love this place. It's easy on the eyes."

"You're referring to North Carolina?" she asked, placing the loaf of French bread in the oven. She then increased the burners to heat the potatoes and peas and stirred the gravy.

"Of course. I was born and raised here. It's home," Tyler said, as he trailed behind her. "What about yourself?"

Katherine stopped stirring the potatoes. She took a deep breath in, another out. "What about me?" she asked, seeming to have more confidence when she had her back turned to him.

"Where are you from?" Tyler asked. "I can't place your accent."

Did she want to go into this now, before dinner? She supposed it wouldn't hurt to tell him her home state. "I was born in Texas."

"The Lone Star State. I've been there a few times for conferences. Big state, friendly people."

Katherine thought if he only knew her parents, he might not be so quick to categorize Texans as friendly. Though she had to admit, most were good folks.

"I left when I was younger and just never lost the accent," she explained, as she put the chicken on a serving platter. She then spooned out the potatoes, peas, and gravy into small serving dishes. She took the bread out of the oven, wrapping it in a clean kitchen towel before placing it in a basket. "I think we're ready. You want to grab the salt and pepper?" She nodded toward the stove.

"Absolutely."

The oak log she'd added to the fireplace gave off a woodsy scent. Fiery sparks snapped, and the orange-yellow flames cast the small room in cozy shadows. She felt the setting was much more intimate now, with the fire ablaze and no other lights on in the room.

Katherine placed the platter and bowls on the table. There wasn't much room, but she managed to arrange the dishes. "Would you like something besides wine with dinner?" she asked.

"No, this is perfect," he said.

She felt blood rush to her face and was glad for the dim light. "Have a seat, and I'll get more wine." Before he could help, she went to the kitchen, needing a few seconds alone to get her act together. She needed to stop assuming every word Tyler said was a come-on. Once again, she attributed it to the fact that she'd been alone for too long.

The dogs were lying on their favorite rugs, and she spoke to them. "You both are getting an extra . . ." She didn't say *treat*, or they'd go bonkers, so she finished with, "dose of love tonight." They watched her and then plopped their heads down, as if they understood exactly what she was referring to.

When she returned, Tyler stood beside the table. "Allow me." He took the bottle of wine from her, refilled their glasses, then pulled her chair out before taking the seat opposite her.

"Thanks."

"Would you like me to carve this? I've had a bit of training," he teased.

"Sure." She couldn't help but laugh. "But I thought you were a psychiatrist."

He took the knife she'd placed on the platter, cutting into the meat with precision. "I had some surgical training in med school."

"I can see that."

Tyler served the chicken, and then she added the potatoes, peas, and a spoonful of gravy to their plates. "Hope you like peas," she added.

"I will eat anything in sight. This smells divine; I haven't had a real home-cooked meal in a while. And to answer your question, I like peas."

They chatted aimlessly between bites about the weather, her dogs, and the upcoming holidays, but nothing terribly personal. When they finished, she returned their plates to the kitchen and then came back with the apple pie, dessert plates, and clean forks. "Apple pie I made this morning." Katherine set the dish in the center of the small table. "No ice cream, though."

"Ice cream can be overrated," Tyler informed her. "But I'm not saying I don't like a scoop now and then."

Katherine didn't explain to him why she didn't have ice cream. The few times she'd ordered it from the gourmet market, it had arrived mushy. Refreezing it hadn't helped. So she'd given up ice cream and didn't miss it, either.

She sliced the pie, giving Tyler an extra-large piece, since he hadn't had anything home-cooked in a while.

"This looks fantastic. I appreciate all this." He gestured to the fire, the pie, the wine.

"I'm glad I had the courage to accept your invitation to dinner." Again, she was glad for the dim lighting so Tyler couldn't see her blush.

"So am I." He took a bite of pie and then winked at her.

He watched her intently. She was tingling in all the right places. A ripple of excitement coursed through her. The possibilities were endless tonight, and she would make the most of them. Fearful of this intense attraction, yet thrilled, she decided she would not discourage him if he insinuated he wanted this evening to end in her bedroom.

"You don't like the pie?" he asked.

She hadn't taken a first bite. "I do. I was just thinking."

He finished his pie, then pushed his dessert plate aside, reaching across the table and taking her hand. Goosebumps traveled the length of her body.

"You can share your thoughts if you like," he told her.

She shook her head. "No, they're not important right now."

"If you say so. Though I believe every thought running through your head is important."

She gave him a slight grin. "I'm not sure I'd go that far."

"Don't underestimate the powers you possess." His tone was serious now. "I mean this in a positive way. The human brain is the most magnificent machine; nothing else compares."

"That's doctor-speak," she said, though she wasn't the least bit offended that he hadn't waited until after dinner to bridge the topic, even though, technically, they were finished.

"No, this is me still. Just common sense."

Unsure how to take this comment, she didn't say anything.

"Doc calls you K. Why is that?"

Talk about a complete change of subject. It occurred to her that she hadn't told him her full name. "K is short for Katherine."

"Katherine." He repeated her name. "Beautiful."

"Thank you," was all she could manage to say.

An uneasy silence filled the small space between them. Katherine recognized the sudden bonelike dryness in her throat, her inability to swallow. She feared she would choke. Suddenly her hands were like those of a ninety-year-old, trembling with age. She hid them beneath the table, tearing her paper napkin into shreds. Her breath came in short bursts, but her throat was too tight, closed. No air.

"Katherine, you're having a panic attack. It's all right. I'm here." Tyler reached below the table, taking her hands in his. Keenly aware of the warmth of his hands, Katherine found his touch jarring yet comforting.

"Focus on me." Tyler spoke softly. "Look at my shirt. See the buttons, my pocket."

She followed his directions, noticing each pearl button, the threads in the blue chambray shirt's fabric, and the double stitching on his pocket. Nodding, she continued to focus on the details of the shirt. His sleeves were folded halfway, the cuffs even, revealing tanned, muscular forearms. His collar was unbuttoned. Her eyes stopped on the patch of dark chest hair at the V of his collar. Quickly, she focused her gaze back on the buttons, unable—yet wanting—to make eye contact with him.

"You're good. Keep concentrating on my shirt," Tyler continued to coax.

Able to take a deep breath as the tightness in her throat eased, she pulled one of her hands from Tyler's. She took her wineglass and downed what was left in her glass. Embarrassed beyond her wildest imaginings, she removed her other hand from his. She licked her still-dry lips, lowering her eyes to the shredded napkin in her lap. After she took a deep breath and slowly released it, her symptoms eased to a tolerable level.

"Better?" Tyler asked.

"Yes."

"I'll get some water." He went to the main area of kitchen, returning with a large glass of tap water.

She guzzled the water like she was dehydrated after weeks in the desert. When she finished, she put the glass down on the table. Searching for the right words, she decided there weren't any, so she went with her truth. "I'm embarrassed you had to see me this way. I don't know why the attack hit me."

"There isn't always an explanation. Accept that."

She shook her head but said, "I know."

"Do you want to talk about this with me now, as a doctor, or would you rather I come over another time?"

"I've ruined the evening for you. I'm so sorry," she said, her dark eyes pooling with tears.

"No, you didn't. Stop thinking that way. This is the best evening I've had in a very long time."

She offered him a droll smile. "I won't question that."

He laughed. "Another time. Let's clean these dishes, and then you can take me on the tour of your house. Unless you'd rather wait."

"You don't have to clean up. You're my guest. You can let Sam and Sophie out for me. I'll only be a few minutes, and then I'll take you on the tour I promised. I'm fine. Really," she added.

"I accept your offer. Should I go out with the dogs?"

"No, just let them out and leave the doors open. They usually have a good half-hour romp before calling it a day."

"Sam and Sophie, right?"

When they heard their names, both dogs jumped off their rugs and ran to the door.

"Come on, you two," Tyler said. "Time for me to get to know you beauties." He spoke to the dogs as though they were human. He opened the door, and the dogs flew outside. "I'm going to watch them, see where they're going," he told Katherine.

"Thanks," she called from the kitchen. Had Doc Baker told Tyler to watch where the dogs went on their nightly jaunts, or was Tyler just curious?

Katherine packed the leftovers in plastic containers to send home with Tyler. She loaded the dishwasher and scrubbed the pots before she realized she'd hardly touched her food. She wasn't hungry. The attacks always stopped her from eating, since one of her irrational fears was choking. Tyler talking her through this attack had shortened it and its severity. Katherine wiped down the counters and the stovetop and checked on the fire. She'd let it burn down until Tyler left and then put it out before she went to bed.

Satisfied, she made a pot of coffee, remembering Tyler drank his black. She took two mugs from the cupboard, waiting until he brought the dogs back in before pouring a cup for herself. Glancing at the clock on the stove, she saw they'd been outside for almost half an hour. Wondering what was keeping them, she went to the open doors to see if they were in sight. She heard the whinnying horses and figured Tyler was checking on them for his friend Carson. Wishing she had the courage to stroll to the stables, she returned to the kitchen and filled her mug with coffee.

Taking her coffee, she returned to the table to wait for Tyler and the dogs. She watched the orange and yellow flames of the fire, the fiery red sparks darting up the chimney. Thinking back to the phone call earlier, she took the burner phone out of her pocket. The call definitely hadn't come from the number Karrie had used. Before changing her mind, Katherine returned to the main kitchen, took a small notepad and pen from her junk drawer, and wrote the number down. She put the paper in her pocket and then deleted the call history from the phone. Later she'd search the phone number to see if she could locate the city and state or maybe do a reverse number check. It also could've been a wrong number. She put the phone back in her pocket after she deleted the number.

Just as she was ready to call Tyler's cell, she heard the dogs barking in the distance. When they trotted through the door, they went straight to the kitchen. They'd had dinner earlier this evening, but she'd probably confused them, as she normally fed them at the same time every day. The dogs must have thought it was treat time.

"Sorry I was gone so long," Tyler said. "I checked the horses."

"I figured as much. Everything okay?"

"Perfect. They seem to be doing just fine. Your dogs seem

to like them. They did everything I asked them to." He closed the door, following the dogs to the kitchen.

Both dogs were standing by the counter, knowing their treats were in the canister Katherine kept stocked for them. She took a beef stick out, breaking it in half. They'd had way too many extra treats today. "Sit." They both did as instructed, and she gave them the treat. "They're well-behaved, though it took some training. I don't know what I'd do without them."

"You've done a remarkable job."

"Thanks. I have to admit that they made it pretty easy."

She remembered the day the dogs were delivered to her doorstep by a courier from the Asheville airport. They were just a few months old, their fur matted, their deep brown eyes filled with fear. It hadn't taken her long to make them feel right at home. She'd found Doc Baker then and made what she hoped was a lifelong friend.

"I have a couple of cats, courtesy of Doc Baker," Tyler said. "Part of an abandoned litter he took in. I believe he kept a couple for himself. Mom and Dad have the only female in the bunch. They're quite entertaining."

"I never figured you or Doc for the feline type," she said, with a newfound admiration for both men.

"I like all animals—dogs, cats, horses," Tyler said with a grin.

"I was never allowed to have an animal as a child. My parents thought they were messy and useless."

She poured him coffee without first asking if he wanted any. He took the cup from her with a "Thanks." He took a sip, shaking his head from left to right. "That's wrong. Your parents, I mean. I'm sorry. All kids need an animal to love, to care for. I think it's good for kids. It gives them a sense of responsibility. I suggest to some of my younger patients that they would do well with an animal. The ones that followed the advice are fine now and don't need to see me anymore."

"You think the animals helped with their treatment?" Katherine asked, now more than just a little curious about his life as a doctor.

"I do."

"These two keep me on track most of the time," Katherine told him. "I need to be able to go outside with them, see where they go when I can't hear them from the house." She explained what had occurred the night before.

"It could have been a wild animal," Tyler agreed when she was done. "It's certainly not unheard of in this area, though I agree it's a good idea for you to learn their stomping grounds."

She nodded. "Can you really help me with this . . . disorder?" she asked.

"Of course I can. I've had many patients with agoraphobia. Maybe not as severe as yours, but to answer your question—yes, it's treatable. If you were my patient, I would suggest you try to recall when or if you suffered a traumatic event right before your behavior changed."

Unsure if she should tell him what drove her to lock herself inside, she decided she couldn't. It was too soon, and tonight wasn't the time. Later, when she knew him a bit better, she would tell him. "I see."

"I assume you aren't ready to talk about your experiences?"

She finished her coffee, got up, and refilled her cup. "You need another cup?"

"No, I'm good," he said. "Am I right? You're not ready to talk about the event that caused your change in behavior?"

Katherine thought he was very, very good at his profession. "No, not yet. Maybe in the future."

"I'm going to put my doctor hat on and tell you the longer you put this off, the worse it will get. You don't want to spend the rest of your life inside."

He was right. But his comment put her on the defensive. "I

went outside earlier. I brought my groceries inside," she told him. "That's the first time since I moved in here. Pathetic, I know."

"No, that's remarkable, especially since you tried it alone. It's more progress than you realize."

"I hope so." She wanted to talk about something other than her mental illness. "Why don't I give you a tour of the house before it gets too late?" She didn't really care about the time, but it was all she could come up with for now. The idea that she would let him "medically treat" her after dinner had been ludicrous, but then again, she thought—why not? She couldn't decide. Not wanting to disappoint him or Doc, she had an instant change of heart. "Then we can talk about me," she said, before she could change her mind again, "and my issues." She would keep her word to Doc.

"If you're sure?" Tyler reiterated.

"As you said, putting it off isn't in my best interest."

"You're already making progress acknowledging this and going out alone. You might not think it's a big deal, but it is." Tyler stood, putting his empty cup in the sink.

"I appreciate those words. I'm so used to living this way, and it's become very comfortable. But it's not normal, and I know that. I've always known it," she added.

"I have no doubt. Now, why don't you show me around this massive place? Ever since this house was built, I've always been curious about the inside."

She nodded. "Then let's get started."

Katherine walked Tyler through the rooms on the first floor. He admired several of the paintings in her living room. She told him most of the art in her house was from local artists. She wanted to give back to her community, even though she'd never really been a part of the day-to-day life in Blowing Rock.

She led him upstairs to the top of the landing, where the windows were floor-to-ceiling like those in the dining room.

"Stunning," Tyler remarked. "You're lucky to have these views."

There wasn't much to show upstairs except all the empty bedrooms and bathrooms. She quickly opened each door, letting him peer into the empty rooms. Two of the bedrooms still had beds left over from the previous owner, but otherwise, there wasn't much to see. After debating whether or not to open the door to her bedroom, she did. Her earlier thoughts of them together in her room for the night were just that. Thoughts. Tyler had given no indication he expected anything more than dinner.

As soon as she opened her bedroom door, she could feel a sense of foreboding, as if something bad was about to happen.

Chapter Eleven

Duckie was gone. She'd placed her against the pillows that morning when she'd made up her bed.

"I think someone has been in my room," Katherine said, glad for Tyler's presence. "I'm sure of it." She scanned the room, her gaze resting on her nightstand. "Damn!"

"What?"

Fear knotted inside her. "My notebook is gone!"

Tyler stared at her.

"You might as well know, since you have to do that doctor-patient confidentiality thing, right? You cannot repeat what I am about to tell you."

"Whatever you tell me stays between us, Katherine. Personal and professional."

"Sit." She plopped on the edge of her bed and patted the space beside her. Tyler sat next to her.

"I'm an author. I write books." Her leg shook uncontrollably. She pushed her boot into the plush carpet so he wouldn't see how nervous she was.

"That explains how you're able to work from home. I wondered if you worked or were just filthy rich." He laughed. "I'm teasing about the rich stuff."

"You shouldn't, because I am what you said. Rich. Oil

rich. Not sure about the filthy part," she added, her voice laced with sarcasm. "My family left me their fortune and their business. I have people who take care of that part of my life. I don't involve myself in its functions at all. I don't have time, even if I wanted to, since I have my writing. And now, someone has my notes for my newest book. Someone has been in my house!" She raked a hand through her hair, twisting the ends around her fingers.

"Okay, then let's call the police. Let them search the property," Tyler said.

Katherine stood up abruptly. "No! I don't want to call the police."

Tyler spoke up, sounding a bit exasperated for the first time that evening. "Why? If someone broke into your home, you were here when it happened. Your life could be at risk, Katherine. I know a couple of officers I can call. They're discreet."

"No, Tyler. No police, discreet or not."

She took a deep breath, sure he thought she was some criminal who was hiding out. She had to clarify her stance on the police. "Look, Tyler, if you think I'm a . . . fugitive or whatever, I'm not. I have my reasons for not wanting the police here."

"Can you share them?"

"I don't know if you're a book lover. It doesn't matter. I'm K.C. Winston, the author. I choose to keep it quiet, as I don't want or need any publicity of any kind." There. It was out.

He appeared astounded. "You're serious? You're *K.C. Winston?*"

She raised her voice enough that Sam and Sophie came running to her side. "Why would I joke about my career?"

"Does anyone else know this?" Tyler asked.

She nodded, her thoughts all over the place. Frustrated, Katherine walked over to the window to see if there was a car or someone on foot, but it was so dark, she couldn't see beyond a few feet. The outdoor lights only covered the outer perimeter of the property surrounding the house.

"I have an alarm," she said, putting voice to her thoughts. "Though it hasn't been on today. I leave the French doors open all the time." Had someone slipped inside her house while she was in the kitchen? The shower? While the dogs were outside? She tried to force herself to remember if she'd heard anything unusual while she'd been busy prepping dinner, but she didn't recall anything. Nothing had seemed odd or out of the norm.

"Do you think someone could've come inside, possibly hid, then slipped away without you knowing?" Tyler asked.

"I'd like to think not, but I can't be one hundred percent sure. This place is huge. It wouldn't be hard to find a hiding spot. Maybe when I was upstairs taking a shower? This is crazy. What would motivate a stranger to take my childhood stuffed lamb and the spiral notebook with my book, outline, and notes? Damn."

Her biggest fear was the public finding her here, then all the accompanying publicity about Adam's death and the men who'd killed him and maimed all those people in Boston. Her parents' tragic ending. It would be a frenzy, with reporters and people prying into her life. No, she did not want her private or professional life made public. If she were being completely honest, her fear of leaving her safe space worried her more than the public knowing who she was and where she lived. It would force her to acknowledge publicly that she suffered from mental illness. Ernest Hemingway. Virginia Woolf. They both committed suicide. Sadly, there were those who already thought authors were just plain crazy. Jack London, the author of one of her favorite novels, *The Call of the Wild*, had also purportedly killed himself. She didn't want K.C. Winston lumped into the insanity category. Not that her work was remotely comparable to theirs, but that's where her mind was going. She paced the length of her bed, while Tyler remained seated.

"I don't need this now. It's crazy. I guess it's fitting, when you think of it. Crazy author. Crazy break-in," Katherine said.

"You're truly K.C. Winston?" Tyler asked again. "I know a kid who reads your books. A former patient of mine."

Katherine stopped, standing in front of him. It didn't matter who she was at this point. "Why would I lie to you? Doc Baker knows. That's why he calls me K." She watched him, a range of emotions changing him from the Tyler she barely knew to a stranger. Maybe this was Dr. Newlon? Admittedly, it was flattering to know her books were known to him.

"I believe you, Katherine. I wasn't trying to imply you weren't K.C. Winston." He took a deep breath. "I was thinking. When I took the dogs out and we went to the barn, I told you the horses were fine. But looking back, I don't believe they were. I'm not a veterinarian, but I've been around horses enough to know their normal body language. Both horses kept flicking their ears. Numerous times. It's possible they saw someone then."

"I don't understand." She sat beside him on the bed, what little fight she'd had in her sizzling out like a deflated balloon.

"I read once that when a horse moves their ears back and forth, more often than not, it's an indicator of fear, anxiousness. For humans, our hearts race," he explained. "Our antennae shoot up. Doc and Carson would know better, but they're not here. It could just be something Carson's horses normally do. Are you sure you didn't hear anything? Did you leave the room?"

"No, I was in the kitchen cleaning the dishes while you were out. But wait—I did jot down a note. I left the pad on the counter in the kitchen." She couldn't explain why she'd written down the number from the burner phone, then deleted it. She knew how silly it would sound, especially to a psychiatrist. Katherine still had the number in her pocket. She doubted there was a connection to Karrie or her Friend-link page. What would that matter now? Surely a wrong call on a burner cell from a number she didn't recognize wasn't linked to this break-in. It all seemed absurd.

"Let's check your desk," Tyler said.

"Why?"

"Possibly whoever was here also took something from your desk. I assume it's where you do all your writing. It could be someone knows who you are."

Katherine didn't like being put on the spot. This Karrie situation wasn't any of Tyler's business. *She* wasn't his business. Katherine didn't want to go into a full-blown explanation. He'd really think she was a loony toon.

"I don't see how anyone could even know where I live. I've managed to get by all these years without any problems," she said. It was odd that just now, when she'd decided to make drastic changes to her lifestyle, her identity may have been discovered. She thought there was more to this than being a well-known author or some deranged person prying through her possessions. Her gut instinct was kicking in, as it used to all those years ago.

Tyler stood and jammed his hands in his jeans pockets. Katherine found him devastatingly handsome; she'd bet all his patients fell just a tiny bit in love with him.

"Let's go downstairs and see if anything is missing," he said again.

She took a deep breath, feeling anxious. "All right," she said, heading downstairs, both dogs at her heels. "I want to check my alarm system first."

Once downstairs, she set the alarm in the kitchen and then turned the outside security lights off. If anyone were lurking on the property, let them do so in the dark. "I should be able to see if anyone was outside. The cameras are backed up on a website." Then she headed into the dining room. She instantly knew someone had been there. "This is not how I left my desk, dammit!" Beyond alarmed, she explained to Tyler, "I left my computer on." Her laptop was now closed, and several handwritten notes that had been beside her computer were gone, too.

"Hang on," she said, pushing papers around the desk. "The flash drive I use to back up my work isn't here, either."

"You're sure?" Tyler questioned.

"Of course, I'm sure! I always use a flash drive, a new one for every book. It's not here." She searched her desk again to ensure the flash drive wasn't hiding underneath anything. "I use different colors. This one is fluorescent pink. It stands out."

She chewed on her fingernail, debating if she should call the police. Let them have a look around the property. Whoever did this could ruin her if word of who she was were to be made public. Any reporter who could dig deep would discover her secrets. Her life as she knew it now would never be the same. Her family tragedy would be a headline again. Adam, too. And other things she could not allow to become public. Such as it was, she didn't want her reputation ruined. "I'm going to call Doc. He has a friend that might be able to look into this."

"This isn't my business, but if you're in trouble, I want to help. If you'll trust me," Tyler said.

"Tyler, this isn't a question of me not trusting you. I have issues from my past. I've isolated myself from the world because of them. I can't talk about it all yet. I know I sound crazy. But I'm not in the kind of trouble you're thinking." She spoke in a harsh whisper, not caring how it came out. Someone had been in her home, and she wanted to find out who was brazen enough to do it.

"Then call Doc Baker. Tell him I'm here, so he'll know you're safe," Tyler added, speaking gently.

She felt a second of remorse for her rudeness. But he'd have to get over it; he was a doctor, after all. He should be used to crazy people.

Katherine nodded, focusing her attention on her cell phone to make the needed call. But she stopped when she heard glass shattering and pounding footsteps on the deck.

Frozen in place, holding her finger to her mouth, Katherine motioned to the stairs with a quick tilt of her head. She took the stairs two at a time, Tyler and the dogs racing behind her. She locked the door as soon as they were back inside her bedroom with the dogs. She leaned as close to Tyler as she could, whispering in his ear, "I think they're on the deck."

His blue eyes grew serious with concern. "I can hear them running."

Katherine mouthed, "Follow me."

When they were safely inside the adjoining primary bathroom, she locked the door. The scent of her orange-blossom shampoo lingered in the air. Water droplets rivered down the glassed-in shower, evidence of her preparation for the evening. It had not turned out as planned.

Still whispering, though this time she didn't step in as closely as before, she said, "The computer at my desk was off, and I have the settings adjusted so it doesn't shut down automatically. Someone must've turned it off when I returned to the kitchen." Her hands trembled, her throat tight from fear. "They had to have been in the house for a while." Just the thought made her sick to her stomach.

Tyler nodded but didn't speak.

"I'm still afraid to call the police," she whispered. "I'm going to call Doc. He'll know what to do . . . he has a connection." She took her cell phone out of her pocket, glad she'd put Doc on speed dial. He answered on the first ring.

"What's up, kid?"

She told him about the break-in, asking if his CIA friend

could help. "I don't want to call the local police. I want to keep this as private as possible. We think someone has been in the house, and they're still on my property." She knew he wouldn't question her about the details until they were face-to-face.

"We heard glass breaking and footsteps." She spoke as quietly as possible, although she wanted to scream as loudly as she could. Katherine knew if she didn't get her act together that maybe next time something like this happened—and she prayed there wouldn't be a next time—she might be alone.

"I'll call Ilene and see if she's available. Stay put, don't touch anything, and don't move until I get there," Doc ordered.

Katherine looked at the time on her phone. Half past nine. Not too late, though she had no clue if Doc's friend went to bed early. "Okay, but hurry. Tyler is here with me now."

"Good. You can trust him, K, with your life. Now I'll get back to you as soon as I can," Doc Baker said. "Remember, stay put. Keep your alarm on."

She hung up, unsure of her next move.

"You said you have cameras? Can you access them on your phone?" Tyler asked.

Katherine's hands shook as she typed in the web address on her phone, then logged into her account. "These aren't super clear. They're small, but all the cameras are here." She held her phone out so they could view the images. As they were time-stamped, she forwarded to the images from the early afternoon and to the camera that focused on the French doors and the deck. There were seven surveillance cameras outside, each directed at the entrances. The most obvious entry point for an intruder were the doors she always left open for the dogs. Nothing looked unusual until 4:45.

"Look at that," Tyler said. "Do you recognize this person?"

Katherine took the phone from him, replaying the image. A person—she couldn't tell if they were male or female—ran through the open French doors. They wore a camouflage jacket with a hoodie and dark denim jeans. She replayed the video again, then hit stop and could see dark boots. The intruder's head was lowered. Based on how they'd disguised themselves, the person must have known she had security cameras, even though they weren't visible unless one knew where to look.

"Forward that time to half an hour ago," Tyler said.

Katherine used the slide bar on her cell phone touch screen, stopping at nine o'clock. That would've been about when they'd heard the glass shatter and the footsteps running across the deck. She let the video play for a few minutes, and then an image of the intruder appeared, a flash of black racing across the deck.

"At least I know they're not inside now. I hope," she said, her voice a bit high-pitched as she tried to steer her thoughts away from what she'd seen. This was the most horrific scare she'd had in a very long time. In all her years of living alone on the mountain, she had never been frightened like this inside of her own home, other than her panic attacks, which were internal. Now, even with all her security cameras, her home violated by this . . . *person*. She wouldn't feel comfortable until they were caught. Without calling the police, she knew the chances of the intruder being arrested were slim, unless Doc's CIA friend could help.

"Let's go downstairs, if you're ready," Tyler suggested. "Your prowler must be gone by now."

"Wait. From what I remember, once you turn off Red Oak Road, it's what . . . a mile or so leading up to the house? I need to warn Doc. He could still be out there."

"It is about a mile, I guess," Tyler agreed.

She speed-dialed Doc again. "Listen, whoever was in my

house has left. They're on foot and could be hiding. Be careful. Watch out for a tall person wearing a camouflage jacket with a hoodie and a backpack."

"Damn it, K! You need the police. I'm getting ready to turn off Red Oak Road now. I'm bringing Ilene with me. If she tells you to call the cops, you better do what she says." Doc ended the call. Katherine knew he was angry with her for not doing what any normal person would do in the same situation.

"Doc will be here in a few minutes," Katherine said. "Come on. I'll make a fresh pot of coffee." Making coffee was the last thing she wanted to do. Now, more than ever, she needed to check her Friendlink page. Surely the break-in wasn't connected to Karrie? But she needed to verify it for herself. Together, Katherine and Tyler made their way, silently and extremely carefully, out of the bathroom. They left the dogs inside to prevent them from racing around. They then crept out of the bedroom and down the stairs. They paused every few feet to listen and observe, but there were no sounds or signs or any other activity in the house.

Finally, they made their way back into the kitchen. After a thorough inspection that didn't turn up anything new, Tyler went upstairs to release the dogs. Katherine waited for the familiar physical sensations that indicated an oncoming attack. Other than a rapid heartbeat and a bit of sweat under her arms, she seemed to be dealing with this. She rinsed out the coffee pot and refilled it from the tap. She dumped the grounds from earlier into the sink, added fresh coffee, then hit brew. She found the mindless task she performed daily comforting, and it helped steady her still-trembling hands. Turning to face Tyler as he reentered the room with the dogs close behind, she said, "I need a minute. Be right back."

"Of course," Tyler said.

Sam and Sophie at her heels, Katherine slipped inside the

small powder room under the stairs. "Come on, you two. Now sit," she commanded. The dogs obeyed. Sitting on the edge of the toilet seat, she took her cell phone from her pocket and logged onto her Friendlink page.

Bigfan216: Hey!
HotandCool: WTF girl! Where you been?
Bigfan216: Just busy.

They were the only two on the page at the moment.

Bigfan216: Any newbies? No one here!
HotandCool: Nope. Same peeps.

This was getting nowhere fast, and she didn't have much time. She wanted to ask about Karrie without coming off as a weirdo.

Bigfan216: Karrie been online?
HotandCool: Nope. Just me and you.
Bigfan216: She was supposed to call. Kinda worried . . .
HotandCool: So call her yourself!
Bigfan216: Sure, I can do that, I'll TTYL.

Katherine logged off the site, flushing the toilet in case Tyler was listening. She looked at her image in the mirror, barely recognizing this version of herself. Her long hair was loose, and she saw fear in her eyes. Yet it wasn't the same fear she'd become accustomed to. "Come on, you two," she said to the dogs and then turned the light off. Returning to the kitchen, she avoided looking at the French door, where the glass was shattered in pieces all over the floor, inside and out.

"You feeling okay? I can give you something for your nerves if you want," Tyler said.

She must've looked as bad as she'd thought. "No thanks, I'm managing." She wasn't really, but he probably knew that already, given his profession. "I hate that this happened while you were here. Not the best evening you've had, huh?"

"I've had much worse, Katherine. I'm just glad I was here with you."

She took two clean mugs from the cupboard, poured coffee into each, and handed one to Tyler. "So am I. Who knows how I would've reacted on my own?"

"My guess is pretty damn well." He smiled, his eyes twinkling.

Katherine realized again that she could fall for Tyler, big time. The question was—could he fall for her?

Chapter Twelve

Sam and Sophie heard Doc's old Ford truck pulling up the long drive, the rattle of the engine coughing up its familiar putter before its final sigh. Both hurried toward the door, but Katherine held back. Glass was everywhere.

"Sit," Katherine ordered the dogs, as Doc Baker and his companion approached. Katherine was instantly struck by the exotic woman at his side. This must be Ilene Silva. "Watch the glass," Katherine warned. "Thanks for getting here so fast." Katherine found it hard to tear her gaze away from the woman. "Please, come in." Katherine stepped aside, then closed the shattered doors. "I have coffee or a drink if you'd like." Her social graces dictated she offer them something, even though this wasn't a social visit.

"This is K," Doc said to Ilene.

Ilene Silva was tall, at least five-ten. Her black skin-hugging dress showed off her slender curves, yet she wore practical black low-heeled pumps with sheer stockings. Her dark brown hair was cut razor straight, then sharply angled toward her chin. Her hair shined as if she'd come straight from a stylist. Diamonds flashed on her hands and around her neck. Her eyes were an unusual aqua color. *Regal* came to Katherine's mind—if you didn't look at her shoes.

Ilene stared back at Katherine like she was a specimen in a petri dish. "I can't say I'm pleased to meet you, so good evening will have to do," Ilene said, holding a well-manicured hand out to Katherine. "Are those your dogs? I'm terrible around animals."

Put off by her rudeness, Katherine ignored Ilene's outstretched hand. This woman didn't like animals. That was an immediate strike against her. Katherine shooed Sam and Sophie upstairs. She then turned abruptly away from Doc and his brusque sidekick. With a newfound boldness, Katherine refused to be intimidated by the woman's commanding presence, probably a remnant of her time in the CIA.

Tyler stood when they entered the kitchen. "Doc, Ilene," he said, and shook both of their hands.

How does he know this woman? Katherine wondered. A dozen questions soared through her mind, but she didn't dare ask them.

"Tyler, you get more handsome every time I see you. How's your mother doing these days?" Ilene asked. Her knowledge of Tyler's mother helped put Katherine more at ease. Possibly Tyler's mother and Ilene were friends?

"You know her—ornery as ever," Tyler said, a grin on his face.

"She's a good girl. I've always admired Cecilia. She's practically a saint, putting up with your father all these years," Ilene added.

Katherine observed their banter and thought it inappropriate, given the circumstances. "Would either of you like a coffee? Something stronger?" she asked again.

"I'm fine. Thank you, Katherine. That's such a pretty name," Ilene said. "Who were you named after?"

"Thanks. I wasn't named after anyone that I know of. Maybe a stray nurse in pediatrics." Katherine was telling the truth; she had no clue who she was named after. Probably one of her father's employees or a name scratched on the wall of a dirty restroom. That was her mother's style. Spiteful and demeaning.

Ilene turned to Doc. "You're right. She's a gutsy little thing, even if she doesn't acknowledge it herself."

Katherine had to respond. "What are you talking about?"

Ilene took charge. "You. Doc told me about you, your situation, and what's happened tonight. Given all this, I'll stick with my initial impression. You're gutsy."

Katherine was unsure how to further respond. So she said what came naturally. "Thank you, I do appreciate the compliment, though it's not true." She offered up a wan smile. They were not off to a good start, Katherine thought. She hated bossy women.

"Never underestimate yourself. Right, Franklin?" Ilene winked at Doc Baker.

Franklin? Katherine realized that before this, she had no clue what Doc's first name was.

"Come on, Ilene. You've messed with K enough for now," Doc said. "You two want to tell us what happened tonight? Why the hell didn't you call the police? You better have a damned good reason, kiddo."

Nodding in agreement, Katherine forced herself to respond truthfully. She gave Doc all of the details of what happened, with Tyler backing her up. "If you want to look at the security cameras, maybe we missed something. I'm not the expert here." She focused her attention on Ilene.

"Can we sit down?" Ilene asked.

"Of course. Let's go to the dining room." Katherine put her cup in the sink, then led the trio to her dining room. She touched a wall panel, and the room filled with light.

"Wow," Ilene said.

"The table is hideous, I know. It was here when I bought the place," Katherine explained, a smirk on her face. "I'd planned on asking Doc if he knew of a church or a charity I could donate this monstrosity to. I just never got around to it." The table was a brushed silver color. Its odd shape reminded Katherine of a puzzle piece. The chairs matched the table; the seats and backs were tufted, the material a maroon velvet, and the chair legs a curved cabriole style. *Hideous* was being nice.

"Are you sure Elvis isn't lurking around here?" Ilene asked. "Never mind. That's crude of me. I apologize."

But Katherine agreed. The former owners may have had an affinity for the King of Rock and Roll.

"Have a seat," Katherine said. "Believe it or not, these ugly chairs are quite comfortable."

Once they were seated, Ilene took charge. "I'll need full access to your security footage. As you said, I might see something you missed. I also want to search the house, top to bottom. Whoever rifled through your desk and turned your computer off probably left fingerprints. I suggest we get a forensic team in here tonight." Ilene paused. "I don't have access to my former contacts in that department, so we'll have to allow the locals to take care of this aspect of the investigation. Plus, you do need an official police report. They can document what's missing."

"No! I can't let the public know about this. Doc?" Katherine turned to him, her brows raised in question. "You explained to her why I can't?"

"I think you should tell Ilene what you want her to know," Doc said. "I've kept my word, K. Now, you need to let Ilene do her job or not. Up to you."

"He's right, Katherine," Tyler chimed in. "Who knows if this will happen again? Your safety is important to me." Tyler stood. "The doors are still open. I'll close them."

"No, Tyler. Leave it. Evidence," Ilene said. "Go ahead, tell me what you can."

Were the two people Katherine felt a kinship with turning on her? "I know it's crazy," Katherine said, and glanced at Tyler. "But there is a part of my life that I've kept hidden for

good reason. If I tell you all, I must be assured it won't leak."
She would tell them what she thought they needed to know.
Doc, Tyler, and Ilene all stared at her.

"Not that I can't trust you. It's the police. If they start nosing around, the privacy I've kept for years will be ruined."
Ilene nodded. "Are you in trouble with the authorities?"
"I wish that's all it was. To answer your question, no. I've never even had a traffic ticket." Katherine was in the clear, unless they found out about her fake identification.

"Then what has happened to you that is so horrible you're willing to risk your safety? Maybe your life," Ilene said, her words much gentler than the tough persona she presented.

"K, you can tell us. I promise you that whatever you say won't leave this room. At least not from me," Doc said.

"Count me in. I took an oath, and I'll uphold it. What you say stays here." Tyler used his index finger to tap his head.

"Listen to your friends, Katherine. I don't know you, but Franklin praises you as much as Stephanie. In my profession, keeping my mouth shut was part of the job. While this isn't a CIA issue, and even though I'm retired, I can sniff around. I haven't lost my skills. However, I highly recommend we call the locals. They're pros and have the resources you need. Up to you," Ilene told her.

"Do you remember the Boston Marathon in 2013?" Katherine asked. Just saying the words made her throat tighten—deep breath in, deep breath out.

"Relax, Katherine. We've all got your back," Tyler instructed. "Take a few more deep breaths, okay?" He watched her, and she saw concern in his eyes as he spoke. "And of course we remember. It was all over the news for weeks. A friend of mine was supposed to run that day but backed out when his wife went into early labor."

"I'm fine," Katherine said. "I just need some water. Excuse me."

"I'll get it," Doc said. "Stay put."

Tyler moved his chair closer to hers. "Deep breathing will help. Later I can teach you different methods, if you want to try them. There's a method that stems from the ancient practice of yoga called equal breathing. When you feel ready, we can discuss it in more detail."

"Here, kid." Doc returned with the glass of water, and Katherine gulped it down, not caring that some dripped down her chin.

"Thanks." She took a few deep breaths and placed her empty glass on the table. "Tyler, maybe you can tell me about this yoga practice another time." The last thing she wanted right now was learn a new breathing technique. "I don't know what the local police can do, but I don't want to call them in." She twisted the ends of her hair, struggling with her decision. The past needed to remain in the past. "I don't want the police here. I'll be fine."

"K, you need to think about this for a minute. You're putting yourself in harm's way. Who knows who's still out there? As Tyler said, they could be here now, just waiting for us to leave. It's more than obvious they've been watching you, the house," Doc said. "You're not safe here."

Katherine knew he was right. She should pack a few things and leave. She'd done it once before, and she could do it again. Irrational fears aside, she wanted to erase this evening from her memory and continue on as she had. Her life was far from perfect, but it was hers. She didn't want to give up her privacy unless her life was truly at stake. She wasn't sure if it was or was not at this point. Maybe this was just some whacked-out person who wanted to rob her—though why would they only take her flash drive and her notebook? It couldn't be that simple. Was it possibly a deranged fan? She chewed on her bottom lip. Someone wanted to frighten her, and that mission had been accomplished.

"I can't leave," she told Doc. Before she lost what little nerve she had, she cleared her throat. How could she explain to these decent, kind folks the nightmares that had dominated her life? She'd always remember Adam, but there was little satisfaction in that. His killer, the brother that had survived, currently awaited a death sentence.

"What about the marathon?" Tyler asked. "What's your connection to it?"

She wished she hadn't said anything. "Just that I lost someone I cared about." The room was silent as three sets of eyes stared at her, waiting for her to continue. "And it has nothing to do with this." She waved her hand at the desk behind her.

"As I said, I lost a friend." She knew it would be easy for them to Google the three who'd lost their lives that day and put two and two together. They must think she was truly out of her mind. She had to clear the air. "I was there the day of the bombings. I saw things no one should ever have to see. Looking back, I realize I was in shock. Who wouldn't be? It was horrific." Just thinking about that day could throw her into a panic attack. After another deep breath, she went on. "After taking care of my friend . . ." She paused. "I returned to my apartment, packed a few things, and well . . ." She raked her hand through her hair. "Here I am."

Ilene asked, "Why here?"

Katherine recalled that day when she'd finally broken down and lost what sanity she had left. She'd taken the first exit off I-95 and drove aimlessly until she spotted a block of fast-food restaurants. She'd pulled her Nissan into the first empty parking space she'd seen. She was unsure how long she'd sat there, crying until her eyes were red and swollen. She remembered pounding her fist so hard against the dashboard that her knuckles bled. The pain forced her to focus on her situation. She'd scanned her surroundings, finding herself in the parking lot at a Wendy's.

"Yes, why Blowing Rock, of all places?" Doc asked. "It's nothing like Boston or Texas."

Katherine nodded. "I know. I didn't realize at the time, but I needed to be somewhere safe."

"Listen up, Katherine," Ilene said. "I've been around the block more times than I care to remember. Lots of people were in Boston that day. What aren't you telling us?"

Katherine felt the heat rise in her cheeks. "That's all there is to tell. I was in shock." She looked down at her out-of-style black booties.

"Listen," said Ilene, "you can keep lying all you want, and if Franklin and Tyler want to listen, that's their choice. But I won't. Either you spit it out now, or I'm leaving."

Katherine wished she had Ilene's spunk. Wished she'd done things differently. She took a deep breath and then slowly released it. "Ilene, you certainly know how to sniff out the truth."

"I know that. Most of the folks I dealt with in DC know that, too," Ilene said, her attention focused on Katherine. "So tell me."

Katherine stared at the floor, embarrassed. She knew what she needed to do.

Chapter Thirteen

After all these years, Katherine hoped her nightmare in Boston could be put to rest. Now Ilene, a former CIA agent, might be able to take away her freedom. At this point, Katherine felt she didn't have a choice anymore.

"Tyler told me this agoraphobia thing I have is usually brought on by trauma," Katherine said, her tone serious. "Which I've had plenty of throughout my life." Pausing, she saw she had Ilene, Tyler, and Doc's full attention. "I'm sure you all saw the destruction, the insanity of that day on the news. I left Boston and never looked back. I believed things would calm down after I left, and wherever I wound up, I would move on with my life."

"And here we are, still clueless as to why you're not willing to call the police," Ilene added.

"I'm sorry—it's hard to think about what happened. I've never spoken about that day to anyone. There was so much devastation . . . people running for their lives . . . I saw a sneaker with a severed foot inside. It was awful." Katherine shuddered and then took a deep breath before she continued. "Before the bombs, before all the confusion, I was in the crowd waiting for my . . . friend. There were so many people, a lot of pushing and shoving, and I bumped into this guy.

Something about him frightened me. It was the way his eyes pierced through to my soul. It sounds crazy, and I know *crazy,* but this guy seemed evil." She took another deep breath. "I stared at him briefly, then quickly walked away."

"Katherine, how does this tie in with your own personal trauma?" Tyler asked her in what she now thought of as his doctor's voice.

"I saw him. The guy, but I didn't know who he was then. I was checking my email the day I moved in here, a few days after the bombings. I freaked out seeing his face splashed all over the news."

She waited for their reaction. She waited for Ilene to cuff her and Tyler to leave in disgust. Doc to order her to find a new veterinarian. They said nothing.

Maybe they didn't understand what she was referring to. "I saw the brother, the one who lived. He was one of the guys responsible for the bombings."

Tyler spoke first. "Damn, K, that's horrible."

"You never reported this to the authorities?" Ilene asked.

Katherine shook her head. "No."

The room was silent. All thoughts of the intruder were set aside for the moment.

"Katherine, you did what you did. I'm sure those two were spotted by hundreds of folks that day. You can't shoulder all the blame. The brothers were on a mission, and no one knew it. You're not responsible for their actions," Ilene said, then directed her eyes to Tyler.

"Ilene's right, Katherine. This tragedy probably caused your anxiety. Don't blame yourself. There's no way you could've stopped it."

Finally, Katherine thought—someone who understood why she'd decided to lock herself away where no one would find her.

"I watched the news, saw when he was captured. But the

lives they took and ruined . . ." Katherine shook her head.
"Maybe had I . . . I don't know, paid closer attention to the
guy, I would've noticed the backpack he carried. An eight-
year-old child was killed. I have nightmares about it, about
what his family went through, and what all the people saw. I
was a coward. Still am. I've been hiding away all of these
years, fearing I . . . I'm not sure, maybe fearing the police
would know what I did—rather what I *didn't* do—and that
they would arrest me."

Doc spoke up. "This is why you don't want the police
here? Listen up, kiddo. You are not to blame for anything.
You've lost some of the best years of your life because of
their actions. Survivor's guilt. There is nothing you could've
done to prevent that tragedy."

Katherine nodded. "I realized that a long time ago. Being
able to control my life as I have keeps me safe. Physically
safe. Calling the police scares me. Reminds me of that nightmare."

"You're a smart woman, K. Do you believe whoever was
in your house tonight has anything to do with those bombings?" Doc stared at her, his blue eyes penetrating like two
shards of ice. He was no longer the jovial old guy with a big
smile and a twinkle in his eyes.

"No, I don't," Katherine finally said.

Picking up where Doc left off, Ilene took charge. "Then
you will let us call the police? I know a few folks on the local
force. They're discreet. Just say the word, and I will make the
call. I don't believe your intruders are related to what happened in Boston, either. I still have a few sources in Boston,
too. When the time is right, I'll help you."

"Go ahead, Ilene—call them. I just don't want my identity
revealed. Is there a way around that?" Katherine pleaded.

"Lie," Ilene said.

"Everyone knows there's a 'crazy lady' who lives in the

house on the mountain. How do we get around that?" Katherine asked.

"How do you know that?" Tyler asked her.

Embarrassed, yet knowing she couldn't keep it to herself, Katherine spoke the truth. "I read the community events website. They have a chat room."

"The people who post on that website are folks who thrive on others' miseries," Tyler said. "Just gossip for lack of anything better to do."

Katherine didn't know if he included her in his assessment of "folks with nothing better to do."

"I'm not including you in that, Katherine," Tyler said, as if reading her mind. "I know you have other . . . projects that keep you occupied."

"I do, and I'm not one of those that spend all their free time looking for gossip about people I don't even know." That was a lie. Katherine cyber-stalked the girls on her Friendlink page. She wouldn't bring the topic up, as she didn't know if Ilene knew who she really was. Katherine needed to get Doc alone for a minute so she could find out. "Doc, can I speak to you alone?" she asked.

"Sure, kid," Doc said. "The kitchen?"

"Fine," Katherine replied. Then to Tyler and Ilene she said, "Excuse us, please, for a minute."

In the kitchen, Doc leaned against the kitchen island. "What's so important that we have to be alone?"

"Does Ilene know what I do? The book stuff?"

"No, I gave you my word," Doc told her.

"Should I tell her? Can she be trusted?" Katherine asked. She didn't know Ilene. She only had Doc's word where the former CIA agent was concerned.

"With your life, K. She'll have your back. Trust me on this. She's everything she appears to be and more. A little rough at times, but she was good at what she did."

"All right, then I want her to know."

Returning to the dining room, they found Tyler and Ilene speaking in low tones. Was there something either of them didn't want her to hear? Katherine wondered.

"Ilene, I have to tell you something about myself that I think you should know," Katherine began.

Ilene nodded, her sharp-angled hair swinging from side to side. "Okay, spill the beans. I'm all ears."

"Do you know the author K.C. Winston?" Katherine swallowed, despising herself for making this sound as though she were someone special, worthy of all their promises.

"I'm not much of a reader. Who is that?" Ilene asked.

"Me. Katherine Celeste Winston."

Ilene's eyebrows shot up. "Wait, I do know who you are! The kids with magic power books, yes?"

Katherine smiled. "Yes."

"The Blowing Rock library has a book club for kids. I was there dropping off a friend of mine, the head librarian, Sarah Waterman. We'd had a night out and drank too much. She left her car at Peckers. Not that it's anyone's business." She looked at Doc, who had a wry smile on his face. "The library has posters of all your books in their book club room."

"You two old gals need to stay away from that watering hole," Doc piped in. "I'd hate to see you or Sarah get pulled over and charged with a DUI."

Unsure of anything at the moment, Katherine smiled. "Sounds fun, Doc. You never told me about Blowing Rock's watering hole." Not that she had any intention of going there for any reason. She glanced at Tyler, and he winked at her.

"You've always had a way about you, Franklin. Sticking your nose in places where it doesn't belong," Ilene chided. "Now, Katherine, tell me about this break-in. And I'd like the truth this time around."

Katherine told her the evening's sequence of events. Her

earlier actions that day had no bearing on that night's break-in, so she kept the GWUP group and their conversations to herself.

"What about that girl from your Friendlink page?" Tyler interrupted. "Earlier, before the break-in, you were concerned about her. I think Ilene could help you with that, too. Find out if she's really in some kind of danger."

Darn! She should've asked Tyler to keep her concern for Karrie private. For all she knew, Karrie could be anyone from anywhere. Gathering herself, Katherine spoke. "I don't see how it could be connected, Tyler. The girl I was telling you about lives in Texas. I doubt she had time for all this; and, she's only sixteen, maybe younger. From what she said, she doesn't have a very good home life."

"Okay, hold up, Katherine. Fill me in. If you want my help, you need to be as honest as possible. When you finish, I'll call the police," Ilene stated.

Resigned, Katherine explained the whole Friendlink page for her readers. She told Ilene about Karrie's emails and the phone call. Most importantly, she explained to Ilene all about the notebook with her book outline and notes and the plush animal, Duckie, and how the dogs had recently brought it inside.

"Did you piss anyone off? Maybe someone you're not even aware of?" Ilene asked.

Katherine took a deep breath and slowly released it. "I don't know. Doc, Tyler, and his friend Carson are the only people I've allowed inside. And now you."

"What about the delivery people? No way you can live as you do without help. Groceries? Post office, FedEx? Are you friendly with them? Do you allow them inside?" The questions flew from Ilene's mouth as she drilled Katherine. "Has anyone tried to force themselves inside? Force themselves on you?"

"No, nothing like that. They've never been inside. They

leave my groceries and mail on the deck by the French doors."

"It's time to call the police. Get the place checked for prints, fibers, or anything out of place. We don't want the locals to take your computer yet. I'll want to go through it first," said Ilene. She removed a cell phone from a pocket in her skin-hugging dress. How she'd managed to keep it hidden until now was a mystery. "I'll use that room off the kitchen."

Katherine knew she wasn't asking her permission. Ilene was sharp. She crossed her *T*s and dotted her *I*s.

Katherine stayed in the dining room, giving Ilene some privacy. Suddenly, it struck her like a lightning bolt—she hadn't felt the slightest inkling of panic since dinner, other than her heart rate was up a bit. Unwilling to overthink why this was the case, she sat silently with Doc and Tyler at the table.

"Are you okay?" Tyler asked.

She nodded. "I am. Which is unusual, I'll give you that. I've been alone for such a long time. Having people around seems to have a calming effect on me." Had she wasted some of the best years of her life hiding for nothing?

"I guess I wasn't enough," Doc interjected, a grin on his face.

"Your mind isn't focusing on your fear right now," Tyler said. "It's common enough. Your next challenge might be more difficult. Leaving your house."

Katherine waited for the familiar body sensations of a panic attack but only felt her heartbeat increase a little more. The dry mouth, clammy hands, and dizziness stayed at bay. She wasn't going to test herself anymore tonight. The person who'd walked right into her house could still be hiding outside. There were dozens of acres that she'd never explored; she'd be a sitting duck if her intruder was still out there.

Ilene returned to the dining room. "I spoke with Detective Davidson. I gave him the basic details. Ray said he'd be here in twenty minutes with a deputy from forensics. No sirens and no marked cars. He promised he'd be discreet," Ilene said, her words succinct.

"Who's the deputy?" Doc asked.

"It's not who you're thinking," Ilene confirmed. "George Gonzalez, though I don't know him."

Katherine interrupted them. "Is there a problem with one deputy over another? If there is, call now and stop this investigation if you don't trust him."

"Tell her," Ilene said to Doc.

"My ex-wife's new husband works for the police department. He's one of the state forensics guys. Comes from Asheville."

Katherine realized she knew absolutely nothing about the personal lives of these three people. They were here to help her. That's all she needed to know right now. "Should I hide my computer?" she asked Ilene.

"Good thinking. I want to look at it first. Franklin, would you take the laptop and put it in that rattletrap of a truck you drive? Under the seat. No one in their right mind would look for evidence in that old heap."

Doc nodded, then stood up. "K, you mind giving me your computer? I'll treat it as gently as I treat my patients."

Tyler stood, as well. "Katherine, use this." He handed her a handkerchief he'd removed from his pocket. "So that you don't smudge the prints."

Katherine hadn't thought of that, but it made sense. Men still carried handkerchiefs? Who knew what else she'd missed during all of these years of self-imposed prison?

She carefully closed out the Friendlink page, then deleted the history. This was her personal property. Ilene didn't need to see her searches. If she tried to find them, there'd be no surprises, but Katherine's private life, which she'd worked so hard to keep that way, could fall apart again if someone was out to get her. The who and why were the big mystery. This had nothing to do with Boston. She felt that in her gut, which she always listened to.

Katherine removed a new flash drive from her desk drawer, saving as much as she could from the hard drive and cramming it in her pocket. She took the charging cord and the electronic mouse she used, located her computer bag in the drawer, and stuffed the slim device inside. "This is my life's work, Doc, Ilene," she said to them. "I want it back ASAP." Katherine decided she could ask for something in return. "With nothing deleted—*nothing.*" Despite her mental issues, she hoped Ilene understood that she meant what she said.

"Of course. I'll take it to my house," Ilene said. "I don't have cat hairs flying all over the place."

"Ilene, I've spent most of my life caring for animals, and I'm doing my best to take care of their needs. I'd bet my last nickel if my cats ever laid eyes on you, they'd cross that rainbow bridge so fast they'd leave a contrail," said Doc.

"Now isn't the time, Franklin. I've told you about my distaste for cats. For all animals with fur. I sneeze, my eyes turn red, and I can't breathe. I do not like you enough to endure that. That's why I won't stay—" Ilene stopped, catching herself before she revealed the obvious.

"Stay where?" Tyler asked.

"Shut up, Tyler," Ilene said, grinning.

Sophie and Sam were growling from their perch at the top of the landing. They came running downstairs to the French doors. "Hey, you two, calm down." Katherine couldn't help looking at Ilene. She knew dog hairs were all over her place, because she hadn't vacuumed in days. But Ilene hadn't sneezed once, and her eyes were perfectly clear. She had Doc wrapped around her little finger. Tightly.

Katherine heard footsteps, then a loud knock at the French doors, even though they were still open. She assumed Ilene had told the cops what door to use, since her house had several other entrances. How did Ilene know that? Probably because she'd come inside the same way. Katherine was getting more paranoid by the minute. Her heart rate began its staccato dance when Ilene let the two officers inside. One carried a large black container that reminded Katherine of a giant bait box.

"Detective Davidson, Deputy Gonzalez, thanks for coming on such short notice," Ilene said. "Ms. Winnie"—she directed her gaze to Katherine—"and Dr. Newlon saw an intruder earlier. They have surveillance videos you might want to view at some point."

Ms. Winnie. Ilene had kept her word. Doc trusted her, so Katherine would do her best to follow suit.

After quick introductions, Deputy Gonzalez took charge. "I'm going to clear the glass first. Don't want anyone getting hurt. I'll check for prints and fibers on the door and the desk. I'll look for tire patterns and footprints or anything suspicious outside. Is there outdoor lighting?" he asked, his attention on Katherine. She eyed his black uniform, the vest he wore with all sorts of gadgets attached in easy-to-reach places. He epitomized law enforcement with his military haircut and muscular build.

Ilene spoke before Katherine could, her intense gaze fixated on the deputy. "Are you sure that's a good idea, George? We don't know if they're out there. Hiding, waiting to do . . ." She lowered her tone. "Whatever the hell they came here to do."

"All the better," Detective Davidson interjected. "He's my best forensics guy. Also keeps his mouth shut."

Katherine watched them haggle. She wasn't so sure of this but kept her thoughts to herself.

Deputy Gonzalez opened his large case and removed several bags, a vacuum, and a camera. "If I find suspicious tracks or footprints, I'll need to make a cast of the prints.

When I'm ready, I'll have you step outside with me, and you can let me know if you see anything unusual or out of place." *What? Surely he knew about my . . . problem,* Katherine thought.

Her hands began to tremble, and her heart felt like it was about to explode. *This is a mistake,* she thought, as panic began its familiar attack, faster than she'd experienced in a very long time. Inhaling, she tried to calm herself with her breathing. She felt the usual clamminess in her armpits and the back of her neck. Her breathing became erratic very quickly. She was hyperventilating, and her vision started to blur. The deputy's mouth was opening and closing, but she couldn't understand him. The floor was about to smack her in the face when someone wrapped an arm around her, placing a paper bag over her mouth. Gasping for breath, she struggled to escape the hand holding the bag over her mouth.

"Frank, my car. Get my bag!" Tyler's voice was loud and demanding. Doc tossed the laptop on the sofa.

Breathe. Breathe. Just. Breathe. The edges of the bag were wet with saliva, but Katherine knew what it was for.

"Come on, girl," Ilene said, helping Tyler try to calm her down, holding her before she hit the floor. "I didn't come over here to see you collapse in a heap. Focus your breathing," she ordered.

Sam and Sophie ran in circles, both dogs whimpering.

Doc bolted back through the French doors, returning with a leather satchel in his hand. He held it against his chest as he opened it. "What am I looking for?"

"Ativan," Tyler said. "Preloaded syringe in the blue plastic case."

"Got it," Doc said, producing the syringe.

"Upper arm, Frank. Quick," Tyler ordered, as he continued to hold Katherine upright.

Katherine felt a slight pinch on the back of her arm and

then, in an instant, a softness permeated through her entire body. She felt light and airy, as though she were floating on a cloud in a dreamlike state. The paper bag fell to the floor, but she didn't care. Everyone was staring at her.

"Dogs," she said, before collapsing into the chair the detective slid across the wood floor.

"K, your dogs are fine," Doc said. "Can you hear me?"

She nodded. Her head felt light as a balloon yet springy like a bobblehead.

"Katherine, it's Tyler. Doc and I are going to help you to your bedroom. You okay with that?" Tyler asked, even though he could see she was starting to feel the drug's full effect.

"Hmmm," she said, her eyes closed, a slight smile on her lips. "Stay."

"Holy crap, Tyler, what did you give the girl?" Ilene asked. "Sodium pentothal? A roofie?"

"Not hardly," Tyler told Ilene. "If you could take over here for a few minutes while we get her upstairs, we can talk after."

"Yes, let's do that," Ilene said in her commandeering way. "Take those dogs with you," she added.

Together, Tyler and Doc managed to get Katherine settled in her bed. Sam and Sophie followed and jumped on the bed, lying on either side of her, protecting Katherine.

As soon as they returned downstairs, Tyler said to Doc, "I'm not going to leave her here alone tonight. I'll sleep on the sofa as soon as the officers finish up. I hope to high hell they're able to figure out what's going on. I hardly know the woman, but I do know there's more to this story. As soon as we find out, I'll do whatever it takes to help her." Tyler stopped and placed a hand on the old man's shoulder. "Were you able to hide her laptop?" he asked quietly. They stood together at the bottom of the staircase.

Doc shook his head. "No, I tossed it in the living room."
Tyler didn't reply.

"You're good for her," Doc said. "In a friendly way, right?"

"Maybe as a doctor. If you're asking me if I want a relationship with her, I can't give you an answer now. I just met her," Tyler said. "Now let's see if we can help those two officers before Ilene chases them away."

Chapter Fourteen

Detective Ray Davidson busied himself writing in a brown leather notebook. Ilene kept a sharp eye on him and his partner. Davidson paid no attention to her. Ilene thought that maybe she should show him around the property, so they could be done with this part of their investigation. Unfamiliar with the house and the mass of land that came with it, but used to taking over, Ilene spoke up. "The girl is down for the night. Any questions, you'll have to deal with me."

"No problem, Ms. Silva," the detective acknowledged, and continued to write. "Give me a minute here." He closed his notebook so quickly that it made a snapping sound. He tucked it inside his navy-blue jacket and then removed a pocket recorder from his other jacket pocket. "Do I have your permission to record our conversation?"

"Good grief, Ray, I'm not the one you need to question. I've just met this woman. You'll have to wait until whatever drug Tyler gave her wears off, so yes, you can record me," she said, adding, "For what little it's worth."

Tyler and Doc entered the room. "Officer," Tyler said, nodding. "Ilene, Katherine is not in any condition to be questioned. Maybe tomorrow afternoon. She'll need several hours for the Ativan to get out of her system," he explained. "I can tell you what little I know, if that'll help."

Detective Davidson had worked his way up the ladder for the past twenty years. At forty-two, he presented an intimidating figure. Six-three, muscular, and lean, courtesy of early morning workouts six days a week. On more than one occasion, he'd used his size and good looks to strong-arm a suspect when needed. Folks accused him of being vain, which he was, to an extent. He'd often been mistaken for the actor who played the superhero Thor in the Marvel Comics movies. His movie-star good looks didn't take away from his skill as a detective. He knew a bit of the backstory behind the woman upstairs. Ilene hadn't used her real name when she'd introduced him. He also knew she was an agoraphobe. Blowing Rock was a small town. People talked. He listened.

"Tell me what you know," Davidson told Tyler, then turned to George and spoke. "Wait a minute before you get started."

George nodded and returned the camera to his backpack.

"I want a few photos inside before you take off," the detective explained.

"Yes, sir." George took the camera out again, waiting for further instruction.

Doc went to the kitchen and emptied what was left of the coffee Katherine had made earlier. He knew where she kept the coffee beans and all the gadgets needed to make coffee. A few minutes later, the freshly brewed coffee scented the large kitchen. He peered out to the living area. "You all care for a coffee?" Doc asked, making himself at home while Katherine slept upstairs.

"Thank you, but no, sir. We're just here to do our jobs," Detective Davidson said.

"Ray, you can have a cup of coffee. I'm not going to run to your boss; you know that. I called you here because you're good at what you do. You know who I can trust. Drinking coffee isn't going to ruin your reputation," Ilene said. "You, too," she told George.

"If you insist," Davidson said, a slight grin on his handsome face.

They gathered in the kitchen, each finding a spot around the large island. Doc poured cups of coffee while Tyler told the officers what had happened as best he could recall. "Once you view the surveillance footage and take a walk through the house, you'll have more of a visual of what I just told you."

Ilene perked up. "There is something else, Tyler. Tell Ray and George about that fan page thing."

Tyler took a sip of coffee. "Right."

"Why would Ms. *Winnie*"—Davidson emphasized the fake name—"have a fan page?" He truly couldn't imagine her being a fan of anyone, unless it had something to do with her agoraphobia. Maybe a support group of others with the same issue?

Tyler glanced at Doc, who shook his head slightly. His way of telling him not to break the doctor/patient confidentiality agreement they shared, even though the knowledge wasn't just a medical issue.

"That's not for me to tell," Tyler said. "From what I gather, Katherine is worried about one of . . ."—he paused—"her friends, a young girl who might be in trouble. Don't ask me what *kind* of trouble. She received a phone call at dinner that seemed to upset her."

"Do you know who her caller was?" Detective Davidson asked.

"No. The phone rang, and she saw the number and hung up without saying anything. Afterward, she seemed antsy. Later, she excused herself to the powder room for a few minutes, and she had the phone in her pocket. When she returned to the kitchen, I could tell she was upset, but it wasn't my place to interrogate her." Tyler would not betray her trust.

"Do you mind telling me why you were here tonight?" Davidson asked.

Doc spoke up. "Is that necessary?" He put his cup in the sink, then took the barstool beside Tyler. "He's a doctor."

Detective Davidson scribbled in his notebook. With the camera dangling from his neck, George leaned against the refrigerator, listening to his superior.

"Ray, the reason I called *you* is your propensity for discretion. You too," Ilene said to George. "I want you to dust for prints, check the perimeter of this massive house, and see what your thoughts are after you view the surveillance video. I didn't ask you because of your good looks. Or yours." She nodded in the deputy's direction. "If you feel you can't be discreet, leave now."

"Tell me what you *think* I should know, Ms. Silva. If there is an online predator, it's highly possible they could be involved in this." Davidson closed his ever-present notebook.

Ilene understood Katherine's reluctance to call the authorities. These two were stiff as boards. She knew Ray but not George. Ray said he was the best and could be trusted. What in the hell happened to "you do me a favor; I'll owe you one in return"? Ilene knew the old ways of dealing with investigations were no longer like they were at the height of her career, but still—she'd expected Ray and his partner to cut her some slack. She hadn't planned on *forcing* them to do what she asked. She'd made it quite clear what she expected. "I know absolutely nothing about an online friend or predator. I just met the woman myself."

"We're getting nowhere, you guys. I wish I had more to tell you but, as Ms. Silva said, I'm a doctor, and I can't talk about my patient. Other than to tell you I just met her yesterday, too," Tyler said. His gaze hardened when he looked at the detective.

"Then your visit yesterday and tonight are medically related?" Davidson pushed.

Beyond frustrated, Ilene raised her voice. "Ray, it's none of your damned business. I asked you here to investigate a break-in, not interrogate my friends. Can you focus on that? Maybe we can look at those videos now?"

"Understood," the detective replied. To George, he said, "See if you find any prints on those French doors and the desk while I look at the surveillance videos."

"Now, that's the Ray I know," Ilene said. "Tyler, do you know how to access the video?"

Tyler took a deep breath and realized he only knew how to use Katherine's cell phone to access the images. "Her cell phone. I saw her put it in her pocket earlier." He wasn't going to go to her room and start feeling around in her pockets. "Ilene, if you wouldn't mind?"

She rolled her eyes. "You're afraid to touch her? Never mind; I shouldn't have said that. Of course I will do it. Give me a minute." She swiftly left the kitchen, her movements as regal and precise as ever.

"She's got quite the mouth on her, but she means well," Doc informed the men.

For the first time that evening, the detective smiled. "Obviously I've dealt with her before. I know how she works."

Tyler relaxed somewhat, satisfied with Ilene's choice. He'd known Ilene since he was in his teens. She'd moved into the house next door to his parents during his sophomore year of high school. His mother had been curious about their new neighbor and made friends with her immediately. Ilene spent more time away from her place than in it. Though he hadn't known her profession at the time, his parents did. He'd been sworn to secrecy when Ilene told him in his senior year.

"Good to know. I wouldn't want to be on her bad side," Doc said. "She's a good old gal. Sometimes." He smirked.

"Old gal!" said Ilene, announcing her return to the kitchen. "I won't forget that, Franklin." She tossed two cell phones on the counter. "That girl is so wiped out. I thought she was dead for a minute, until I checked her pulse. Tyler, you might want to check on her."

"I will. She'll be fine," Tyler told her. "It's how the medication works."

All eyes were on the cell phones in the center of the island. Detective Davidson spoke first. "Since these phones are evidence, I can't let you keep them. Is there a paper bag I can use?"

Ilene grabbed the phones with the same crumpled napkin she'd used when she took them out of Katherine's pocket. "This is not on the books, Ray, or have you forgotten? Maybe I *should* speak with your superior, as you seem to have a memory issue."

He shook his head. "My bad. I'm used to normal, routine investigations. Sorry," he said, a bit sheepishly.

Ilene placed both cell phones back on the counter. "As long as we're clear, and this is *off the books,* let's see the damned video. We're wasting too much time. Tyler, can you access the security footage? Is there a password or anything else I don't know?"

"I'll try," Tyler said. "She used her iPhone, not that other phone. She had it in her jeans pocket."

"She did; the iPhone was in her back pocket. This burner phone was in her front pocket." Ilene's curiosity was piqued as she wondered about the burner phone. Was there more to Katherine's story than what she'd told them?

Tyler scanned the apps on Katherine's iPhone, stopping when he saw the app for the security cameras. He clicked on it, surprised when he wasn't asked to enter a password. He was sure when he watched her open the app in the bathroom earlier that she'd logged in using a password. Apparently, she never signed off, which made sense, as she'd been frightened. He opened the footage. "Here it is," he said, and gave the phone to the detective.

Ilene stood closer to Ray so she could view the footage. "Stop," she said after viewing for a minute or so.

"Ms. Silva, I see it too." Detective Davidson used his thumb and forefinger to expand the screen, then clicked on the photo of the figure wearing the hoodie. He continued to scroll through the images, clicking various images and enlarging them. Then, when he had finished, he emailed the pictures to his own phone. "I have a friend who can run these through facial recognition," he explained. "See this?" He held up one of the screenshots he'd enlarged for them to view. "The side of the face when they're looking at the cameras. I'm pretty sure this is a man who didn't realize his hoodie wasn't completely hiding that part of his face. Or maybe he's unaware of the camera. I won't ask if any of you all recognize this guy. It's hard to tell, but technology is pretty damn good. With luck, my buddy will enhance what he can, then run it through the program. George will put a rush on the prints. I'll have to get all of your prints to compare to any unknowns."

"Mine are already on file," Ilene said.

"Doctors have to have background checks, so I have prints on file as well," Tyler told him. "I never thought they'd be used in an investigation, but they're all yours. I assume you know where to locate them." He said this last part a bit sarcastically. The cop was overbearing, and Tyler wasn't sure he liked the guy. He found him arrogant.

"Same," Doc said. "It's been several years, though prints don't change."

The detective had his recorder on the counter, recording every word they said. The green light stuck out like a sore thumb. "I need Ms. *Winnie*'s permission to contact the security company."

"Ray, stop with the act. You know who she is—the crazy lady on the mountain. I'm not going to give out her personal information, like her name. She's a recluse for a reason. You can ask her what name she goes by when she's awake." When Ray asked Ilene for a favor, she'd make sure to run him through the wringer, as he was doing now.

"Sorry—don't take it personally, Ilene. I'm trying to help out. I'm just set in my ways," Ray said. "Give me a break here, okay?"

"Just do something. I promised I could fix this. I told Ms. Winnie I'd do whatever I could, and I want you to continue to refer to her as such until she decides to tell you otherwise." Ilene turned to Doc Baker. "Right, Franklin? You know I always keep my promises."

Doc raised his brows. "Of course. You haven't let me down yet."

George returned to the kitchen. "I've finished the prints. Not too much—broken glass, just a couple of panes. Appears it was hit by something."

Tyler couldn't help it; he had to speak up. "Ilene, don't refer to her as 'the crazy lady on the mountain.' It's demeaning," he said. It wasn't right, and here they all were, in her home, while she was knocked out on medication, talking about her as if she didn't exist.

"Don't be so touchy. It's nothing personal." Ilene snickered.

George cleared his throat. All eyes were back on him. "I'm going outside to see what I can find."

"Thanks, George," Detective Davidson called out. "He's a workaholic. What about this fan club thing? I want to take a look at her computer. At least let my forensics guy see if he can find anything threatening."

"No, you can't take her computer. It's a work thing. We wouldn't want to overstep our boundaries. It will have to wait until she gives her permission," Tyler said.

"Exactly what type of work does Ms. *Winnie* do?" Detective Davidson asked Tyler.

Doc took over. "It's a computer tech job. I don't know all the details, but as long as I've known her, she's worked from home." He didn't elaborate any more than necessary.

Tyler glanced at Doc. "I'm not sure what company she's employed by. Apple, Microsoft, maybe?" Tyler knew this wasn't true, but it kept Katherine's computer out of their hands for now. He wasn't a whiz with computers; couldn't access hers even if he tried. But he was smart enough to realize she wouldn't want her Friendlink page up for review without her permission.

"Since this is off the books, I won't insist," the detective said. "If you find any threat directed at Ms. Winnie, I'd like to know. Wouldn't want to discover I missed any hint of a stalker or an unhappy boyfriend."

Tyler agreed. "I may be speaking out of turn, but I don't believe any of her Friendlink"—he almost said *fans* again, but caught himself—"connections are responsible for this break-in." And Tyler felt sure there wasn't a boyfriend involved. It didn't take a detective to figure out that Katherine hadn't been in a relationship for a long time. She'd said as much earlier. As a psychiatrist, he was an expert on human behavior. While he hadn't performed a clinical evaluation, it wasn't required in this particular situation. She had panic attacks and was an agoraphobe. In her own way, she'd been up-front about this with him and Doc. From his short time with her, she appeared to be a high-functioning, successful author. Her success was real, not imaginary, as it might be with one suffering from a delusional disorder or psychosis of any kind.

Again, he hadn't an ounce of her medical history to make a real diagnosis. She'd been traumatized, and her way of protecting herself was to remain in her safe space. Which happened to be a mansion on one of North Carolina's many magnificent mountains, close enough to the Blue Ridge Parkway to have a view most would envy. Tyler could see how easy it was for her to live as she did. With modern technology and a fortune at her disposal, Katherine's lifestyle was manageable until tonight, when her personal space had been violated.

"Let's hope not. Internet scams are on the rise. Folks have been fooled too many times. Men prey on women. Some have gone as far as to stalk and kill. Women aren't always the victims; men are often victims, too. I don't like telling you all this, but be aware," the detective continued.

Doc shook his head. "No, she's too smart to be taken in by an online romance or whatever they're calling it these days. Dating games."

George returned to the kitchen with his black box closed up. "I have enough to work with. I took the liberty of walking around the area, looking for anything out of the ordinary. This is a huge property. I can't cover it all on foot, though I didn't see anything suspicious in the areas I searched, other than her horses are in a tizzy."

"I'll check the horses," Doc said. "They're here temporarily while a fella's new stables are being finished. Tyler, you know more about Carson than I do. It's been a while since I've spent time with him. Is he capable of this?"

"Never," Tyler said emphatically. "He's as clean as they come."

"You sure?" Ilene asked. "Those are the kind that usually have something to hide. Remember Ted Bundy, a good-looking man in the prime of his life."

"Of course—who doesn't remember that whacko? If Tyler is sure, then you should be, too," Doc said to Ilene and Detective Davidson. "I'll be back. I want to see for myself what's got them into such a, uh . . . *tizzy*," he said, emphasizing the last word.

"George and I will come with you, just in case," Detective

Davidson said. "I think we've done as much inside as we can. I'll send someone over in the morning to replace the glass. Ilene, as soon as I have any information, you'll be the first person I call. When the lady wakes up, maybe she'd be willing to talk to me tomorrow? Off the record."

"I'll ask her," Tyler said. "I can contact you through Ilene."

"Not necessary," Davidson said, removing a card from his jacket. "Here, call me when she's ready. My personal cell number." He took a pen from his pocket and jotted the number down. "Keep this private if you can."

"I'm a doctor. I keep my patients' personal lives private. Thanks." Tyler wanted to say *this woman I care about*, but that was too much too soon. The detective was not his style. However, he'd owe him, if he could figure out who had broken into Katherine's house.

Chapter Fifteen

Ilene and Tyler waited in the quiet kitchen, while Katherine continued to sleep upstairs. Doc soon returned from outside, minus the two officers.

"I didn't see anything out of place. Those horses might've, though. Both were bucking; their eyes were wide and fearful. I'd let Carson know. He might've purchased horses that have a history," Doc said to Tyler. "Something or someone frightened them. I did my best to calm them down. They'll need a good run first thing in the morning."

Tyler said, "Katherine's intruder probably scared them. I checked on them earlier this evening. They were agitated, ears back, jumpy. When I saw the intruder on the surveillance videos, I figured that might've been what scared them."

Doc nodded his head. "Most likely, that's what's stirred them up. I didn't see any injuries or signs of poisoning."

Ilene spoke up. "This might not be what you two lovesick admirers want to hear." She cleared her throat. "But I want to do a background check on Katherine. Something about her bothers me. The idea that one could spend years in isolation as she has sounds insane."

They sat around the kitchen island, and no one spoke for a moment.

"That's wrong," Tyler finally said. "Unless she's committed a crime, you shouldn't check up on her, Ilene, especially given her fragile mental state. She's been so badly frightened. I wouldn't want her to think our concern is an act."

"I agree with Tyler," Doc said. "She's decent, down-to-earth. Just because she's intentionally stayed inside her home doesn't make her completely crazy."

Ilene rolled her eyes, then laughed. "She's gotten to you both. I promise I won't do a background check. Yet," she added. "So what's next?"

"You both can go," said Tyler. "I'll stay with her. The dogs need someone to feed them and let them out. No way will I leave those French doors open. I'll find a piece of wood or something to cover them. Then I'll call Carson and let him know his horses are acting out of character. He would never purchase a horse if he thought there were bad bloodlines."

"I hope not," Doc said. "Those beauties are worth a small fortune."

"Carson knows what he's doing. He's the best. I'll call him." Tyler checked his watch. "In a few hours. This can keep for now. Let the guy rest."

"Speaking of . . ." Ilene began. "Franklin, let's get out of here. I'm tired, and there isn't anything more we can do here. Tyler's got her so doped up, she'll be lucky if she wakes up by tomorrow evening."

"Thanks for the vote of confidence," Tyler said. "I know it's still hard for you, Ilene, but I am a doctor now. Not the kid next door playing loud music just to tick you off."

"You are still a kid to me," she acknowledged. "With a medical degree. Take care of that woman, all right?"

Doc shook his head. "Ilene, unless you want to walk home, put a plug in that hole beneath your nose."

Tyler raised his eyebrows. "I'm not sure I'd want a ride from him, Ilene. There's a crude man hiding behind that fake smile."

Ilene laughed. "You're right. He is not the charmer he pretends to be." She took Doc Baker's hand. "That's why I like him."

Doc rolled his eyes, a giant smile on his face. "Women," he said.

"Can't live with or without them?" Tyler asked, even though he didn't believe the overused cliché.

"I wouldn't go that far," Doc joked. Then, in a more serious tone, he added, "Be careful, Tyler. Whoever broke in could still be out there. Stay close to K, all right?"

"Sam and Sophie aren't going to let anyone near her tonight. I'll check on her after I fix the windows," Tyler promised.

"Upstairs, in the third bedroom on the left, there's a toolbox, some laminate, and I'm pretty sure I saw a few pieces of pressed wood last time I was up there," Doc said.

"What were you doing in her bedroom?" Ilene asked.

"Not what I do in yours," Doc said. "Let's go; it's too darn cold. An old man's bones can only take so much."

"'Night," Tyler said to their retreating forms. Ilene and Doc had been in a relationship for a long time. Both tried to hide it for reasons unknown to him, but he thought they made the perfect couple.

As soon as they left, Tyler went upstairs to check on Katherine. Sam and Sophie hadn't budged, though both were wide awake, eyes on their dog mom. Tyler smoothed Katherine's long hair away from her face. Seeing her so vulnerable, yet relaxed, he thought she looked even more beautiful. Tyler checked her pulse, then pulled the covers up and tucked them close to her. Both dogs relaxed, their heads on their paws.

"I'm going to take care of her," Tyler told them, patting both dogs on the head. He had feelings for Katherine. How and why so soon, he didn't know. She was delicate, pure, and new. He'd never felt this way before, especially in a matter of hours. She had reached his heart and, at this point, he wished for more. He could only hope she allowed him to help her live a normal life again.

Assured that all was well for the moment, Tyler located the spare room. He wasn't sure where the light switch was located, so he used the flashlight on his cell. Locating the switch on the left side of the door, he flicked the overhead light on. Sealed boxes were stacked against the far wall. It wasn't his place to look inside. On the opposite wall, he spied a few scattered tools alongside a pile of mismatched tiles and several oddly shaped pieces of wood. Then he saw the laminate Doc suggested he use as a temporary fix until Katherine could have the glass replaced. He found what he needed to cover the two panes and headed downstairs.

With the razor knife, Tyler cut the laminate to fit the missing windows. He carved the fake wood around the edges, hoping it would snap in place, and fortunately, it was close to perfect. He locked the door, then went into the kitchen and grabbed a barstool. He positioned the stool beneath the doorknob so if anyone tried to get inside, he would hear them before seeing them. Satisfied, he was tempted to reach out to Carson and let him know what happened. But as he'd told Doc, it would keep. Tyler walked through the dining room, making sure all of the windows were locked. He'd done the same upstairs before coming down.

Back in the kitchen, he used Katherine's iPhone to turn the alarm system on. He checked the current video footage and didn't see anything unusual. In the small area off the kitchen where they'd had dinner earlier, which seemed like days ago, Tyler saw orange-red embers still burning in the fireplace. With the poker, he spread the bits of ember in a thin layer, watching as they cooled. Then he returned to the kitchen in search of baking soda. Katherine had a well-stocked pantry. He smiled, remembering that she said she liked to cook. He found a large box of baking soda. He once more shoveled the embers into a thin layer, then sprinkled baking soda over the top. He watched as the glow faded into tiny swirls of smoke. Satisfied, he returned the poker and shovel to the stand, glad that he had remembered to check the fire.

He spied the containers of leftovers Katherine had placed on the counter and put them in the refrigerator as she'd intended. He scanned the kitchen, searching for anything out of place or unusual—which would be tough, given that he wasn't too familiar with the house. He decided other than the broken panes on the French doors that everything was in its place. The dirty pots, pans, and dishes could wait.

Tyler was about to head out of the kitchen when he heard a buzzing noise that stopped him. After a visual sweep of the kitchen, he saw the burner phone on the island. It continued to buzz. Normally he wouldn't have taken it upon himself to answer someone else's cell phone, but these circumstances weren't normal. He opened the flip phone and said, "Hello."

"Can I speak to Darby?"

"Sorry, no one by that name lives here," Tyler answered.

"Really?"

Tyler took a deep breath. "There is no one by that name here, really," he said emphatically.

"But this is the number Darby called me from. I told her about my dad and the notebook. I think he's going to do something to K.C. Winston."

The caller had Tyler's full attention now. "What are you talking about?"

"He says he wrote all of the GWUP books and is working on a new one. I wanted to tell Darby. She's up on all the latest books."

Suddenly it clicked. *Darby.* That was Katherine's online alias on her Friendlink page. Tyler couldn't reveal her true identity, so he went with the truth. "Oh, well, she's asleep. She wasn't feeling well earlier and went to bed."

"Are you her foster dad, Walter?"

How far was he willing to go with this? Should he play along? Knowing what was at stake gave him no other choice. "Yes, I am."

"Could you please tell her that I called? Maybe she could call me back as soon as possible? It's really important."

"Sure, let me . . . uh, get a pen and paper." Tyler saw the pen and pad of paper on the counter. "Okay, what's the number and message?"

He wrote her number down, even though he already knew it, as it had flashed on the cell phone. "I'll have her call you tomorrow," said Tyler. The girl was clearly scared; he could hear the fear in her voice. But nothing she said made sense to him. Katherine had told him about Karrie and her circumstances, but he hadn't given them much thought until now. This kid was frightened, and Katherine was right to be concerned.

"Tell Darby it's urgent, and I really mean it," the girl told him. "She can call me anytime, okay?"

"I'll see that she gets the message," Tyler promised.

"Bye," the girl said, then ended the call.

Debating whether he should try and wake Katherine up, since he knew she was concerned about this young member of her Friendlink page, Tyler looked at the time. She still needed a few more hours of sleep, as far as he was concerned. The Ativan hit her hard; Tyler was almost positive she'd never had any kind of benzodiazepine, hence her almost immediate sedation. As a medical doctor, he knew some of his patients reacted differently to medication. He would simply let her sleep it off. He'd call the office in the morning and have Liz, his secretary, cancel his in-office appointments. If there were emergencies, Liz knew to refer them to either his father, which wasn't a possibility now, or Dr. Rose Smith, a good friend and colleague. He would call Rose first thing tomorrow and have her cover for him.

Tyler put the burner phone and Katherine's iPhone in a drawer that stored her flatware and tore Karrie's phone number from the pad and put it in there, too, just in case the phone hadn't stored the number. He didn't trust those cheap phones, but knew in an emergency they worked okay.

It was now after two a.m., and he was tired and anxious after the night he'd been through. Anxious not for himself, but for Katherine. There was something about her that went straight to his heart, a feeling he had never experienced before. He'd been in a couple of long-term relationships, if you could call eighteen months long-term. Hannah Logan had had an issue with his profession and always thought he was psychoanalyzing her. She was a nice woman, but with her insecurities, in addition to the constant complaining, they had both agreed the relationship wasn't going anywhere.

He hadn't dated for several months when he met Trudy Rollins. She was gorgeous and knew it. She was a flirt and a spoiled brat. They'd had a good time for a few months, but Tyler knew she wasn't what he wanted in a woman for a real relationship, so he'd broken it off with her. Trudy had been mad for a couple of weeks until she met another guy. Tyler hadn't heard from her since.

Katherine had an effect on him. He'd felt it the first time he saw her, which had only been yesterday—though again, that seemed like a lifetime ago. It was more than physical attraction. She was beautiful, kind, and smart. She loved animals. He was pretty sure she was attracted to him. It would be hard for her to commit to a relationship with her agoraphobia, but he wouldn't let that deter him. He'd spent twelve years training to be a medical doctor and another two in a fellowship for psychiatry. Tyler would help Katherine overcome her fears. He'd done it for dozens of people, and that made his choice of profession more gratifying than anything. He loved his work, but he knew when to turn it off.

The sofa in the living room called to him. He took off his shirt, tossing it on the back of a recliner. Katherine had soft pillows and plush throws on the back of her sofa, making it pretty darn comfortable. Tyler tucked himself in. Very comfortable, indeed. He gave in to his exhaustion and was asleep in minutes.

Chapter Sixteen

Katherine struggled to pull herself out of the deep fog that engulfed her. Turning her head from side to side, she opened her eyes but was unable to fully awaken. Was she having a nightmare? She didn't know why she couldn't wake up. Did she die? Was this her journey to the other side? How did she die? She didn't feel any pain. Giving in to the deep desire to sleep, she relaxed, not caring if she were dead or alive.

She felt something warm and wet on her face. She was unsure how much time had passed since she'd first opened her eyes. Her vision was blurry as she tried to focus on her surroundings. "Dog," she managed to say. Again she felt wetness and warmth on her face. An odd smell, too. Dog breath.

"I see you're finally waking up," Tyler said. "Down, Sophie; down, Sam."

Katherine's eyes opened wide. She tried to concentrate on her surroundings. Looking from left to right, she realized she was in her bedroom. "What happened?" she managed to ask the voice in the room. She didn't remember inviting Tyler into her bedroom. "Why are you here?" Should she be frightened? Had she done something crazy?

"Katherine, it's me, Tyler. Remember, we had dinner last

night? You made a delicious roast chicken and the best apple pie I've ever had."

Slowly her brain began to function with these prompts. "Tyler?"

"I'm right here." He'd been sitting in the chair opposite her. He walked over and sat on the edge of the bed.

"What happened to me?" Tears glistened in Katherine's eyes, then rolled down her face.

Tyler placed his thumb and index finger on her face, gently blotting her tears. "You had a bad panic attack last night. I gave you a shot of Ativan."

She tried to recall the previous night's events, but only bits and pieces came to her. "Tell me."

"You're having trouble remembering. It's the drug. Sometimes benzodiazepine's effects on the brain are the results of an increase in GABA, which is an inhibitory neurotransmitter. It blocks messages between nerve cells. It basically slows down the nervous system. People hallucinate and forget. That's probably what's going on with you."

Katherine smiled. "I have no idea what you're talking about, but I'll have to take your word that you do. You're the shrink."

"You were about to faint. Like I said, I gave you the shot, and it knocked you out almost immediately. Doc and I brought you upstairs, tucked you in bed, and now you're awake."

"I'm afraid to ask what time it is," Katherine said, as she tried to sit up.

"It's almost lunchtime."

"Wow, I have to get up, I need to . . . I have a lot to do. Sophie and Sam, have they been out?"

"They've been out, fed, watered, and had a couple of treats. Doc told me what they ate and where to find it," Tyler said. "Sit up for a bit. I'll bring you a coffee. Get your bearings, then you can get up if you feel like it."

"Thanks." Katherine had never met a guy who was this

thoughtful. He still wore the same clothes he'd had on last night. He must've stayed. Bits and pieces of the evening came back to her. The break-in. The man with the backpack. Her flash drive. Who would do this to her? And more so—why? She didn't have any family, no close friends. She'd been safe in her home, alone, all these years. What had changed?

Katherine went over her daily routine. It was the same every day. Get up and let the dogs out. Make coffee. Feed the dogs. Shower. Get dressed. Work. Maybe have something to eat. Go to work. Let the dogs out. Have dinner. Feed the dogs again. Look at her Friendlink page.

Karrie.

Hadn't Karrie said her father had a notebook that contained the first GWUP book? Though that was impossible. All of her notebooks were here in the storage box she had stashed in the back of her closet. She'd checked them herself. But she realized that she hadn't actually *opened* each spiral notebook. And were the notebooks still there? Did the thief take those, too? Katherine hadn't even thought to check last night.

She eased her legs to the side of the bed, put both feet on the floor, and stood. Katherine took a deep breath and slowly walked across the bedroom to the closet. The storage box was exactly as she'd left it. She removed the plastic top and took out a few of the spiral notebooks. They were hers, in her handwriting. Surely her notes for the first book in the series was in here, too. She searched through every notebook she had but didn't find it. Karrie could be right.

Katherine was puzzled—and ticked off. How had someone, maybe Karrie's father, gotten into her home and found her notebooks? Not having left her house in years, she knew it was impossible for anyone to just walk inside, search her home, and take what they wanted. But isn't that what had happened the night before? While she had a guest. She was no longer safe in her own home.

Katherine put the notebooks back in the storage container, her thoughts all over the place. A wave of dizziness overwhelmed her. She crawled into her bed, easing beneath the covers. She wished the effects of this drug Tyler had given her would wear off. She had so much to do.

A tap sounded on the doorframe. "Hey, I've brought coffee. You awake?" Tyler asked.

Katherine slid out from beneath the blankets, leaning against the headboard. "Yes, I've been up. I had a wave of dizziness hit me when I was in the closet, and I figured I was safer in bed."

Tyler placed a cup of coffee and a plate of toast on her night table. "No sneaking around just yet. Doctor's orders. I wasn't sure if you're a breakfast person, but you need to eat something. It'll help absorb the drugs in your system. When you're ready to start moving, that will also help. Drink lots of water, too."

"Yes, Doctor." Katherine couldn't help herself, despite her circumstances. She took a sip of coffee. "This is good. You found my special assortment of Keurig pods."

"I did. I'm somewhat of a coffee connoisseur. It's what I live on some days," Tyler told her.

"I like that. I'm a bit of a coffee nut myself," she said, then realized she'd used the word *nut*. Had Tyler caught that? He probably thought she was nuts anyway, so what did it matter?

"I figured as much when I saw that swanky coffee machine. I wasn't sure how to use it, so I went with the Keurig."

"The JURA? Late-night shopping. It's nice, though. Makes two espressos at the same time. I have four coffee machines," she teased. "Three too many."

Katherine knew this small talk about coffee was just to avoid the elephant in the room. She needed to get her act together and find out who had broken into her home, who had her notebook, and how they were able to get inside her house. This was nice, though. She hadn't been this relaxed in such a long time. She hesitated, because right now, in this moment, she actually felt at ease.

"Don't you have work to do today?" she asked. Anything to prolong the inevitable.

"I had my secretary Liz send my appointments to a colleague of mine. Rose is a good friend. We've had to do this many times over the years, so it's not a problem."

Katherine wondered just how good a "friend" this Rose was. "I wish you wouldn't have. I don't want to mess up your day . . . your week, your life. I'm good here. I promise." That was a lie, and she knew it. She wanted him here, though she hated that he'd had to change his work schedule to babysit her.

"It's fine, Katherine. None of my appointments were matters of life or death. Rose can handle them. She's an excellent doctor."

Again, Katherine wondered if Tyler and Rose's relationship was more than that of just professional friends. It wasn't her business, but this was the first man she'd been around, other than Doc, in more than seven years. When she actually thought about the number of years she'd purposely locked herself away from the world, it was shocking. She didn't have any friends, no family, unless there were distant relatives from generations back that she was unaware of. Her choices had placed her in this insane life. Looking at it now, she could see why the folks from the community website called her "the crazy lady on the mountain."

"I'm so sorry you got caught up in this mess," she said, reaching for a piece of toast.

"I'm a big boy. If I didn't want to be here, I wouldn't be. I spoke to Doc earlier. Detective Davidson called and said they got a good set of prints from your desk last night. They're running them through IAFIS, so whoever was in your home, if they have any type of criminal record, they'll find out."

Katherine knew any hope of keeping her identity secret was most likely futile. She would have to deal with it one way or another. "What is that—the letters, what do they stand for?" She should know, but she didn't.

"Integrated Automated Fingerprint Identification System."

"I'll stick with the acronym," she said. "Do you know how long it will take for the police to have a name? I've never personally been involved in a criminal investigation." She reached for a second slice of toast. Katherine realized just then how protected she'd been her entire life, even before she'd decided to lock herself away from the world. At thirty-seven, she was as naïve as she'd been in college. She had been the only virgin in her graduating college class. Not that it was a bad thing, but it was unusual in this day and age.

"No, I'm sure they'll call when they have any information. For now, you need to relax and get the Ativan out of your system. I'm going to get you another coffee and some water." Tyler took her empty cup and plate, leaving her bedroom without giving her a chance to respond. Katherine decided she liked that about him. He took charge without being overbearing. Unlike her dictatorial father.

He had not been a kind man. Not once did he ever put her on his knee, take her to an outing, or tuck her into bed at night. Nothing. In his words, he simply "bled oil." Katherine could almost believe it, because he had no heart, nothing to pump blood through his veins like any normal person. His death had been tragic, but fitting for a man like him. She hated herself when she had that thought, but it was her true belief. Her mother had been cold, too. She could be nice when it suited her, but that was rare. Though she didn't deserve to die the way she did. Katherine despised these memories. It made her remember the other bad things she did not want to remember.

"Piping hot," Tyler said, as he held the mug of steaming

coffee. "You'll have to teach me how to use that fancy machine sometime. I like an espresso now and then."

"I'd love to," Katherine said, then wished she could take the words back, or at least the *love* part. "It makes a regular old cup of coffee, too," she quickly added.

"Good to know. How are you feeling?" Tyler asked.

Katherine thought for a moment before answering. "Honestly, I feel better than I have in years." And that was the truth. Maybe it was the aftereffects of the drug, or having Tyler there; maybe a combination of both. Whatever it was, she wanted it to stay.

"That's great, K," Tyler said, using Doc's nickname for her.

"I'll finish this cup, then I'll clean up and come downstairs," she told him. "I can't remember a time that I stayed in bed this late."

"I slept late for a week after I finished medical school."

"Tell me about that. Where did you study? Why did you choose psychiatry?"

"I went to Duke for four years, then Yale Medical. After I finished medical school, I did a two-year fellowship at Yale. Fourteen years of books, no sleep, and no social life. Sounds fun, huh?" he joked.

"No, it sounds like you knew what you wanted to do, and you were dedicated. Adding another two years, that's tough, but I think you're a tough guy." She truly did.

"Thanks. I don't know about tough, but I am dedicated to my career, my patients. I've been in practice long enough to know that I have a right to a life outside of work, and I do. I suppose growing up with a father who was a psychiatrist rubbed off on me. He would come home and talk about his day. Of course, he never revealed anything about his patients, but he had a way of telling a story about his work that I knew was his way of getting the day off his chest. Because there are times when a patient can be, well, let's say *trying*.

Dad's storytelling was his relief, and I believe it still is when he has a rough day. I keep telling him it's time to retire, but he won't listen."

"If he likes what he's doing, why should he quit?" Katherine asked.

"He's getting old," Tyler stated.

"And isn't he riding motorcycles?" she teased, remembering his accident.

"That's not that half of it. He's a daredevil. I suppose as long as he doesn't kill himself when he's working, that's probably the safest place for him to be."

Sam and Sophie were lying quietly on the bed. "These two are mesmerized. They're so quiet," Katherine said. "I believe they like you."

"And I like them, too. You'll have to meet my cat Pickles sometime. What a furball, but funny as ever. He's quite the entertainer. A show-off."

She laughed. "Pickles? Where did that come from?"

"His eyes are green, like a pickle. Just wait until you see him, then you'll understand. He's the brightest shade of orange, too."

"Maybe you should've named him . . ."—she thought for a minute—"Mango? They're orange on the inside."

"A little late for that, but that's a good name. I'll remember that if I decide to get Pickles a friend."

She gave him a sad smile. Would she ever be able to leave her home to visit Tyler to see his silly cat? Or, was she doomed to remain inside forever, imprisoned by her own fear? She needed to get a life. She wasn't safe here. Until they found the person who broke into her home, she'd feel better if she had another place to stay. She had such a fear of the outside, but her fear of being alone in the house without Tyler would be worse.

"Are there hotels in Blowing Rock?" she blurted out.

"No, but I know a couple of folks who rent their homes

out on Airbnb. Lots of hotels in Asheville, if you want to drive a few miles down the road. Are you thinking about leaving, Katherine? If you're afraid to stay here, I'll stay with you. Or, you could stay at my house. I've plenty of room, a huge yard where Sophie and Sam can run around. No strings, though," Tyler said. "You're in a very difficult situation, and that's putting it mildly, however cliché that sounds."

Katherine took a sip of her coffee. Could she leave all of this behind, even if it was just temporarily? Could she actually force herself outside in order to go to another place where she would feel safe? If she did, her entire world would change.

"I'm not sure. I don't feel like I could stay here by myself now. I know I sound like a whack job . . . no, I *am* a whack job." Tears pooled in her eyes. She used the edge of the sheet to wipe them away. "I feel so frigging helpless. I have everything in the world except my freedom. It's insane, I know. I want to go out and be like I used to be. Tyler, I really want you to help me. I'll do whatever it takes," Katherine told him. It was all a bit unbelievable, since she'd only just met him, but she felt she'd known him much longer. Maybe in another life, if she even believed in that sort of thing.

He sat on the opposite side of the bed. "Katherine, the mind is a mysterious machine. It controls everything we do. What we think and feel. How we react or don't react. I'm sure you understand. If you're determined to face your fears head-on, I promise you will be the best version of yourself. At least I hope so, because, like I said last night, I'm a bit smitten with that woman, and that isn't changing. But I promise during our sessions, I'll be your doctor and nothing more. You'll be able to come and go as you please. No grocery deliveries. No ordering fancy coffee machines from the Internet. You will be able to go out and do these things yourself. Getting there might scare the crap out of you—pardon my language—but I'm just telling you like it is, because I've seen my patients go through this. I've also seen them get to the other side of this disease. And when they do, their life renews, and they can live again. So I can help you get started and guide you, but you're the one that will have to do all of the work."

She took a deep breath. "I'm ready. I want to start today. I'm going to shower, and then I'll be downstairs in fifteen minutes." She shoved the sheets aside and got out of bed. Tyler steadied her when a wave of dizziness washed over her.

"I'm here, so no need to be afraid," Tyler told her.

"I'm so embarrassed. I feel like a two-year-old, but I'd like it if you stayed," she said.

"While you shower, I'll go downstairs and make us another cup of coffee. If you need help with anything, give me a shout."

"I owe you so much, Tyler. I'm not sure I could ever pay you back. Yes, to the coffee, even though you're probably exhausted. Did you get any rest?"

"I slept on your sofa and had a decent night's sleep. I woke up a couple of times, but went right back to sleep. In medical school, you learn to sleep whenever and wherever you can. It took me a while to learn, but now I'm a good sleeper, kind of like these two." He patted the two shepherds on the bed.

"Then let me shower and get on with the day."

Tyler followed Katherine to her luxurious en suite. "This is the fanciest bathroom I've ever seen," he told her as he looked around. "I didn't pay much attention last night, but wow. Lots of stuff."

"There's a sauna if you want to use it sometime. The tub is good to soak in. I prefer the shower. It's like a dang rainforest, there are so many shower heads hitting you from every direction. It's all a bit much, I know, but I love this place and my fancy bathroom. Now if you'll excuse me," she said, raising her eyebrows and giving him what she hoped was a sweet and slightly sexy smile.

Tyler's face reddened. "Uh, yes, sorry. I'll just step out and go let the dogs out again. And make more coffee."

"Okay. And Tyler . . ." She stuck her head out of the partially closed door. "When I'm finished with my shower, you're welcome to have a shower and a shave if you want." She closed the door before he could answer.

Katherine found it hard to believe how her life had changed in a matter of hours. If she and Tyler were to become a couple, she had Doc to thank. It had started with a phone call. If Doc hadn't told Carson about her stables, where would she be?

The intruder. What would she have done on her own? Called Doc, as that's what she did when she was in any situation where she needed someone. But now she was determined to handle her issues by herself. She was a middle-aged woman. A professional. A published author with thousands of readers. She was a multimillionaire. And here she was, letting life pass her by.

No more, she thought, as she stood under the warm water. Today was the first day of the rest of her new life.

She used the tangerine body wash she'd purchased online. The smell really did rejuvenate her, just as they'd advertised. Katherine would write a good review for the small shop in Blowing Rock that she'd ordered the body wash from. Taking her hair out of its braid, she washed it with an herbal shampoo she'd ordered from Amazon. It was nice, but nothing she would take the time to review.

When she finished her shower, she dressed in a pair of Levi's and a black long-sleeved T-shirt. Her Nikes were back in her closet, thanks to either Doc or Tyler. Their kindness really did overwhelm her. She took the sneakers, grabbed a pair of socks, and slid her feet inside. It felt good to actually wear shoes.

When she reached the bottom of the staircase, she waited for a moment, watching Tyler in her kitchen. He looked like he belonged there. His movements were effortless, as if he knew her kitchen inside and out. She felt like today was her first Christmas, and the break-in, and all that went with it, didn't matter right now. She was beginning to feel like her old self. No rapid heartbeat. No tightening in her throat or dry mouth. Her hands weren't shaking. She didn't feel as though she'd die if she stepped outside. Was she really agoraphobic? Or had she used that as an excuse in order to keep herself safe? Either way, she really did need Tyler's help.

"Hi there," Katherine said as she walked through the dining room. "Are you making more coffee, I hope?"

"No, I was putting the dinner dishes in your dishwasher," Tyler said.

Reality set in for Katherine. "I'm so sorry, Tyler."

He wiped his hands on a paper towel, then took her hands in his. "Katherine, please don't apologize. You have nothing to be sorry for. I'm here because I want to be, okay?"

She couldn't grasp why anyone would want to hang out with the "crazy lady on the mountain." Apparently, Tyler was a bit crazy. Didn't they say psychiatrists were a bit loony themselves?

"Katherine?" Tyler said.

"Sorry, my mind was wandering."

"Let's have that coffee, and then we'll talk." Tyler handed her a fresh mug of coffee, then waited for his to finish brewing.

Katherine sat down on a barstool at the kitchen island. Tyler sat across from her. He was the first to speak. "Are you one-hundred-percent sure you're ready for treatment?"

"I said I was," Katherine stated. "I won't go back on my word." She hoped like hell she wouldn't. Now she had someone to fight for, other than herself. Though she wouldn't admit that to him. Not yet, as her feelings for him were new, fresh. She had enough sense not to reveal them yet, if at all.

"Good. Then if you're sure, I want to start today," Tyler said.

Maybe she'd spoken too soon. With the break-in and her missing notebook and flash drive, she'd assumed they wouldn't start therapy until the investigation was completed. But she'd given her word, and right now that was all she had.

"Okay, let's do this." Katherine waited for the familiar sensations to paralyze her, to send her into a deep vortex of fear. There was nothing. No dry throat. No rapid heart rate. No sweaty palms. No choking sensation. "Tyler, I have to tell you this. When I talk or even think about my panic attacks, I usually have one, almost on demand. It's not happening now. Is there a medical explanation for that?"

He smiled at her. "There are many factors, K, and I'll take you through them one at a time as needed, with your permission."

"Sure. I need to do this. I'm ready now," she said, leaning across the island and getting as close to him as the space allowed.

"All right, then there is one test we can do now, if you're willing."

"Tell me what it is," she said, fearful but ready.

"I want you to go outside with me."

Katherine had known this was coming, and she waited for the dread to consume her, but the familiar panic didn't come. She waited a full minute before giving her answer. "Let's give it a go." She downed the rest of her warm coffee and stood up.

Tyler walked over to her side. "Now, if at any time you feel any sensation that makes you uncomfortable, I want you to tell me. It doesn't matter what it is, even if you think it's insignificant, I want to know. That's part of your therapy," Tyler said, then took her hand.

"Do you always hold your patient's hand?" She smiled.

"No." He grinned back at her.

They stood in front of the French doors. Sophie and Sam stood beside them. Katherine noticed the makeshift repairs to the two windowpanes. "You did this?" she asked before they opened the doors.

"Yes. Are you trying to stall, Katherine?"

"No, I'm not." She dropped his hand like a hot potato, went to the door, and swung it open. Before she could stop herself, she stepped outside onto the deck. Then, to her utter shock and amazement, she walked down the steps circling around to the front of her house.

Standing there, the sight of her home from the outside was the most beautiful thing she'd ever seen. She waited for the panic to come, but all she felt now was excitement.

"Oh geez! How magnificent!" Katherine had no clear memory of the view from this standpoint, but seeing it now was mind-boggling. She turned around, her eyes scanning everything, trying to take it all in, all that she'd prevented herself from experiencing for seven years—the joy, the scents, the sounds—it was out of this world. There truly was a God, she thought. She had doubted him as a child, but no more.

"K, you're going down in the record books as the most successful case of agoraphobia on record. How do you feel?" Tyler asked when he joined her.

She saw the amazement on his face. Fighting off the urge to jump in his arms, she held back, though her smile was as bright as the sun that shone in the sky. "I feel like the biggest idiot on the planet, that's how I feel. Why now? Before today, I couldn't even *think* about going outside. I've tried stepping onto the deck many times, and I would run back inside because I was afraid, and I'd have a panic attack. Sometimes I could stop them—but why this, why now? Did that shot you gave me last night have some magic potion in it, or what?"

The dogs were as ecstatic as she was, both jumping up and down. She bent down to their level. "It's a miracle, right?" She scratched them between their ears, and then they took off running so far, she lost sight of them. This is what they were used to; she'd been clueless. What if something had happened to them? Of course she would've called Doc, her safety person.

"What about going for a drive?" Tyler asked, a sexy smile on his face. His blue eyes really did match the sky, she thought, knowing how cliché it sounded, but she didn't care. It was true. His dark black hair was no longer sleek. Her first impression of him had conveyed professionalism, but now his hair was messy and even sexier. He took her hand again. "So, do you?"

She raised her brows. "Do I what?"

"Do you think you'll be able to get in my SUV, which is parked around the other side of the house. And yes, before you ask, we can take Sam and Sophie. So, are you up for a ride? You wanna see the town where you live?"

She wasn't sure what to do. "What if the people who broke in last night return?"

"Trust me, they won't," Tyler said, still holding her hand.

"You can't know that for sure, Tyler."

"I want you to look at me, and don't take your eyes off of mine. Can you do that?"

If he only knew what her thoughts had been a moment ago. "Of course," said the new Katherine.

"Okay, there are six professionals watching your house as we speak." He touched her cheek. "No looking around. I had Ilene do her thing last night. No one will get within a mile of your house, I promise."

Katherine couldn't say a word.

"I'm going to be blunt, so if I hurt your feelings, I'll apologize when I'm finished," Tyler said. "Who did this to you? Someone has beaten you down so badly that you have no faith in humanity. Whatever I did—and will continue to do for you—is because I want to. I really like you, Katherine. I like you more than any woman I've dated. I don't really know you, but it's easy to see you think so little of yourself by the way you question what others do for you. You're kind and beyond beautiful. You are smart. You're a bestselling author. You're a fantastic cook. You love Sam and Sophie and take excellent care of them. That's all I know about you, but I want to get to know more. You're broken; and I want to help put you back together. Not as a doctor, but as a man." He backed away. "The doctor part is secondary, for when you decide."

Stunned, she just stood there like a lawn ornament. She wrapped her arms around herself, against the beginning of an autumn chill. Words were her life, but at the moment she couldn't think of a damned word to say.

"Are you pissed off?" Tyler asked. "I'm sorry, okay? But I meant every word I said. I want to be with you, get to know you better. We can figure out everything as we go, K. Do you mind if I call you K, or would you rather I call you Katherine?"

She shook her head, turning away from him, knuckling away her tears so he wouldn't see how his words affected her. He was right. For one man to discover those things about her in such a small amount of time was precious. Before he walked away, she turned to face him. "I don't care what you call me, Tyler. I'm not sure if your ability to see through all my craziness is due to your profession, or if you're just the sweetest guy in the world. Probably a bit of both." She wiped away another tear that had spilled down her cheek. "I am grateful for all that you've done for me in such a short time. Why would I be upset? You've brought me back to life. How can I thank you?"

Tyler had positioned himself a few steps away from her. Now he stepped forward and took her in his arms, holding her so tight, he felt her rib bones. Afraid he'd hurt her, he loosened his embrace.

Katherine could no longer hold back her tears. She didn't care if Tyler or the people guarding her property saw her. She'd lost seven years of her life, by her own hand. Working with Tyler, she hoped to understand why she had done that to herself. She was unsure of everything, but all that mattered to her now was the freedom she'd rediscovered. And she had two people to thank for it: Doc and Tyler. It didn't matter if he denied it; she knew if she hadn't met Doc that she would still be hiding behind her computer, living her life via the Internet and spending her evenings pretending to be a sixteen-year-old girl named Darby.

Karrie! She felt as though the wind had been knocked out of her. "Tyler, last night I was supposed to make a call to Karrie, the young girl from the Friendlink page. I had one of those disposable phones so I could call her without giving my identity away. Did you find the phone?"

"I saw your phone last night. Karrie called you. She seemed pretty upset. I'm sorry I didn't tell you sooner. I was so focused on you that I forgot."

She pulled away from his embrace. "What did she say? Was she all right?"

"She wanted to speak to *Darby*. Apparently, she thought I was your father, Walter. I told her you didn't feel well and had gone to bed early, said you'd call her back. She was upset. She was worried about K.C. Winston. She said it was urgent."

"Shoot," Katherine mumbled. "Something is going on with that kid, I feel it in my gut. I just can't figure out what it is. She says she's sixteen, but I'm not so sure that's true. I'm thinking thirteen, fourteen. She just seems . . . I don't know, like a scared rabbit."

"I'll get the phone and you can call her back," Tyler said.

"You must think I'm out of my mind. I don't know why I got involved with this kid, but I have, and I need to finish what I started. I need to call her now, Tyler. I want to find out what this girl needs, and possibly help her, but I don't want to reveal my identity just yet."

"Let's go," he said, then called out, "Sophie, Sam. Come."

The shepherds came running back, stopping when they saw Katherine. They were panting, saliva dripping from their muzzles.

"You two need water," Katherine said. "Good dogs." She rubbed their heads affectionately. "They like you, Tyler."

He smiled. "The feeling's mutual. You trained them well. Let's go get that phone, and then we can plan our day after we figure out what's going on with Karrie."

The dogs ran back up the stairs to the deck, which was their routine. Nothing new to them, but new to Katherine. She was awestruck at the vast land around her. She could walk her property lines now and find those trout streams the realtor had told her about. She would jump in piles of leaves, because she was surrounded by hundreds of sugar maples, oak trees, dogwood, and hickory trees, all of which she recognized from the research she'd done during her first autumn in North Carolina, stuck inside. Now she could go outside, walk the trails, and discover what she'd neglected for seven years.

"How are you feeling?" Tyler asked, as they walked back to the house.

"I think I believe in miracles. I feel like myself, my old self. I don't understand why I'm"—she thrust her hands out— "able to be here. I haven't felt the slightest symptom of a panic attack. Normally when I think about it, I go into full panic mode. I don't understand what's happened."

"You experienced a series of traumas last night—it's possible they jolted something inside of you, similar to how the initial trauma caused you to go inward."

As they made their way up the stairs to the deck, they saw the dogs waiting for Katherine to open the door. She was a bit hesitant to go back inside.

"How do you feel?" Tyler asked her again, as he opened the French doors.

The dogs raced ahead of Katherine and headed straight to the kitchen. Katherine trailed behind them. "Sit." She took two beef sticks out of the jar, giving each a treat as usual. She didn't want to stray from their routine.

"I want to make that call now," she said to Tyler. "I need the phone."

"Of course." He opened the drawer where she kept her flatware and pulled out the burner phone, giving it to her along with the number he'd written down. He placed her iPhone on the counter.

Katherine was embarrassed that she had pretended to be a teenager, and she didn't want to have to change the tone of her voice in front of Tyler. "Do you mind giving me a moment?"

"Not at all. I'll go take that shower," he said. "If the offer still stands?"

"Of course. My home is yours." Katherine might've rushed her words, but she meant what she said. Tyler had given her so much more, he could have her house if he wanted.

"Thanks. I'll shower while you can make your call." He smiled at her and went upstairs.

Inside the downstairs powder room, Katherine closed the door, sat on the toilet seat, and dialed Karrie's cell phone number. Karrie answered on the second ring. "Hey, Karrie, what's going on? My foster dad said you called last night, that it was important." Katherine hoped she sounded like she had the last time they spoke on the phone.

"Darby, you need to help me. I'm serious—my dad is insane. He's losing it about K.C. Winston. I don't know what to do. I'm afraid."

Katherine didn't know, either. Still uncertain if this was real or just a prank, she was inclined to go with the latter. "Where is your dad now?"

"At work, I think," Karrie said. "I have to go; the bell is ringing. Call me after three. I'll be out of school then. I'll be in my room doing homework. If he comes home, he won't be suspicious."

"Karrie, like, this is crazy. Suspicious of what? That you have a friend? Like, what do you want me to do? I can call the cops, like, now if you want me to," said Katherine in her fake Darby voice, purposely overusing the word *like*. "Is he hurting you?"

"No! You can't do that. Look, I have to go. Call me later this afternoon." Karrie hung up.

This was beyond strange. Katherine went back to the kitchen and waited for Tyler. Karrie must have an emotional problem Katherine couldn't fathom. She couldn't make sense of anything she said. Her father was mean, she got that. But how was he connected to her books? Why did Karrie think *Darby* could help her? Did she know more than she was telling Darby? Did Karrie know she was K.C. Winston? If so, what was the connection between Karrie's father and the books?

"How did your call go?" Tyler asked. He smelled of her tangerine body wash and shampoo. His wet hair was slicked back. He hadn't shaved, which Katherine thought was sexy. He wore the same clothes as before, but Katherine didn't care. He was striking, a man who most likely turned heads when he walked into a room. She would bet on it.

"This girl, Karrie . . . I don't know if she's suffering from an emotional problem or if she's a little drama queen." Wasn't Katherine in a similar situation herself? "I asked her if she wanted to me call the police, and she adamantly told me no, I couldn't do that. Said her dad was at work. She asked me to call her after three this afternoon. I think she's lying about being in school. She told me the class bell was ringing when I spoke with her, yet I never heard any bells, or any other voices in the background. I think it's strange."

Tyler ran his hand through his damp hair. "What is your gut telling you?"

Taking a deep breath and slowly releasing it, Katherine shook her head. "I can't pinpoint an exact reason she'd be doing this. None of it makes sense. She's a kid living in Dallas, and her mother passed away a couple of years ago, according to her. I did find an obituary online that seems to corroborate all that, if she's the person she says she is. I just don't understand the *why*s and *what for*s."

"Do you want me to see if Ilene can do a background check on her? Did she ever say what her father's name was?"

"No, but it's in the obituary." Katherine saw her cell phone sitting on the counter. Picking it up, she did a search, and within minutes, she had pulled up the obit. "Here, have a look." Katherine handed Tyler the phone.

"Okay, so this could be the girl. We need to find out why she's afraid, but let's leave it for now so we can focus on your progress. You've made such a drastic turnaround, Katherine. I don't want you to do anything that would jeopardize this unheard-of recovery. Do you still want to go for a ride? See Blowing Rock?"

"Would this count as part of my therapy?"

"Absolutely. You aren't the first patient to ride in my car. Though you are the first patient to overcome your agoraphobia in such a short amount of time."

"I wouldn't call seven years a short amount of time, Tyler. Something in my psyche clicked, or so you tell me. Right now, I don't feel an ounce of fear."

"I'm not factoring that in. When you said yes to treatment, what, two hours ago, you actually went outside on your own. Let's try and move forward from there. You need treatment, K, because something caused you to hide away for a good portion of some of the best years of your life. We need to find the cause of it. So even though this miraculous thing has happened, we don't want you to have a setback."

She nodded. "That makes me uneasy, I can't lie. I never want to go back to the way I've been existing. I'll do whatever it takes. If I need to be in a hospital for therapy, I'll go. I have to start making up for lost time."

"I'll come to you for your therapy for now. No hospitals needed. A positive attitude makes a difference," Tyler said, then asked, "You want to see Doc's place?"

"Yes, I owe it to him. Let's go. Sam and Sophie will be thrilled. I'd like to surprise him, if that's okay with you."

"It's perfect. Let me call to make sure he's at the clinic. He makes a lot of house calls," Tyler said.

"Of course," Katherine said. She hadn't thought of that, but again, she hadn't been out in public since the day she walked through the main entrance to her mansion on the mountain.

"He's there," Tyler said, getting off his cell phone. "I told him I just wanted to let him know you were doing okay. I don't normally lie, but this is worth a little fibbing. Something I seem to be doing more than I should," he said, grinning.

"I'm ready when you are," Katherine said. "Anything I should do with the dogs? They've never been in a car with me, just Doc's old truck."

"Don't let that fool you. Doc has a red Mercedes-Benz convertible and a Range Rover. I think he also has a couple of Harleys, maybe an old Indian Cycle, too. He drives the truck because he doesn't want animals ruining his precious vehicles. Before you get the wrong idea, Doc is a car buff, the same as my father. They're a lot alike—good, honest men. Makes me feel guilty for not caring about cars and trucks as much as they do."

She went to her desk, still covered in fingerprint dust, and took her wallet out of the drawer. "I don't know your father, but from the little I've heard, he seems like a nice guy. Doc's best friend. That can't be bad." She wanted to meet the senior Dr. Newlon sometime soon, though she kept that thought to herself. "I'm ready to go, Tyler."

"You'll get to meet him soon. Follow me," he said, taking her hand. "I mean, you're coming with me." He squeezed her hand. "Doctor's orders." He winked at her.

Walking around to the east side of her house, she saw how the driveway circled completely around her home, leading out to Red Oak Road. She breathed in the crisp, cool afternoon air, a briskness that promised a cool fall evening.

Tyler drove a black Ford Bronco. He opened the hatch for Sam and Sophie. They jumped in the back, as if they'd done it before a million times. "See? They like me," Tyler said as he opened the passenger door for her. "How are you feeling?"

"Surreal," she said as she slid into the passenger seat. "Nice wheels, though not quite as fancy as Doc's, according to you." Her parents had always purchased a Mercedes-Benz E-Class every other year. Looking back, she knew they were snobbish. But that discussion was for another time, when she and Tyler were better acquainted.

Tyler nestled into the driver's seat, adjusted the seat belt across his chest, then cranked the engine. "I'm not a fancy car guy, remember? I'm just a Ford fan. K, your seat belt. It's against the law to ride or drive without using them."

"Sorry, it's been a while," she explained, her voice more serious than it had been all day.

"You sure you're ready for this?"

"Positive, Tyler. Let's go," Katherine said. Words she thought she would never say again, and now she spoke to them without fear.

Tyler shifted into gear, and they headed down the winding driveway. Katherine was leaving her house and didn't feel the least bit frightened. If she counted all the Christmases she'd spent alone and rolled them into one, it couldn't compare to the excitement she felt now, as Tyler maneuvered the twists and turns leading to Blowing Rock. She pushed the electric window button, letting in the cool air. Her extra-long hair, still a bit damp from her shower, tangled around the passenger-side mirror, but she didn't care. Just being out with Tyler was the ultimate gift. If she had a panic attack, so be it. She knew she would survive.

When they reached Red Oak Road, Tyler turned to her. "You sure you're up for this?"

"More than you could imagine," she said, untangling her twisted hair from the side mirror. With her hair now intact, she closed the window. "That's a bit dangerous. Not ready to lose my hair yet," she teased, then had a thought. "Tyler, I know this is completely crazy . . ." Why did she continue to use that word? "Is there a hair salon in town?" She sounded like she'd been in a coma, that everything in the outside world appeared new to her. For seven years, she'd been content with her hair. Now wasn't the time to be vain.

He laughed. "Hey, we're not just a bunch of country bumpkins out here," he said, then reached across the seat and took her hand. "We have a couple of salons in town, K. I'm sure either would love to get their scissors on all that gorgeous hair."

She squeezed his hand. "Good to know, for the future."

"When the fall foliage is at its peak, people from all over the country come just to get a look at the red oak trees on either side of the road," he said, turning onto Red Oak Road.

"Hence the name of the road," Katherine said. "I've never seen it, since the house is too far away. I'll make sure that I see the trees this year."

"You'll make up for lost time," Tyler said. "I feel it in my bones."

"Thanks for the vote of confidence."

Katherine tried to take in as much as she could. To her left, she saw hundreds of red oak trees, the same to her right. Ahead was more of the same. "And I thought I had the best view around."

"They're all good, no matter which direction you're looking in," Tyler said. "One of North Carolina's bonuses."

Signs advertising BLOWING ROCK'S FORD DEALERSHIP and POOR MAN'S AUTO REPAIR came into view as they drove toward town. Katherine wasn't sure how many miles they'd gone, and she was about to ask, when Tyler's cell phone rang, startling her.

He pulled onto the shoulder before answering. "Dr. Newlon." He spoke in a very professional tone. "Yes, I see. Thank you." He ended the call, then pulled back onto the highway.

"Everything okay?" Katherine asked. "Do you need to get to your office?"

"No, I'm fine. Rose is taking care of my patients."

He'd waited a beat too long to answer, so she knew something was wrong. For the first time since she'd walked out of her house, Katherine felt the tiny fingers of panic tickle their way up her spine, raising the hair on the back of her neck.

Chapter Seventeen

Katherine clenched her fists, closed her eyes, and took a deep breath in. She then slowly eased it out, as she'd practiced so many times. *In. Out. In. Out.*

"K, are you okay?" Tyler jerked the Bronco to the side of the road for a second time, shifting into park. "Katherine, look at me."

She shook her head. "Home," she managed to mutter. "Take me home."

"Dammit, no. You are not going to drop out of life, Katherine. Not now, not when you've just gotten a taste of what's beyond the end of your driveway. You're having the fight-or-flight response because you feel safer at home. Relax. I'm right here, and I promise nothing is going to happen to you on my watch. Breathe deep. Deeper," Tyler instructed. "Exhale slowly."

Katherine nodded, following his instructions. Her heart-beat slowed a little; her fear was manageable now. What had caused that instant relapse? When she could speak, she said, "I don't understand. One minute I'm my new—old—self, and the next I'm ready to hide."

Tyler turned in his seat as much as he was able so that he could face her. "It's very common. Panic attacks come out of the blue. You of all people should know that. Don't let it discourage you, K. You have already accomplished so much more than many of my patients. Many took years to get where you are now."

"Truly?" she asked.

"When you get to know me better as a man and a doctor, you'll see for yourself and come to your own conclusions about me, but I'm not a liar. Yes, I am telling you the truth, but I can't reveal my patients' identities. It would be unethical."

Katherine listened to his words. But it didn't matter what he said, just that he spoke. She had realized what had prompted the attack. She was unsure if she should reveal the truth to Tyler. They had only known each other for a few days. How could he affect her so?

"You stopped talking after you got that phone call. I think that's when it started." She was embarrassed, especially at her age, so she turned away.

Tyler reached across the console, gently cupping her chin and turning her face toward him. "K, I'm sorry you had another attack. If hearing me run my mouth all the time helps, then call me a mockingbird."

She leaned into him, and he kept her chin cupped in his hand. "Okay, Mockingbird."

He grinned. "You're sure you want to continue?"

She had the choice to opt out or go the full distance. "I'll continue."

"Wise decision." Tyler removed his hand, then cranked the engine again.

Katherine guessed there would be many more episodes such as this.

"All of this will help us work on a treatment plan," Tyler said, holding true to his promise to keep talking. "For now, let's plan what we can do to surprise Doc." Tyler came up with several suggestions, each one more outrageous than the last. Katherine realized he was trying to distract her and make her laugh, and he succeeded. Katherine felt calm listening to Tyler. He had a ripe sense of humor, and she liked that about him.

"I need to turn around," he said, pulling to the side of the road yet again. "We passed the turnoff to Doc's a mile back."

"You're kidding," she said, laughing. But she couldn't help wondering if he'd missed the turnoff for another reason.

"Are you distracted because of the phone call?" She knew it wasn't her business, but she'd heard a change in his tone. Professional, yes, but there was more. If he wanted her to know, he would tell her.

"Actually, it was Detective Davidson."

Alarm bells ringing, Katherine now had to know. "Did he find out who broke into my house?"

Tyler turned onto a dirt road. "He's waiting on more results to come in."

She sighed. "That's reassuring. I'm glad Ilene convinced me to call him."

"Here's Doc's clinic." Tyler pointed to a large brick building.

Katherine was surprised at the size of the place. She had thought Doc Baker had a little mom-and-pop operation, especially when he came to her house in that old beat-up truck.

Tyler parked the Bronco in the back of the parking lot. "Stay here with the dogs—don't let them out, or Doc will know something is up. I'll tell him I brought in Pickles because he was acting funny, and now he won't let me touch him for whatever reason. Then I'll have him come out and examine him. He'll know the surprise when he sees you. I'll be right back."

Katherine checked the time on her cell. Almost four. She was an hour late returning Karrie's call. In her excitement, she'd forgotten to bring the burner phone. Her personal cell was off-limits in this situation. She realized she hadn't been on her Friendlink page today. Using her cell, she logged on and saw that only two girls were active. Blondebookbabe and HotandCool. Before they could start chattering, she clicked out. No Karrie. Most likely she was waiting for Darby to call. And she would call, but later.

Anxious to see Doc's reaction, Katherine spoke to Sam and Sophie, who waited patiently in the back. "Good dogs," she said to them. For never having traveled with her, they were being well-mannered in Tyler's vehicle. She thought about hiding so Doc wouldn't see her as he came closer to the SUV, but decided that was too juvenile. Besides, the dogs would give her away as soon as they spotted Doc Baker.

Sure enough, before Katherine even saw Doc, the dogs started whining, so she knew he was close by. Katherine stepped out of the SUV, a huge smile on her face. Doc wore his usual jeans and dress shirt, though he also wore a white doctor's jacket she'd never seen him in before.

"What in the world are you doing in my parking lot? I suppose Tyler performed his magic on you? I'm sure glad to see you, and those two, out of the house," Doc exclaimed.

Katherine nodded, tears streaming down her face.

Tyler let the dogs out of the car, and they took off.

"Sam, Sophie!" Katherine called.

"They're going to find the other dogs. I think they want to play," Doc said. "The few times they've been here with me, they frolic around with the other dogs that are out of their kennels. I board a few dogs for friends. I don't lock them up, before you ask." He smiled at her. "You know if I knew your dad, I'd tell him how proud of you he should be. All in one day! Tyler told me what you did. Heck, *I'm* proud of you, kiddo." Doc gave her a hug. "I'm honored you chose to come see me first. Come inside, and I'll show you around." Doc placed an arm across her shoulders. "How does it feel to be out of your safe space?"

"Like thirty-seven Christmases rolled into one," she said, as they walked to the front of the clinic. Tyler caught up with them just in time to hear her say it.

"Why thirty-seven? Why not a hundred and thirty-seven?" Tyler teased, as Doc opened the back door using a code and keypad.

"You both know that I'm thirty-seven, so that's why I used my age. I never had too many Christmas celebrations as a child, or when I was in college—"

"K, you don't have to explain," Doc interrupted.

"I need to. My family is from generations of big money. But they had no instinct to share their money in a charitable way. I have all their money and the refineries now, and I plan to do something with it once I figure out who needs it most. They died tragically—fittingly for my father, as he was a bastard. Mom wasn't all warm and fuzzy, either, but she didn't deserve to die so horribly. They were on safari in South Africa when their guide got too close to a group of lions, and they attacked. Everyone perished except one woman, but I heard she was maimed so horribly that she frightened people. Being here with you guys, not locked away in my house, not being ignored by my parents, not being bullied at school, is better than all of the Christmases I've experienced." She waited for either to react, to tell her to have some wine with her cheese, but they didn't.

"Good grief, who treats their child like that?" Doc asked.

"I just wanted to get that off my chest before going inside. A clean slate. Forget about it, and I will, too," Katherine said.

Doc nodded and pulled the heavy door aside. "Welcome to my world."

Tyler followed them inside, but hadn't spoken since hearing Katherine's story.

"I'll show you where I operate on my patients first," Doc offered.

Katherine followed Doc until they reached a large room occupied with long tables with lights above them.

"We use this space for minor surgeries, mostly spaying and neutering," Doc Baker explained. "I have two techs, but they're gone for the day. Steph and Bethany are staying here tonight, since it's Friday. Both love animals, maybe more than I do. I stay with them, so it's basically a family get-together."

"This way," he said, and directed them to a room across the hall. "I have six exam rooms, all basically like this one." He stepped out of the room, since there was barely enough room for the three of them. "And this is my family area."

"Nice," Katherine said. "A mini apartment."

"I spend much of my time here, so when I had the place built, I figured I'd need some place to rest my old bones. Sit down while I get us a cola."

Katherine thought that Doc's home-away-from-home suited him. It contained a small round dining table, maybe made from hard rock maple, with four matching chairs with red-and-white-checkered cushions. In the center of the table sat a red napkin holder and matching salt-and-pepper shakers. Across from the table was a mini kitchen, including a small stovetop with an oven and a microwave. An old Mr. Coffee maker was on the countertop. Katherine figured that might be the reason Doc liked her coffee so much. In the living area were two dark brown leather sofas, each with an end table and lamp on opposite ends. A large table in the center between them was covered with magazines.

"So, tell me how this came about," Doc said, as he handed Katherine and Tyler sodas and glasses of ice.

"Frank, let's not put off the inevitable, okay? Katherine needs to hear this," Tyler said.

Katherine almost choked on her sip of soda. "Hear what? I thought this was a tour of the clinic."

Doc looked at Tyler. "He's right, kid. Go on, Tyler. It's yours to tell."

"Detective Davidson did get a hit on the fingerprints," Tyler admitted. "I didn't tell you because you looked so peaceful. I didn't want to ruin your first day out, even though I just did anyway."

"It's fine. Who is it? Is it someone from around here? Do either of you know this person?" She looked both men up and down.

"No," Tyler said. "It's the name of the father in that obituary. Jameson Thurman."

It took Katherine a full minute to absorb this news. Karrie was right. Her father was insane. But how could he be in North Carolina, when just a few hours ago, he'd been at work?

"Karrie thinks he's at work—I'm not sure where, but that's what she told me. The break-in was last night. Do you think he's still here?" Katherine asked.

"I'm not sure. That's why I had Ilene put those watchdogs in place. They're trained. Special Forces and then some. That's all I'm at liberty to disclose to you. If he's lurking around your place, he won't be for long. Right, Doc?" Tyler said.

"Yes," said Doc.

"What's next? What do I tell Karrie?" Katherine was shocked at this news. But hadn't Karrie warned her?

"Let's go down to the police station and talk with the detective," Tyler said. "He can give us more details about what Jameson was charged with previously."

Katherine hadn't even thought of that. So Karrie's dad was not only mean and abusive; he was a criminal, too.

"I can look after Sam and Sophie, and introduce them to the girls, if you wouldn't mind," Doc Baker offered.

"Uh, sure, they need to meet other people," Katherine told him. "Doc, I cannot thank you enough for sending Carson to use my stables. If not for that, I would still be inside." She truly couldn't express how grateful she was. "I'll call when I can," she told Doc. "You have that special food for the dogs, right?"

"Yeah, kid, don't worry. I plan to spoil them while they're here."

Back in the Bronco, Katherine had more questions for Tyler. "Why didn't you tell me Detective Davidson knew who those fingerprints belonged to? Am I so unstable I can't take part in this investigation?"

Tyler shook his head. "Of course not. I think you're brave as hell. We should go back to your place to get your burner phone before we go to the police. See if Karrie's tried to call you again. If not, try calling her and see what story she comes up with."

Five minutes later, they returned to Katherine's house. "Doc's place is close. No wonder he always gets here so quickly," Katherine observed.

Tyler parked behind the house again. Katherine decided that this would be his spot if he were to become a regular visitor. Once inside the house, Katherine quickly located the burner phone. In and out in under five minutes, Katherine was eager to put this nightmare to rest.

On the drive to the station, Katherine decided it was time to explain who she was to the detectives and to the folks in Blowing Rock if she planned to continue living amongst them. She would definitely give the folks on the community website something to gossip about. Rather than seek revenge for their petty gossip, she would do something special for them instead. She wanted to be part of this community and hoped they would accept her.

"How do you feel?" Tyler asked for the tenth time that day, interrupting her thoughts.

"Strange. Excited. A little sad."

"All normal emotions. This is good. Don't keep issues bottled up; it's damaging. Most people do just that, keep everything in. The next thing you know, they explode. Not necessarily in a mass shooting kind of way, but they throw something across the room, say mean things to someone they love, just because they happened to be there when they couldn't take it anymore. They hurt people and destroy relationships."

"I understand. I've had my moments. When I lived in Spain, the girls at the boarding school were so hateful. They mocked my accent and teased me when I had to stay behind at Burgess Hill for most of the holidays. There were moments I wanted to pull their hair and scratch their eyes out. Instead, their bullying ways inspired me to write the GWUP books."

Tyler parked in front of a small white brick building, shut the car, and turned to Katherine. Taking her hands, he said, "You are amazing. You took those negative emotions and turned them into something that has delighted so many. I have no doubt now that you're going to be fine. Remember, I won't ever let anyone hurt you."

"My knight in shining armor." She squeezed his hand.

Once inside the police station, Katherine saw it resembled others she'd seen when working at the *Globe*, though on a much smaller scale. A woman in her mid-fifties with short-cropped, dark brown hair was busy clicking away on her keyboard. Bulletproof glass separated them. Tyler tapped on the glass.

The woman jumped, placing her hand over her chest. "Oh dear Lord, rest my soul, you scared the bejeezers out of me. Now what can I help you with, Dr. Newlon?"

"I'm here to see Detective Davidson," Tyler said. Katherine was surprised the lady knew Tyler. But he was a doctor, and this was a small town. Katherine wondered if this woman was a patient of Tyler's. She wondered if his patients all knew one another. Did they compare visits? Medications?

"Of course, Dr. Newlon. He's waiting for you. You can go on back, sugar," the woman said. Then she looked at Katherine as if she were an annoyance. "Ma'am, how may I help you? Did you schedule an appointment with one of our detectives? Or do you need a permit for a yard sale? We only issue those on Fridays, and only two per year per person."

It was time. Katherine couldn't pass up this opportunity. She couldn't have chosen a better place than the police station to reveal her identity. "Ma'am . . . I'm sorry, what is your name?"

"I'm Miss Lucy Anne," the receptionist replied.

Tyler stood to the side, giving Katherine enough space, so it didn't appear that they were together. Miss Lucy Anne hadn't seen them enter together.

"What a pretty name," Katherine continued. "So, Miss Lucy Anne, there's this rumor—and I do hate to repeat rumors, but I have no other option. Do you know of the 'crazy lady on the mountain'?"

"Ohmygosh!" Lucy Anne said it so fast that Katherine had trouble understanding her. "I have heard of her, yes. She's a recluse, doesn't leave her house. Some say she stares out the window all day and talks to herself. Such a waste, her living in that mansion. How in the world can she afford that place?"

Katherine glanced at Tyler. He gave her a slight nod.

"Miss Lucy Anne, could you please do me a favor? I'm sure this news will spread quickly, with you working on the police force and all."

Lucy Anne's brown eyes opened wide. She reminded Katherine of a cow.

"I would be more than happy to help you out. I didn't get your name, either." She pronounced "either" as *eether.*

"That crazy lady on the mountain is me. Katherine Celeste Winston, also known as K.C. Winston, the children's author. If you could pass this info around, I'll donate a book to the library in your name. Heck, I'll even sign it for you."

Miss Lucy Anne seemed to be at a loss for words. She stared at Katherine, then walked around her desk to the reception area where Katherine waited. She got as close as she could without touching her. She stretched her thick, flabby arm out in front of her, her index finger pointing at Katherine like a knife. "Listen up—I don't spread lies around this town. I don't know why you think I would do such a thing, but you need to leave now."

Tyler moved toward her, but Katherine held her palm out, indicating she didn't need him to intervene. "No, Miss Lucy Anne, I won't leave. I'm with Dr. Newlon, and we have an appointment with Detective Davidson." She turned her back on the woman, confident that she would spread the word about the "crazy lady on the mountain" as soon as they were out of sight.

Taking his cue, Tyler took Katherine's hand, guiding her through the ugly cement block halls, painted a dull gray like many of the police stations she'd been to before. They were all the same: ugly and depressing. They passed two doors before she saw the plaque on the door of Detective Davidson's office. Tyler gave a quick knock.

"Come in." Detective Davidson stood when they entered. "Have a seat." He motioned at the two utilitarian steel-gray chairs placed in front of his matching desk.

As soon as they were seated, the detective opened a file folder. "This Thurman has quite the record in Dallas. I can't imagine why he'd travel this far to break into your home. Do you have any idea why, Miss Winnie?" Katherine did not like this man. She felt the old Katherine emerging. Sort of like how the Hulk transformed when he was pissed off.

"No, Detective, I do not. And please don't call me Miss Winnie. You may call me Ms. Winston."

The detective leaned back in his chair, his muscular arms across his chest. "Ms. Winston then. Do you have any idea why this"—he picked up the folder, using it to fan himself—"guy from Texas would come all the way to North Carolina just to break into your home?"

Katherine wouldn't let him get under her skin. "Isn't that your job to figure out? I'm not a detective."

No way was she going to play a role in his intimidation game. She wasn't a criminal, though he made her feel like one. She wondered if he treated all victims like this. She guessed in his youth, he'd been the type who stole girls' lunch money and pulled their pigtails.

Tyler spoke up. "Tell us what other crimes he committed, Detective. I seriously doubt Ms. Winston has any clue about this man's identity. She's the victim here, as I'm sure you know."

Detective Davidson began. "He committed arson and served eighteen months in juvie when he was fourteen. At sixteen, he stole three cars from a Home Depot parking lot. He worked there, which was one of the terms of his probation after his arson conviction; he had to hold down a job. All three vehicles were recovered, minus their catalytic converters. He was sent back to juvie for a year. He's currently a suspect in a string of home invasions in White Rock.

"In yet another incident, three women claim he attacked them when they were coming home from working a late-night shift at three separate local bars in Irving, Texas, on three separate occasions. You want me to continue? There's more if you do. This man is bad news, any way you look at him. So, I'll ask again—why would a thief travel this far when the Dallas area has been his prime location all these years?"

If this man was Karrie's father, Katherine needed to know. "Is he married? Does he have children? Any family you could reach out to?"

"We're working on that now, *Ms. Winston*," the detective replied.

The way he said her name made her feel dirty. He reminded her of her father. How could Ilene vouch for this condescending jerk?

"This is off the books. Otherwise, I would use all my re-sources, and I might have more answers for you," he added.

"Then get the investigation on the books now. I don't care who knows about it. Better yet, maybe you and your fellow officers should alert the public that we have a criminal on the loose. Isn't that what small-town police officers do in a situation like this? Or do you call in the big guys?"

"It depends."

"On what? If the person has a reputation as crazy? Loony? A nutcase? I could go on, but I'm sure you know what I mean. I believe the safety of a young girl might be at stake, so use all the resources you have. You have my permission. If you need more, let me know. I'll pay. Money is no object." This was more of the new version of herself. Normally she would think flaunting her money in this way was tacky. But now that it suited her current situation, she would do what she needed to protect Karrie. If her story were true. She felt it possible that the blood of Karrie's evil father might flow through her veins.

"Why do you believe there is a young girl involved? Is there something you aren't telling me?" Detective Davidson asked. "Hiding evidence or witnesses is against the law."

"Tyler, let's go. I can't sit here any longer. I'll have my attorney activate Winston Oil Refineries' best investigators. I'm sure they can get the job done without making me feel like I've done something wrong." Katherine stood, then turned her back on the misogynistic moron. She didn't wait for Tyler to follow her. If he didn't, she'd find a way home herself.

She reached the main entrance before Tyler caught up with her. Outside, the sun had set, and it was downright cold.

"Katherine, slow down," Tyler said.

Standing beside his Bronco, she waited for him to unlock the door. "I didn't mean to make a scene back there. He was just so damn condescending, treating me like I did something wrong! And that receptionist! I'm sorry . . ."

Tyler held up his hand to stop her. "No need to apologize. I'm not a fan of Davidson, either. And Miss Lucy Anne is harmless enough. Just a big gossip. I think you hit a sore spot. But I'm glad to see you standing up for yourself. I don't claim to know the old Katherine, but I say she's coming back."

Katherine smiled. "I actually think I'm a new, improved Katherine. I've missed out on so much and was treated so poorly for so much of my life. I won't go back there." Katherine shuddered. "Can you put a little heat on? It's been forever since I've actually experienced being outside. I'm freezing. I need to acclimate to this weather."

"Of course. Turn it as high as you want."

"Thanks, but this is fine. I remember what it was like to be in an overheated car. In Texas, there's not much cold weather. Sometimes I would go out with my mother and her driver, Teddy. I remember once, in December, a cold front hit Texas. I must've been ten or eleven at the time. I don't recall what the temperature was, but she had the heat up so high, it made me physically ill. I threw up in the back seat. She slapped me in the face and had Teddy take me home. She was so angry, she made me clean myself up, and then I had to clean up the vomit in the car. I couldn't complain, because she'd been in a mood that day, and I'd had enough of her wrath. There wasn't any help at the house to watch me. She had to take me with her, and for days, all she said was I'd ruined her Christmas. I didn't receive any gifts that year."

"No wonder you've been hiding. I might've resorted to doing the same if I'd had a parent like yours." Tyler backed out of the parking spot. "Why don't you and I have dinner? We can drive to Asheville. While we're there, you can get a jacket or whatever you need. Call Doc and tell him we're going to Asheville for dinner. Also tell him what a jerk Detective Davidson was and that you want this investigation made public. You can keep Ilene's men stationed at your house on your dime. Will that work?"

"Absolutely." Katherine made the call, explaining what had happened. When she finished, she realized she still hadn't called Karrie back. "Doc is good with it all; he'll tell Ilene what happened," Katherine relayed to Tyler. "I'm going to call Karrie now."

"Are you sure it's not too late?" Tyler asked.

"I don't care what time it is. If this Jameson Thurman has returned home, she's going to be faced with the brunt of his anger. If I can prevent it, I don't mind pretending to be Darby."

Tyler glanced at her, then placed his hand on her leg. "How do you feel? I need to know before you make your call."

"Like myself. I'm good, I promise." She laid her hand on top of his. Katherine couldn't believe this change had happened so fast. Being with Tyler had a lot to do with it. Before she had a chance to change her mind, she dialed Karrie's cell. It rang several times before going to voicemail. Expecting to hear Karrie's voice message, she was surprised when a gruff male voice said, "Karrie is grounded and does not have phone privileges." Then the automated female voice said if she wished to leave a message to press one. Katherine hung up.

She told Tyler what the voicemail message had said. "It must be her father, but does that mean he's home? You said she called the night of the break-in. She had her phone then. This is weird."

"I agree. Let's try to figure it out over dinner. Listen, I need a change of clothes. My place is close by, do you mind?" Tyler asked.

"This day has been focused entirely on me. I don't mind at all." Actually, she was curious to see where he lived. Plus, she wanted to meet Pickles.

Still heading in the same direction, Tyler turned left. He clicked a button on the car's visor, and two large gates in front of them opened.

"Talk about fancy," Katherine said.

"It's too much, I agree, but I have drugs at my place. Prescription medication for emergencies. Can't be too careful these days."

His driveway went steeply upward, then curved to the right. Katherine saw the driveway rounding off as they reached the front of a large brick home. It was Colonial style, with evenly spaced windows and large columns on either side of the main entrance. Kathrine smiled. "Nice, Tyler. And classic."

He drove the Bronco close to the entrance, then shut the engine off. "You want a quick tour?"

"Yes, but let's do it another time. I'm worried about Karrie." She hoped that he didn't take offense.

"You're right. Come inside for a minute while I get changed. I'll have you over again as soon as we get this business with Karrie and her father resolved."

As soon as Tyler opened the door, lights came on, showcasing a grand staircase curving up to a landing. "I'll just be a minute." He ran up the stairs with the energy of a young boy, which reminded Katherine that she didn't even know Tyler's age. Not that it mattered. She watched him turn to the right, and then she could hear drawers opening and closing and water running.

Tyler's home was beautiful, yet it lacked the lived-in look she'd tried to create downstairs at her place. She doubted he cared about little details such as throw pillows, sweet-smelling candles, or soft blankets tossed about.

Tyler returned, running down the stairs. "Okay, let's go have dinner or do whatever else we need to do. I think we should see if we can locate where Thurman's been staying, try to figure out if he's still here. Check the airlines in Asheville."

While dinner with Tyler would be her first choice, Katherine needed to solve this Karrie thing and move forward with her life. Knowing Lisa Pratt-Stevens, all Katherine needed to do was call and ask, and Lisa would track down any information she requested. "I didn't see Pickles." It was totally off topic, but Tyler had talked up his kitty, and she wanted to see the furry little guy.

"He's at my mom's today, frolicking with his sister. I'll make sure he's here next time. Here, put this on for now, until we can get you some warmer clothes." He gave her a blue sweatshirt with DUKE UNIVERSITY embroidered on the front and back.

"Thanks." She slipped it over her head. It was too big, but warm enough for now.

"You sure you're up for this?" Tyler asked. "If you need to do whatever makes you feel safe, you'll tell me, okay?" He was so close to her, she could smell the mint toothpaste he'd just used.

She nodded. "I will."

Outside, Tyler unlocked the Bronco, then opened the passenger door for her. "Katherine." Tyler said her name differently than others, as though it were special. Time stopped for a moment when he lowered his mouth to hers. His lips were firm against her own. She responded with equal passion that had lain dormant far too long. He wrapped his arms around her waist, pulling her close to him before ending their kiss. "We're going to finish this. Later." He brushed her hair away from her face. "I want to say words to you that I shouldn't right now. I know you've come a long way in a very short amount of time, and I don't want my personal feelings to interfere with your recovery."

"I understand, but I believe . . ." She hesitated. "*You* are part of my recovery."

There, she'd said it. She'd leave it alone for now, because

she should, but when the time was right, she would let Tyler have a place in her life. She didn't expect him to elaborate on her admission, so she eased into the seat and buckled up while Tyler started the Bronco. They headed back the way they'd entered.

"I'm going to call my attorney and ask if she can help us out. Everything she touches turns to gold, but I'll tell you more about that another time." Lisa had been on speed dial ever since Katherine had first hired her after firing her father's attorney. She hit number three on her cell, and Lisa answered on the second ring.

Katherine delved right in. "I need a favor. Can you check the airlines in Asheville and see if a man, a Jameson Thurman, was on any flights within the past week or so, headed my way? Or headed back to Asheville from here. Also, a young girl, Karrie, with a K. Karrie Lynn Collins. She's about fourteen or fifteen. They would've left out of Love Field, or possibly a smaller airport in that area that flies into Asheville. Check Raleigh and Charlotte, too." After further confirming the details with Lisa, Katherine ended the call. "She'll get right on it. So, what's next?"

"Like I said, if this Thurman is staying locally, there aren't many choices. A couple of folks rent their homes out on Airbnb. Let me make a call. You need to eat something first. Are you hungry?" Tyler asked.

"A little."

"You won't mind having a bite at Willie's Hot Dog Palace? It's on the edge of town."

"Sounds fine to me." Katherine didn't care where they ate. One, she was out of her house, and two, she was with someone she cared about, and was pretty darn sure he felt the same.

"Then we're going to have our first date at Willie's. It'll be easy to remember." He grinned at her, then reached for her hand. "Willie's son-in-law, Kyle Avery, rents his place out, since he travels a lot for his job. He works for a Napa winery. He has another place in Winston-Salem. I think that's his home base."

Fifteen minutes later, Tyler parked in slot number seven, according to the number on the sign displaying the menu. "Can I help you?" came a very Southern voice from the nearby speaker.

"It's Tyler. Is Willie around?"

"You don't want no food?" the Southern voice asked.

"Yes, I do, but I need to speak to Willie first, if he's around."

"I'll tell him," the Southern voice said. "You wanna order now?"

Tyler turned to Katherine. She smiled, her palms outstretched. "Burger, fries, and a vanilla milkshake?" she suggested.

"Perfect." Tyler ordered for them both.

A few minutes later, Willie tapped on the driver's-side window. "Hey there, Dr. Shrink, what's up? Lulu said you wanted to talk." Willie had to be in his late seventies at least, Katherine thought, as she peered across Tyler's shoulder. Willie's hair was almost as long as her own, though it was as white as snow, and he had a matching lengthy beard that reminded her of the singer Charlie Daniels. He wore a pair of faded coveralls and a red shirt with a picture of a smiling hot dog that read, "Welcome to Willie's, where the dogs eat dogs." She couldn't help but laugh. There was so much to discover in Blowing Rock. She couldn't wait to see the town she lived in.

"Is anyone staying at Kyle's?" Tyler asked.

"You ain't gonna use your own place?" Willie stretched his neck to get a glimpse of Katherine. She smiled and gave him a finger wave.

"It's not what you think. I'm serious, I need to know. It's

kind of important," Tyler said, in what Katherine recognized was his doctor's voice.

"Yep, he's got some folks there now. Not sure when they're leavin', but I can find out for ya." Willie's accent was similar to Lulu's.

"No, no. Don't bother them. I was asking for a friend, so no worries. Thanks, Willie." Tyler stuck his hand out of the window to shake the old guy's hand.

"You're welcome, son. Now let me get in there so I can fix your dinner." He walked away from the Bronco, giving a half-wave.

"Old Willie is a good guy. Country all the way, but he and Lulu are good people," Tyler explained.

"I'm sure they are," Katherine agreed. "Tyler, do you mind if I ask your age?"

"I don't mind. I'm forty-three and counting."

"Okay, that's good. I mean I really don't care about age, but I was just curious."

"There's usually a follow-up question. 'Why aren't you married and settled down with a family?' My stock answer is I haven't met anyone I want to share my life with."

Ten minutes later, a young girl wearing tight jeans and a red shirt identical to Willie's roller-skated over to the SUV, carrying a tray high above her head. Tyler turned the key over so he could lower the electric window.

"Hey, Tyler. Poppy said to tell you the burgers are a full pound," the girl said.

"That's my man," Tyler replied, removing his wallet from the center console and taking out three twenties. "Keep the change, Tressie."

"Thanks," she said, and then skated away.

"She's Willie's granddaughter," said Tyler.

Katherine and Tyler ate in silence for the next fifteen minutes. When they finished, Tyler returned the tray before they left. Back in the Bronco, he explained, "Kids take off with the trays still on their windows. Raises the price of a burger. They don't realize it yet, but they will soon enough."

Katherine had never thought about money in the sense most people did, because she'd always had access to everything she needed. Though her childhood hadn't been pleasant, she'd been given the best of everything. Shoes, clothing, books—whatever she'd asked for was hers. What she didn't get was attention from her mother and father. Looking back, she knew it had never been her fault. They had been older than most parents when she was born, and she'd upset their lifestyle in ways that a child naturally would for a wealthy couple used to traveling the world whenever they pleased.

"Are you ready to see who's staying at Kyle's?" Tyler asked, interrupting her thoughts of the past.

Was she? If this is what it took to put this craziness to bed so she could begin a fresh start, she was game for just about anything. "I'm ready. I want this over with."

"You're sure? We don't have to."

"Let's get it over with."

Tyler pressed down on the accelerator as soon as they were on Red Oak Road. "Kyle's house sits off the road ahead. I'm pretty sure whoever is staying there will see us if we park in the drive. The windows face the road. If this Thurman guy is there, he'll be watching."

"It's worth taking the chance. Let me out so I can walk to the back of this place. Maybe I'll see Karrie." *This is so ridiculous*, thought Katherine. She wasn't Nancy Drew, and Tyler wasn't one of the Hardy Boys. Did the Hardy Boys even have first names? If so, she didn't remember them.

"We'll both go on foot," Tyler said, as he pulled the Bronco off the road. "We can walk from here. No one will bother the car, and if they do, we'll deal with it later." He got out and shut his door quietly.

Katherine opened her door, careful to close it without making too much noise. "How far is this house?"

"Right there." He pointed to a white house with dark shutters framing the large windows. Tyler took her hand. "Stay close to me."

"Okay." Katherine's heart began to pound. She feared she was on the brink of another panic attack. When nothing happened, she motioned Tyler to go on. She was good.

When they reached the property, what little bit of light the moon provided was now blocked by dozens of lush trees. Tyler motioned for Katherine to stay close to the side of the house. Every sound they made seemed to be amplified. Once they reached the edge of the house, Tyler glanced around to the back. He nodded, which she interpreted as meaning they were still safe. Rounding the corner behind Tyler, Katherine jumped when she saw a light in the window.

"Shhh." Tyler placed his index finger on her lips, mouthing the word *bathroom*. Katherine nodded. Her adrenaline pumped as they waited for someone to shut the light off. Maybe a minute passed, and then the light extinguished. She breathed a sigh of relief until she heard glass doors glide open. She stopped. Holding her breath, she tapped Tyler's arm. He held his hand palm up. There again came a whooshing noise, a subtle, almost whispering that indicated whoever had opened the door had now closed it.

Katherine's senses were hyperalert. Had the person gone back inside? Or were they now outside? Watching. Waiting. Ready to attack.

Chapter Eighteen

Katherine swallowed. Her throat was dry as dust, a sure sign of an oncoming attack. Taking a deep breath while trying to be quiet wasn't easy, but she managed. Tyler turned to face her. "You okay?" he mouthed.

She nodded. As she anticipated what she knew came next, her cell phone buzzed in her pocket. Grappling with the device, she hit the end button. She'd put the phone on silent mode but forgot to dim the screen. If this idiot intruder was here, she would shove this phone down his damn throat. She visualized it, and it had a strangely calming effect on her. Was she a sociopath? No better than the person who broke into her home?

Tyler placed his hands on her shoulders, physically moving her away from the sliding doors. "Stay here," he whispered, and then disappeared without giving her a chance to ask where he was going or what he was doing. Fearing they would get caught, she removed her phone from her pocket now that she was away from the sliding doors.

Lisa had called and left a message, but Katherine didn't dare listen now. She felt like a sitting duck at the county fair, just waiting for some punk to blow her feathers off. Why was she having all of these insane thoughts?

Unsure how long she should wait, Katherine surveyed her surroundings. Shadows moved by the fence at the edge of the back lawn. She kept to the side of the house as she inched closer, hoping to see who was there. Not Tyler. He was too tall. Reaching the corner of the house, Katherine knew she had to find Tyler.

Katherine feared this Jameson might've overpowered Tyler—stabbed him, choked him, or some other method of killing a person. If the worst had happened, then Katherine would confront him directly. Brave thoughts, but could she really act on them? As she decided she had no choice, Tyler emerged from the shadows.

He tapped her shoulder, scaring the life out of her. "What are you doing? I've been visualizing a chop shop inside, with you being the chop-ee," Katherine hissed.

"There's an open window on the other side of the house. I saw it when we were heading over."

"Did you see or hear anything useful?" she whispered, her voice hoarse. She needed a drink of water.

"Let's get back to the car."

"Okay, but why now?"

"Follow me," he instructed.

Katherine stayed close to Tyler. When they reached the Bronco, he opened her door, then hurried around to the driver's side. "Look what I found," he said, pulling a square piece of paper from his back pocket and handing it to her.

"We need to take this to the police," Katherine said when she realized what she held in her hand.

"I know, and we will," Tyler replied, as he pulled onto the main road. "Not Detective Davidson. Ilene trusts him, but I don't like the guy."

"Where did you find this?"

"On the front porch, stuck under the screen door. Look at the date."

She used the flashlight on her cell phone to read the date

on the boarding pass. Three weeks ago. "I haven't said this to anyone, but I will now. For years, starting right after my parents died, I have always felt a presence, like someone's been watching me." Saying it out loud made it real. She put the pass in her back pocket.

Did he believe her? Or was this paranoia? She had never left her home for over seven years, and yet she'd always felt someone was watching her. It was one of the reasons she never walked around without at least a robe on. For all of the deliveries she received, she was always fully dressed. No lying around in a sleep shirt all day. She didn't go braless; she behaved like she was being watched. "I know it sounds crazy."

"It doesn't, because whomever this person is"—Tyler nodded at the slip of paper in her hand—"has been planning this for a very long time."

"But why? What are they planning, other than claiming they wrote the GWUP books? My editor and publisher know me. We Zoom often."

"You said you had a car at one time, right?" Tyler asked.

She had no clue where he was going with this but answered, "Yes. I still have the old thing in the garage. It's been there since the first day I arrived."

"I'll have Doc check to see if it's worth keeping. Do you remember the make and model?" he asked.

"Of course I do. A 2005 Nissan Altima. Before you ask, I still have the keys along with the title. Where are we going?"

"To your place. I want to see your car and look around. Make sure Ilene's men are still in place."

When they reached the end of Red Oak Road, Tyler turned into the long driveway. Katherine could still see her house in the distance, even though it was dark. She hadn't seen her home from this perspective since she'd first moved in. "Can you stop for a minute?"

"Sure."

Katherine got out of the car, focusing her attention on her house. If the lights were on, anyone could see inside. Especially her office, the former dining room with its floor-to-ceiling windows. She had no window coverings, because she had been sure no one could see her. Not that it mattered, but something Tyler said had triggered something in her mind. Back in the car, she asked Tyler, "You said you always wondered about this place, that when you drove by, you could see the house all lit up or something like that. Do you remember?"

The SUV bounced up the long winding drive. "Yes, I remember telling you. When the other folks lived here, they never shut their lights off. From the main road, anyone could see . . ."

"Are you thinking what I'm thinking?" Katherine asked him. She needed to know he didn't think she was as loony as those people on the community events website.

"Let's get you home. I'll call Doc and see if he can bring Sam and Sophie home. If not, I'll pick them up. I need to check on Carson's horses before I call it a night."

Tyler parked in the same place as before. Katherine felt very uneasy returning home in total darkness without Sam and Sophie by her side to warn her. Not that she'd knowingly ever put herself or her dogs in danger, but they could hear things she couldn't.

"Ask Doc if he wants to bring Steph and Bethany," said Katherine. "There's plenty of apple pie left if they want. I'll make coffee, espresso, whatever, while you and Doc take care of the horses." She knew she was babbling, something she did when she was nervous.

Katherine hadn't been this kind of nervous in a long time. It was much different than a panic attack. She could handle it, but she didn't want to do it on her own. She needed people around her. She wanted to fill this monstrosity of a house with noise—laughter, cries, barking, meowing, sounds of the living. That was the answer to her panic attacks. She knew it. When Doc was around, she was usually fine, and then she met Tyler. They clicked instantly. She had told Miss Lucy Anne where to go without being afraid. Sort of. Detective Davidson definitely knew she wasn't a fan of his.

Those events had happened because she was making them happen. Being with people mattered to her. It came as a shock, because she'd never been around people much. Alone as a child, then sent away to boarding school, then college. Her work at the newspaper exposed her to all sorts of people. She'd loved her job. Loved Adam, who would always hold a special place in her heart. Then the bombings. And she ran away when her life as an adult woman with a promising career was just beginning.

She needed to be with people. She ran up the stairs to the deck when she remembered she had left her wallet in the Bronco. "Tyler, can you bring my wallet? It's on the floorboard. My keys are inside."

She waited for him to answer. "Tyler?" She called his name again, and this time, she heard the worry and fear in her own voice.

Taking her cell phone out of her pocket, she used the flashlight to search the area below. "Tyler, are you there?" She walked to the edge of the steps, preparing to search for him, when she felt her jeans rip. "Damn!" Apparently, she'd caught her leg on an S-type hook that the previous owners had left.

In the dark and alone, fearing something bad had happened to Tyler, she hit the number one on her cell. Her safety person. Doc. He didn't answer, so she left a message. It wasn't like Doc to avoid her phone calls. Then again, he was with family, so he'd probably given up his phone for the evening. But what about her dogs? She hadn't planned on leaving them with Doc all night. He knew that. He also knew she would be sick with worry if she couldn't get in touch with him when her dogs were in his care. "Darn jerk!"

"Hey, that's just plain rude," Tyler said. "I'm not perfect, but . . ."

"Tyler! Are you all right?" She raced to the bottom of the steps. "I thought something had happened to you. I promise I wasn't calling you a jerk! I was just saying it because, well, I tried calling Doc, but he isn't answering, and I didn't know where you were."

"Hey, calm down." Tyler reached for her, wrapping his arms around her. "I was in the garage. Didn't you hear me tell you where I was going?"

Had she? No. Did he really tell her or was he just saying that to protect himself? He was a professional, and he knew how to do that type of thing.

"Though to be honest, I was halfway there when I thought I'd better let you know where I was. I didn't mean to frighten you."

"Are you sure you're not playing head games with me? If you are, please leave." She stepped away from his embrace. "I'm scared and confused, Tyler. I don't know who to trust, or who not to. This entire world is new to me. I know I sound nuts, and I sometimes think I am. My thoughts are all over the place. I'm not agoraphobic. I need to be with people. I need to hear life, see life, and most of all, I really, really want to start living my life. If I can't trust you now, then just go."

Tears streamed down her face, but she didn't care who saw her. If this was what a nervous breakdown felt like, she was in the throes of one right now. Her thoughts were like shooting stars. One went off in one direction just as another shot off in the opposite direction.

"Katherine, listen, I am going to call my mother. She'll come and sit with you. She can reassure you that I'm not a stalker or a serial killer or anything else that you think I might be. Is that okay with you?"

Katherine didn't answer him. Instead, she walked upstairs and, using her fist, she punched the laminate Tyler had used to cover the windowpane. She reached inside and unlocked the door. Once she was inside the house, she started turning on every light. Upstairs and downstairs. When she returned, Tyler was in the kitchen, making a pot of coffee. "Doc is on his way with the dogs. He said he was bringing Steph and Bethany over."

Jolted back into reality, Katherine sat down on a barstool. "Did I just whack out or what?" she asked Tyler, confused.

"Not really. You've just had a dose of life, I think. I'm taking responsibility for my part in this, because I shouldn't have left you alone in the dark. I did shout out to you, but I was too far away for you to hear. I'm so sorry."

"Can we forget this ever happened?" she asked, as a fresh round of tears gushed down her face. Tyler stuck a tea towel in his belt loop and went over to her.

"It's okay, Katherine. You're gonna be all right. I'm never going to let anything happen to you. I'm so sorry I screwed up. It's my fault." He used the tea towel to wipe her tears.

She laughed and felt snot on her upper lip. "Good grief, turn your head." She took the towel from him, wiped her nose, then tossed the towel aside. "I never cry, and now I can't seem to stop."

"Listen, this is all new to you. You went from day to night at the speed of light. You're going to cry, be confused, pissed, happy, sad, and glad."

"Good thing you went to medical school, because you aren't much of a poet," Katherine said. "Me, either. I can write novels, but poetry, no."

They sat in silence while the coffee brewed. Katherine had humiliated herself, but she didn't feel judged by Tyler. She needed him. More than he knew. She'd flipped out, as she'd taken too many hits today. But she wasn't going to continue down that pity road. She was done.

"So, how bad was the garage? I haven't been in there since I parked the Nissan all those years ago," she said.

Tyler nodded. "I see."

"What?"

"There is no other way to say this other than to tell you straight out—there is no vehicle of any kind in your garage."

She laughed. "That bad, huh?"

He got up and poured them each a cup of coffee. "I'm not joking, Katherine. I'm serious. There isn't a car in your garage. It's clean as a whistle. No tire tracks, gas smells, or oil stains. Any normal things that would have been there if a car was stored there this long."

"I have the title and a set of keys." She hurried across the room to her desk. Opening the drawer where she kept important papers, she searched until she found the title to her car. She'd kept the keys in the drawer under her desk as a reminder that someday she would drive again and see the world. Now that day had arrived, and she apparently didn't have a car. And she couldn't find the keys.

"Someone has been in my house. More than once," she said when she returned to the kitchen. "Look." She handed Tyler the title paperwork. "The keys are missing. I put them in a drawer, and I've never moved them."

How could Katherine have gone about her day-to-day life and be oblivious to a person violating her space, stealing her car? Maybe it would be wise to allow Tyler to place her in an institution, where she could be treated around the clock. She'd been so engrossed in her self-imposed exile, focusing on her dogs, work, and the Friendlink group, she'd unknowingly allowed her home, her safe place, to be violated.

Tyler glanced at the title. "I see this is your vehicle, registered in the state of Illinois. Somebody knows your routine. They know where you are in the house. When you take a shower or when you sleep or whatever, they must come inside and take what they want. Do you have any idea who might be behind this?" Tyler's tone was deadly serious.

"No, I swear. I don't know anyone here. Just Doc, you, and Carson."

"What about the delivery people? Do any of them know you had a car? Where you kept your keys? Did they come inside any time?"

"I don't think so, but I'm not one hundred percent sure. They'd have to be pretty sneaky to get past Sam and Sophie."

"Or they are well-acquainted with the dogs. Do Sam or Sophie seem overly eager when you have a delivery?"

"Not really. They bark at everyone, though the kid from the Apple Blossom Market brings them treats when he delivers, but not every time."

"Think back to the last time he was here, if you can remember," Tyler coached. "When you made dinner, did you order any groceries that day?"

"Yes, I ordered a couple of things. I never normally go out to get the bags until he leaves, but yesterday—or the day before?—he had treats for the dogs. I'd been brave that day, because you were coming for dinner, so I stepped outside as he was giving the dogs a treat. Royce, that's his name. He saw me and said it was nice to finally put a face to the name. I agreed, grabbed the bags, and came inside, feeling like I'd just conquered Mount Everest. That was it. He seems like a nice kid."

"I know who he is. He is a good kid. I doubt he's been breaking into your house."

"There is no one else. I really don't have any idea who would do this. Maybe someone local who is down on their luck?"

"Could be. Something to check into. When we were at Kyle's, the Airbnb house, I saw a garage in the back, an unattached one. There was a vehicle inside. It looked either gray or silver. It was hard to tell, since it was so dark out." Tyler looked at her title again. "Your Nissan is silver?"

She nodded. "Yes, it was a great car, with good gas mileage. It had the works. Sirius Radio. The first car I bought with my own money."

"Someone is going to pay for this, Katherine. I'm going to make damn sure of it. Now, what about your attorney? Have you heard back from her yet?"

She'd forgotten all about Lisa. "Yes, she left a voicemail, but I haven't listened to it yet. With all the excitement going on, I didn't play it back. Let's listen now." She took her phone out of her pocket and clicked into her voicemail. Lisa's voice was clear and succinct: "Call me, kid. I think I know who's screwing with you."

"That doesn't tell me anything," said Katherine. "Lisa knows I don't have any close friends. She is aware of my living situation. If she has a name in mind, maybe it's simply a stranger from here, and she was able to find them faster than that jerk detective. No—*defective*," she couldn't help adding.

"You trust her?" Tyler asked.

"With my life." And she did. Lisa's references had been top-of-the-line. Clean as a whistle.

"How did you meet this woman?"

"She came highly recommended to me after my parents died. Their attorney was an old bastard. I remember him trying to touch my breasts when I was eleven. As soon as their last will and testament was read, I fired him immediately."

"Would *he* resort to this type of behavior?"

"Unless he crawled out of his grave, no. He died not long after Lisa took over. He had a massive stroke," she told him. "Lisa said he lingered for days."

"I guess we can definitely count him out then."

"I can't imagine anyone wanting to do this. Do they truly

believe they're going to get credit for my work? It's insane. Plagiarism happens, sure, but nothing on a scale like this. I'm calling Lisa. I need to know who she suspects, a name, or anything I can give to investigators."

Tyler refilled their coffee mugs. "I wouldn't call in your investigators just yet. You don't want to alienate the local authorities."

"I really don't care. If Detective Davidson is representative of the police force, then I'll have Lisa fly my people in." More and more, Katherine sounded like her father, a powerhouse. There were times such as now that she understood why he'd had to be so forceful.

Katherine hit speed dial, and Lisa picked up immediately. "Hey, Lisa. I got your message, but it was so cryptic. Were you able to find out who this Jameson Thurman is?"

Listening to what Lisa had discovered was mind-blowing. Never in a million years would Katherine have even thought of it. She ended their call and just sat there, staring at her phone. She had no words. Lisa had to be mistaken.

"K, what's going on?" Tyler asked, sitting down next to her. "You're white as a ghost."

She didn't answer. Memories of that day came back in full force. While they weren't as clear as she'd have liked, she realized that she had known what she saw was wrong, but had no one to explain it to her. So she hadn't said anything. Ever. Not a word.

And now, knowing what she'd just learned, would she have reacted differently?

"You're scaring me, and I don't scare easily," Tyler said nervously.

Katherine took a deep breath, blowing it out so forcefully that strands of her hair landed in her mug. "This is so frigging out of this world, I'm not sure I want to repeat it. I'm going to have one of the company investigators look into it before I go any further."

She wanted to tell Tyler, but her gut told her to keep this bit of information to herself until she was one hundred percent sure. Sighing, she removed part of her hair from her mug. "I'm sorry. I can't repeat what Lisa told me until I . . ." She couldn't even say the words out loud. "Research."

"Okay, I get it. You don't trust me completely yet. If this Lisa has information on someone who might try and hurt you, I would carefully consider keeping it to yourself."

"Tyler, I'm not even sure I believe what she just told me, but there is a way to find out if it's true." Wouldn't Tyler know? As a doctor, he probably had all kinds of resources available to him. He had helped her regain control of her life; the least she could do was trust him. "Okay, but this stays between us. Do you know anyone who could do a DNA comparison quickly? Like ASAP," she added for emphasis.

Katherine took the boarding pass they had found at the rental house from her pocket. She handled it carefully so as not to smudge any prints or DNA. "Can you get DNA from this? I realize we've handled it, and maybe someone at the airport did, as well, but I need to know."

"Maybe. It depends. But even if we can, it's useless if you don't have a comparison. We know Jameson Thurman is staying at Kyle's, and it's possible that the car in the garage belongs to you. I'm not sure how DNA evidence would help, unless we could get his print from inside the house or the garage, just to prove he's been here."

She nodded. "Right." Katherine thought about Karrie, about losing her mother. If what she thought were true, this kid was in danger.

Jameson Thurman. His name bothered her. There were no Thurmans in her past that she could remember. It could be an alias. People changed their names all the time for a variety of reasons. It was his first name that really bothered her.

"Does the name Jameson mean anything?" she asked Tyler.

"It does. It's a brand of Irish whiskey brewed in a distillery for the last couple hundred years. Very popular in Ireland."

"Is it expensive?"

"It's been a while since I've imbibed, but I think it's just average price. Good whiskey, but not top-of-the-line," Tyler said. "You want Doc to stop at The Pony Keg? I'm sure they stock it there."

"No, I don't want to drink it. I'm not a whiskey drinker."

"Where is this leading, K?"

"You asked me if there was someone in my past that might want to . . . I don't know, get even, hurt me in some way. There is someone. I just need a DNA test to prove it."

Before Tyler could reply, Katherine heard Doc's old beater truck coming up the driveway. "We'll talk about this later."

Katherine stepped inside the pantry, found a brown paper bag, and placed the boarding pass inside. She didn't want to lose what little evidence she had to prove what she was ninety-nine percent sure of.

Sam and Sophie came barreling through the French doors. When they saw Katherine in the kitchen, they jumped on her, licking her face, whining as if they hadn't seen her in twenty years. That was the thing about animals. Their love was always unconditional.

"Hey, pups, I missed you two," Katherine said as she calmed them. "I bet neither of you has had a treat today." Sam and Sophie immediately sat while she took a treat from their special jar.

Doc grinned at her when the dogs were settled. "I wanted to ask before bringing them inside. Stephanie and Bethany want to meet you. Before you ask, no, I didn't reveal your secret."

Wishing she'd had time to clean up, Katherine figured they might as well see her looking as crappy as she felt. Doc had been like a father to her, and she wouldn't do anything to disappoint him. "I would love to meet them. I'll heat up the apple pie I made yesterday."

"Sounds good to me," Doc said.

"What can I do to help?" Tyler asked.

"Find someone who can do a DNA test. Fast," Katherine said.

"Done," Tyler replied. "I'll take care of this tonight."

"Okay. We'll discuss details later," said Katherine.

Doc looked puzzled and intrigued, but he didn't question anything. "I'll just go and get the girls," he said.

Katherine took the pie from the refrigerator, making sure there was enough to go around. She placed it in the microwave to warm. She then took out the dessert plates she'd purchased online, yet never used. The plates were light green with mountains etched in the glass. They reminded her of the view she had while sitting at her desk when she was working. "Tyler, in the drawer to your left, please grab the forks." He did as instructed.

Katherine used the kitchen island as a table. No way would she allow the girls in the horrendous dining room. In due time, they could see the atrocity. She set the plates out, and Tyler placed the forks beside them. "Napkins," Katherine said, opening the pantry where she kept them. She took a stack from its wrapping, placing them in the empty holder she usually kept stocked on the island. It was where she ate most of her meals, drank her morning cup of coffee, and wished for a life that she didn't have.

Although now, she had a life and, so far, she wasn't off to a great start. *Except for Tyler*, she mentally reminded herself. If not for his patience and kindness, she wouldn't be serving pie at nine o'clock on a very eventful Friday night.

Doc returned with his daughter and granddaughter. "Katherine, this is my daughter Steph, and this little stinker is my granddaughter."

Steph was not anything like Katherine had imagined. She'd assumed she would fit her image of a schoolteacher: perfect hair, glasses perched on the tip of her nose, a stiff white blouse tucked in a navy pleated skirt. But she had long blond hair, deep blue eyes, and she wore a pair of jeans with a T-shirt that read, BAKER'S BEST.

"It's so nice to finally meet you, Katherine," Steph said, leaning in to give her a hug. She had a soft voice, but her accent wasn't quite as pronounced as Lulu's. "This is Bethany, my daughter." Katherine initiated a hug with Bethany, because right there on the spot, she had decided she would reveal who she was.

Bethany was a replica of her mother, though she wore black leggings and a long pink hoodie with pink Converse sneakers.

"I'm glad I finally got to meet you both. Doc said we had a lot in common," Katherine told her new guests. "I've made an apple pie, if you want a slice. We're eating in the kitchen."

"Who in their right mind would turn down apple pie?" Steph asked, following her to the kitchen. "Hey, Tyler, what are you doing here?"

Obviously, Doc hadn't mentioned that Tyler would be there. "I'm about to dig into a slice of the best apple pie you'll ever eat," Tyler said by way of answer.

"He had dinner with K yesterday," Doc explained to his daughter.

"Oh, I am so happy for you. Tyler never has a date; he's always working, picking folks' brains apart," Steph said.

Tyler laughed along with Doc. "Spot on, Steph."

As soon as they were all seated around the kitchen island, with slices of apple pie, coffee, and a glass of milk for Bethany, Katherine decided it was the perfect time to surprise Stephanie and Bethany.

"There's an elephant in the room, and I need to send it on

its way." Katherine smiled at Tyler, and he winked back. "Bethany, your grandfather tells me you like reading. Is that true?"

Doc shot Katherine a look she hadn't seen before. Fear, maybe?

"I do like books, more than most of my friends," Bethany said, her accent more pronounced than her mother's.

"I hear you're a big fan of K.C. Winston's books."

Doc grinned, giving Katherine the thumbs-up sign.

"Yes, I love those books. Those girls are awesome. I've read them all twice. I have to, because when they come out, I read them in one day, then I get mad at myself for reading them so fast, so I just start over," Bethany gushed.

Bethany was Katherine's first in-person fan. "What would you say if I told you I know the author?" She was dragging this out just to see the excitement on the young girl's face.

"OMG, I would ask if she would sign all my books. Do you really know her?"

"I do."

Stephanie spoke up. "Exciting, right, Beth? You can tell your father when he calls. He's deployed with the Reserves right now," she explained to Katherine, "but when he's home, he's a teacher. We all love books. Except Dad. He and all those expensive cars he likes to make the drag in."

Katherine didn't have a clue what "make the drag in" meant, but it didn't matter right now. "Okay." She took a deep breath. She felt nervous herself, but in a good way. "I'm K.C. Winston."

No one said a word.

Then Bethany's eyes filled with tears. "Really?"

"Doc?" Katherine looked at him so he could confirm what she'd said.

"It's been one of the hardest secrets I've had to keep from

you, sweetie. I've known this lady for a long time. She's smart and loves animals, and she's a heck of a cook," said Doc.

"Y'all aren't joking?" Bethany asked, looking at Doc, then Tyler. People she knew and trusted.

"She's the real deal," Doc said.

"There's so much mystery surrounding you," Stephanie told her. "Our public library always orders several copies of your books. They get snapped up like grapes off the vine. I take Beth to Asheville so we can purchase the books at our favorite bookstore. Why do they always put the books out on a Tuesday?"

"Actually, most books are released on a Tuesday. It gives some of the important newspapers time to compile their charts and, usually on weekends, the sales are noted by how they place on the list. I think distribution factors in there, too." Katherine knew more, but it was boring, and she didn't want to get into that technical aspect of her work. She had nothing to do with that end of publishing.

"Do you have any copies of your books?" Bethany asked.

Katherine smiled at her. "It's silly, but no. Once I finish one story, I move on to the next. I do see the artwork and approve the covers." She would have Gayle overnight copies of all the books so she could sign them for Bethany.

They all discussed Katherine's books for another hour until Doc said it was time to leave because his old bones were tired. He had arranged for Katherine's window panels to be replaced first thing the next day.

"Thanks, Doc. You're the best," said Katherine.

"So say the shirts." He nodded at Stephanie's shirt.

"I get it now," Katherine said. It was their last name. "Do you have them at the clinic?"

"No, just these two. If you're good, I might let you wear one. Girls, this old guy is tired, and I still have the animals to take care of. Tyler, K, I'll see you two later. Call me if Dewayne doesn't show up on time." He was the best window man in town, according to Doc.

After goodbye hugs and promises to Bethany, Katherine was exhausted. Tyler insisted on staying on the couch again, and with Jameson Thurman still out there, Katherine was glad to say yes. She would have preferred him in her bedroom, but so much had happened already tonight, and she hoped there would be plenty of time in the future for that. This certainly was turning out to be the busiest, strangest day she'd had since moving to North Carolina.

Chapter Nineteen

Early the next morning, Tyler took her to Asheville Memorial Hospital. The drive to Asheville wasn't long at all, which was a good thing, because Katherine was anxious to see if they could get some DNA results. Katherine felt like she was a spy during the Cold War era. But this was real, nothing fictional created by herself or another author.

"How long will this take before we have the results?" Katherine asked.

"Not as long as it used to take. A matter of hours, if we can find DNA on the boarding pass that matches what's on file."

Katherine hadn't known Jameson's DNA was part of his criminal record. Detective Davidson hadn't told them that it had been taken when he was arrested the year before for driving while intoxicated. He'd lost his driver's license yet stolen her car. On their way to Asheville, Katherine and Tyler had stopped back at Kyle's house. Sure enough, Katherine's Nissan was parked in the garage.

Katherine had asked Lisa to dig deeper into Jameson's background. Sure enough, he'd been arrested as an adult. Lisa had emailed his record along with his DNA results. Katherine would triple Lisa's yearly bonus. She'd earned it.

*   *   *

"You're my fiancée, if anyone asks," said Tyler.

Katherine nodded. She was glad she'd showered and changed clothes. She walked through the hospital's private entrance as if she belonged there. "Whatever it takes."

They walked through several long hallways. The sound of monitors, respirators, and moans could be heard from behind closed doors. The lights were so bright that Katherine doubted the patients could sleep. Doctors were paged over the intercom system. The smell of alcohol and bleach permeated the place. "I hate hospitals," she whispered to Tyler.

"Me too," he said, looking at her with a sly grin. "If my patients wind up on the seventh floor, it means I'm not doing my job."

"Are any of your patients here now?" she asked, even knowing he couldn't give out that information.

"None," he said, taking her hand. He pushed a button on the wall, and a large set of metal doors opened.

The room ahead of them was packed with medical staff. Katherine stopped. "I'll wait." She felt frightened for a moment.

"You can't. I need your DNA."

"I'm a little nervous, that's all."

The doors closed behind them, and Tyler walked Katherine across the lab. She saw tubes of blood and slides of something being placed in a black light mini refrigerator. She'd hated science and chemistry in school and college.

Tyler squeezed her hand. "This is Fuller's office. This won't take long."

Drawing a deep breath, Katherine plastered a smile on her face as they entered Tyler's college pal's office.

"Dude," said Fuller, standing up from behind his desk. "Been way too long. Dude."

Dude? So Fuller was one of *those* college roommates, thought Katherine. Fuller had dreadlocks and a full beard.

He was much shorter than Tyler; in fact, he was the polar opposite of Tyler.

"This your chick?" Fuller nodded at Katherine.

"No, I'm not his chick," Katherine said primly.

Fuller held both of his hands out in front of him. "I'm cool, no worries. We're all super cool, like, minus subzero cool."

On the drive over, Tyler had told Katherine that Fuller was a genius with an IQ above two hundred. He hadn't told her that Fuller was an emotionally underdeveloped dude.

Tyler was laughing. "I can't believe you still sport the locs."

Katherine wanted to add, *dude*. "I'm in kind of a hurry," she said instead. "I'm pregnant with triplets, and I pee every ten minutes."

Tyler looked over at her, ready to burst out laughing, but he played along. "Triplets. It was a shock to us but, what the heck, let's get it over with."

"My man! Yo' a one-shot dude! Congrats, man." Fuller looked at Katherine's midsection. "Cool, you aren't even fat yet."

Katherine's eyes tripled in size. "Can we just get on with it?" she asked.

"It looks like you did already! Cool, though, man. I'm in. You should name one after me."

"They're all girls," Katherine stated, hoping he'd stop with his *dude* act and do what they needed him to do.

Fuller motioned for them to follow him to the lab behind his office. He put rubber gloves on and removed a swab from a sterile package. He swiped both sides of Katherine's mouth. Tyler handed over the boarding pass. Lisa had already forwarded over the records of Jameson's DNA.

"I'll do this, dude, and let you know what I find. Cool like ice with that?" Fuller asked Tyler. "Two hours, max."

"Okay. We're going to wait in the cafeteria and grab a coffee then," Tyler said.

"Cool," Fuller said, and then went to work.

One hour and fifty-two minutes later, Katherine learned she had a half-brother named Jameson Thurman. Which meant that Karrie was her niece.

On the drive back to Blowing Rock, Katherine didn't say much. She was remembering what she had never wanted to remember.

Katherine crouched down behind the leather chair when she heard the door to her father's office open. She should've listened to Miss Audrey. She told her and Tracie that no matter what, life or death, they could not go inside Mr. Winston's office. Katherine didn't care. She hated her dad, and all she wanted was one of those ink pens that he used when he signed papers. It was all swirly and curly, and she wanted a pen for herself. Maybe she'd write on the walls. She would really be in trouble then. Hoping he'd hurry up and leave, she squeezed her legs tight, because she needed to use the bathroom. There was a knock on the door, and then it opened. Katherine peeked around the side of the leather chair. It was the woman with the red hair.

Her father walked across the room and yanked the woman's arm. "Didn't I tell you not to come to the house? Damn you, if my wife finds out you've been here, there will be hell to pay. And if I have hell to pay, Helen, trust me, you will as well. Until you give birth to that bastard you allowed yourself to get knocked up with, stay home. Don't go to the office; don't come back here. Until you pop that little prick out, we're done. Maybe you'll remember to take your birth-control pills next time. Now get the hell out of my sight!"

Tears streamed down Katherine's face. The memory of that day had finally surfaced, and she knew why. A dozen scenarios played in her head. Why would her father deny his own son?

"You okay?" Tyler asked.

"No. I'm not sure I'll ever be okay. I knew my father was cruel and controlling, but this? I've had family all this time, and I didn't know."

"What about Jameson? How do you want to handle that situation?"

"He needs to be punished for breaking the law. If I had to guess, I'd say he's been holding a grudge against me his entire life. I would've felt the same if I was in his place. A billionaire for a father who cared nothing for him. It's sick. I think I should reach out to him before I call in the authorities."

"Are you sure?"

"Yes, I need to do this. If I can right just one wrong that my father created, then I'll try my best."

"I'll be right there beside you, all the way. If you want me to be."

"I'll always want you beside me, *Dude*."

Epilogue

Six months later . . .

Katherine had never been more excited and nervous at the same time in her life. She had imagined this so many times but, honestly, she'd never believed it would happen to her.

She adjusted the three-carat platinum diamond on her left hand. "How do I look?" she asked Stephanie.

"Gorgeous as usual," Stephanie told her. "Tyler's a lucky guy."

Katherine had her hair cut to her shoulders with several layers added in. She'd purchased new makeup and a pair of diamond earrings for her special day. She found out that a day shopping with Stephanie and Bethany was like going on a world tour. It was as if she'd had an entire life makeover. In reality, she had. She adjusted the buttons at her wrists; she didn't want them getting in the way.

"Are you sure this is going to be successful? It's scary," Katherine said.

Stephanie adjusted Katherine's collar, then fluffed her now much-shorter hair into what she called the "sexy messy look."

Bethany came barreling through the doors. "K, they're

starting to go a little crazy out there. Do you want me to introduce you like we practiced?"

"Is she here?" Katherine asked. She was afraid to hear the
answer, but when Bethany grinned and then hugged her so
tight that she couldn't breathe, Katherine had her answer.

"Go on, you introduce me, and I'll be right behind you,"
Katherine said. Her hands were shaking, and she felt tears
pool in her eyes. Stephanie handed her a tissue.

"Don't you dare cry—you'll ruin your makeup. You can't
let your fans think you're not as tough as the Girls with Unusual Powers. They're your babies. Now go on, break a leg,
or whatever it is they say at book signings."

Katherine felt lightheaded as she walked down a short hall
before stepping onto the stage. Bethany spoke into the microphone. Katherine knew this would give her gold status on the
popularity rank. When Doc and Stephanie had mentioned
Bethany was being a bit shy during her first year of high
school, they'd planned this so she'd be a true rock star.

"Hey, y'all," Bethany said into the microphone. "Is everyone excited this afternoon?"

The crowd cheered and hooted.

"How excited are you?" Bethany encouraged.

The audience grew louder by the minute as Katherine
waited until her name was called. She wasn't the only one
who needed to shine today. In the front row, she knew she'd
finally see the girls that she'd formed such an attachment to.
Her niece Karrie would also be there. They'd had an instant
friendship, despite the crimes her half-brother Jameson had
committed against her. No doubt he had issues. Tyler had
promised to work with him as soon as Jameson was done
serving his latest sentence. Katherine hadn't pressed charges,
but the District Attorney had. Those charges were minor
compared to what they could have been had she persisted.
Jameson had been shy when he and Katherine finally met face-
to-face. But like Katherine, he could now finally stand up and

claim his heritage. It was only right that she share what their family had possessed for generations before them. She would never give Jameson full reign over the refineries, but there would be a place for him in the business.

Katherine's hands were sweaty. She wondered if she would have to sign as many books as anticipated. When word of this event was made public, the publicity team had gone crazy. Katherine hadn't realized so many of her readers would turn out for the event. They had been forced to change venues from a bookstore to the Asheville Stadium, where concerts were held. She peered around the curtain. It was packed. Her heart started beating so fast, she thought she would have a panic attack. *Please, not now.* Katherine took a deep breath; then, when she heard her name, she stepped out onto the stage, waving her hands at her fans. Tears ran down her face as they clapped, shouted, and whistled. Then they began to chant.

"Winston! Winston! Winston!"

Katherine had sent special invitations to the Friendlink group—even Walter. Once they all confirmed they would be able to attend K.C. Winston's first book signing, she sent each a round-trip, open-ended airline ticket. They would be seated in the front row, as well. Rows would be called by number, and anyone who wanted their books signed would finally have their chance.

"Finally, fans, I am thrilled and truly honored to introduce my friend, K.C. Winston, the author of Girls with Unusual Powers!" Bethany exclaimed.

Katherine let the tears flow. This is what she wanted. She wanted people. She wanted noise. She wanted friends. She wanted to live. As she looked out at the crowd, she thought that all of the days she'd spent alone were worth this moment. Seeing the culmination of what she loved doing come to fruition in ways she'd never imagined, she waved at her friends. Tyler and Doc were in the front row with Karrie,

Lola, Ashleigh, and Melissa, who was sitting next to Walter, who stood up and blew her a kiss.

Scanning the hundreds, maybe thousands of fans, Katherine stopped when she saw two women in the third row, seated side by side. Her mouth opened, and she stood stock-still on the stage. She blinked to clear her vision. The two women were not figments of her very wild and crazy imagination. She remembered Audrey. She hadn't changed much.

It was the woman beside her. She had red hair, just like Jameson and Karrie. Her face could only be described as a nightmare. It all came flooding back. The attack in Africa. She knew this woman.

Her name was Helen.

Katherine's Carolina Apple Pie

Flaky Pie Dough for 2 crust pie (or use store bought)

Ingredients:
- 2 cups all-purpose flour
- 1 teaspoon salt
- $\frac{2}{3}$ cup plus 2 tablespoons shortening like Crisco (cold unsalted butter will also work)
- $\frac{1}{4}$ cup cold water

Instructions:

In large bowl, combine flour and salt with fork or whisk.

Cut in shortening with pastry cutter or fingertips until it looks like coarse crumbs.

Add cold water and work mixture with your hands until it can be formed into a ball. Be careful not to overwork dough to avoid a tough crust. If dough is too dry to form ball (sometimes level of humidity may affect it), gradually add more water, a tablespoon at a time.

Divide dough into 2 flattened balls.

Lightly flour work surface, rolling pin, and top of flattened ball. Each flattened ball will be rolled out to about $\frac{1}{8}$ inch to fit in a 9-inch deep-dish pie pan.

Filling Ingredients:
- 6 cups peeled, cored, and thinly sliced apples (such as Granny Smith or Honeycrisp)
- $\frac{1}{2}$ cup to 1 cup apple butter
- 1 teaspoon orange zest
- 1 cup dried apples, coarsely chopped
- 1 tablespoon lemon juice
- 1 cup granulated sugar
- $\frac{1}{4}$ cup all-purpose flour
- 1 teaspoon ground cinnamon

¼ teaspoon ground nutmeg
⅛ teaspoon ground cloves
2 tablespoons unsalted butter (dotted on top)

Instructions:

1. Preheat oven to 375°F (190°C).
2. Roll out one of the pie crusts and place it in a 9-inch deep-dish pie pan.
3. In a large bowl, mix together the sugar, flour, cinnamon, nutmeg, ground cloves, and orange zest.
4. Layer ⅓ of the sliced apples into the pie crust.
5. Sprinkle with some of the sugar mixture and a portion of the dried apples.
6. Repeat the layers until all the apples, sugar mixture, and dried apples are used.
7. Drizzle the apple butter evenly over the filling.
8. Sprinkle with lemon juice and dot with the unsalted butter.
9. Roll out the second pie crust and place it over the filling. Trim the edges and crimp to seal.
10. Cut a few slits in the top crust to allow steam to escape.
11. Optionally, brush the top crust with milk or an egg wash for a golden finish.
12. Place the pie on a baking sheet to catch any drips.
13. Bake for 50-60 minutes or until the crust is golden brown and the filling is bubbly.
14. Let the pie cool before serving.

Don't miss *Smuggler's Cove*, the first book in #1 *New York Times* bestselling author Fern Michaels's Twin Lights series, featuring siblings Madison and Lincoln Taylor, whose Jersey Shore inheritance plunges them into a world of mystery and mayhem . . .

Growing up, Madison Taylor and her younger brother Lincoln lived in privilege, but their sheltered existence abruptly ended when their father was arrested for fraud and the family assets were seized. Since then, Madison has carved out a new path, studying fashion and working her way up to editor-in-chief of *La Femme* magazine, while Lincoln teaches wealth management at a small college outside the city. Both have separated themselves from their family and their past—until an unexpected bequest arrives from their late uncle.

Madison and Lincoln are now the new co-owners of a marina at Smuggler's Cove on the Navesink River. Instead of a fabulous, Hamptons-style property, Smuggler's Cove offers little beyond a dilapidated dock, a few gas pumps, and a handful of clam boats. Madison's plan to sell the property goes awry when a dead body is found floating under their dock and transforms their new inheritance into a crime scene.

Suddenly, Madison is swapping her city-girl wardrobe for cargo pants and flannel shirts, while she and Lincoln receive a crash course in small-town Jersey Shore life, complete with quirky characters, pirate legends, and a mysterious treasure map. They're discovering more about themselves and each other every day, but with a mystery to solve, and big decisions to make, these are lessons they'll need to learn fast . . .